THE INSECT HOUSE

SHIRLEY DAY

BLOODHOUND
— BOOKS —

For my dad.

"There is only one corner of the universe you can be certain of improving,
and that's your own self."
— **Aldous Huxley**

CHAPTER ONE

HELEN

Drop an egg in the chicken coop, and the hens make quick work of it, even if the egg's been fertilised. Those hens just gobble it right up, then peck around for more. Helen had discovered this cruel little gem of evolution all on her own. She had been eight, maybe nine, and carrying too much; the lock on the run was broken as always, and she'd been forced to manoeuvre around the half-arsed gate using her legs for arms like an octopus. The procedure had been too ambitious, even for someone as determined as Helen, and a single egg had gone falling, falling to the ground, smashing on the packed earth. Funny how time slows down when you're in the middle of a disaster, and disaster it was. Because, despite the large house looming over Helen's young shoulder, watching from the background like some master of ceremonies, Helen's family were not rich people. The money had been long spent. There was a family bible somewhere. A crest with dead personages branching out over the front page. But who really gave a fuck? That kind of entitlement, in the seventies, was all beginning to be a bit of an embarrassment. Besides, the once grand farmhouse had faded just as surely as those illustrious hyphenated names. Given enough time, everything lost muscle to bone.

Despite its grandeur Helen's childhood house had been more of a shell than a home, a maze of cold corridors, leaking taps, and fridge-like rooms. It didn't matter who your great-great grandfather was if your belly sat empty; a dropped egg was an event you could not afford. Back then, the egg would have been the jewel of their supper. Her stomach had given out a long lonesome cry as she bent double, quick to scrape the jellified object back into her fingers. But hens could always move faster when there was something tasty congealing in the dust. Despite Helen's lightning drop to her knees, and the cruel crack of skin against dry mud, she'd been rewarded with nothing more than a better seat to view the carnage from, as the greedy birds pecked down every last gloop.

Yet, that one little show of survival had turned out to be more life lesson than anything Helen had skated through at the local primary. A learning curve that stayed with her all through her life: hens ate their own. It was a lesson that could perhaps be extended to the wider world. When push came to shove, morality, loyalty, well it could all go hang.

Now in her fifties, Helen could sacrifice a dropped egg or two. In fact, it amused her sometimes to watch the chickens scrabble over each other's backs, tearing into the yolk, or each other if necessary. Sometimes she'd just stand in the pen, break a few eggs and watch. But this morning, she was not in the mood to play. It had just turned seven. The house was still in darkness, just a hint of light piercing the dark horizon sharp as a pin at that line between what should be sea and sky. She usually liked the dawn – the possibility of something fresh. She hoped each morning for something different. Any slight variation in routine would be enough; she asked for so little these days. But this morning, the new light left her cold. No, that was wrong, disappointed. It felt as if the dawn itself should be offering more, somehow. That there should be more of a fanfare. Because today something major was at last approaching. Something monumental. Today really was going to be different.

Last night she had hoped for a blood-red sky. Shepherd's delight? Isn't that what they said? But no. The coast had been petulant. Obscured by a thick layer of sea mist, the house was wrapped in its arms like an unwanted present, forgotten. And now this. Disappointed, she peered out into the darkness at the apologetic creep, creep, creep of light up over the marshes.

'Fuck it,' she muttered, gathering the eggs into her basket as she swung the coop door open, way too hard. It didn't protest. It didn't sag on its hinges or need her to 'octopus' it back into shape. It worked. Everything worked now, or near enough. Everything, that was, apart from Helen, and today the man who had broken her intended to make his return. So yes, the day's arrival seemed... understated.

Back in the kitchen, Helen was pleased to find herself alone. It wasn't always the case. Sometimes there would be a presence in there, a hangover from the past eager to get under her skin. But today, not so. The kitchen was empty. The air thick with the heavy warm mix of Aga and dogs. Helen put the eggs in the tray she kept on the dresser. The day's routine had begun. With or without a decent fanfare of 'arrival', the usual fences would need to be jumped. She could do it all with her eyes shut. She took her washbowl from the side, placing it in the Belfast sink to fill. Holding her age-wrinkled hand under the tap as she tested for the right temperature. The movements were automatic, distilled into a graceful art from constant repetition. From upstairs, she could make out the usual heavy sounds of Tim, her husband, waking. Tim was not a big man, yet when he woke, he seemed always to have gained a few extra pounds, as if gravity had caught up with him overnight. Perhaps it was the age difference – he was a decade ahead of her. Or maybe, Helen thought to herself, gravity sticks to us as we grow older. From her own experience, this seemed a reasonable observation. The bed was certainly getting harder to extricate herself from in the mornings, and sometimes, just sometimes, when she sat in a chair, she could barely get the momentum to stand. Gravity or lethargy or perhaps a sense of hopeless, endless inevitability had to be at the root of this gradual slowing. But this morning, she had risen before it got light. She had not slept. She had stared at the ceiling tracing the familiar cracks in the plaster with her dry eyes, noticing to herself where this or that leak had left a blossoming stain as she counted off the baritone ticks of the grandfather clock. Today everything would become clear.

She shut off the taps. The bowl was full enough. Too much and it would spill; Helen had quite a walk ahead of her. She grabbed a clean flannel from the stack under the sink, lifted the bowl gently then off she went sailing into the house. Despite her age, a handful of forgettable digits more than fifty, she was a graceful woman. There had been no need for ballet lessons and deportment; Helen had always walked well. Even as a teenager, she had avoided rounded shoulders, being proud of her figure. Perhaps it had paid off because now there were no rheumatic pains or injuries to worry her body out of shape. She secretly despaired of modern women: the actresses, the singers, the icons for this helter-skelter generation, as they stooped and slouched and shimmied their large backsides. Helen was different, a dying breed. A branch of women that sailed and glided and 'entered' a room. As opposed to barging into it in a pair of ripped jeans, stealing the family silver, and vomiting over the rug. She would leave all those modern excitements to the young.

4

She rarely went to events anymore. It was uncertain whether the events still happened, and she wasn't invited, or if Tim's academic cohort had grown tired of Tim. He was an easy man to grow weary of. Regardless, she would continue to sail and glide and enter: to move with pointed elegance from corridor to corridor until her movements ceased altogether, and her slight, pale body exited the grand skeleton of the house in a thin oak coffin, swaying gently from side to side. The thought did not distress her. Everyone has to leave eventually. Provided it was done with grace, she could cope.

The maze of corridors sprawled off from the kitchen, each tentacle strung with variations on the same theme; dark-smelling wood for eddies of stale air to get trapped behind, hard stone floors and uncluttered walls stretching out in front of Helen like cold, dead arteries. It was true that everything was now 'fixed'. The roof didn't leak. Those stained blossoms and cracks that she ran her eyes over every morning had long dried. The attic had been insulated. Even the central heating could effectively warm small pockets of localised air around the radiators. Each and every improvement had been implemented by Tim, courtesy of his professor's salary. Yet despite Tim's grudging financial involvement, he had been unable to stamp his personality on the place. The house remained disdainful of all attempts to make it homely, a fact Helen was thankful for. Helen was not a *Homes & Gardens* type of woman. Deep down, she had always felt there was something just a little crass, a little nouveau about comfort.

She took the second staircase to the first floor and set off, once again, down another long, narrow corridor. This one was darker. The windows upstairs were cut into a patchwork of small diamonds set at wonky angles into the lead. The arrangement meant that the light up here was forever stunted, never given the opportunity to play full beam. The dark hallway snaked off in front of Helen, leading away from the master bedroom. It was still 'the master'. They still slept together. From habit? Or warmth? Or perhaps simply because neither of them had the enthusiasm to hire a decorator and upgrade one of the other rooms? She wasn't sure. But over the years, she had grown used to Tim's snoring, and he had never stolen the blankets, so perhaps there was no point in changing the arrangement.

As she walked towards her mother's room, she could hear the shower pumping loudly behind her. It had been fitted ten years ago: the latest electrical pump. They'd replaced it three times. Tim had aspirations to be a power-shower kind of a man: fresh, and the noise was truly impressive, but despite the constant updating of the pump, the water flowing through the old pipes refused to hurry. Perhaps the fashionably large shining chrome head helped Tim feel for a few brief minutes as if he were a part of the twenty-first century, helped him forget that he was slowly moulding away in rural nowhere, like everything else within these four walls.

Mother was waiting for Helen in the room at the end: a lifeless, crumpled bag of bones. Despite daily bathing and garment-changing, mother was beginning to smell. Helen pinched her nostrils together from the inside, an automatic reflex. She didn't even have to think about doing it anymore; it happened automatically as she stepped over the threshold. Placing the bowl on the wooden cabinet that stood sentry beside the bed, Helen leant across her mother and pulled the two top corners of the sheet down. There was still a little warmth escaping from the body when fully exposed. Sometimes even a slight twitch, depending on how cold it was in the room. Helen knew that one day, maybe soon, the warmth would be gone. She'd roll the cotton shroud down, and her mother would have vacated. But today, even as Helen grasped the cotton corners, she could feel a tiny stirring of life, just the faintest pulse, fluttering like a trapped bird. She didn't feel disappointed. Not exactly. Though the thought did flit through her mind that it would have been hugely convenient if the old lady had copped it during the night. But life was rarely *convenient*.

Starting at the top, Helen folded the sheet neatly into five equal turns. The movement practised to perfection. She placed her flannel into the bowl with its tepid water and wrung it through. Every action had been done so many times before. If she didn't do it all in the right order: the chickens, the wash, she would forget what day it was, be gobbled up by time. Routine was the scaffold for her day, remove it and her life might just disintegrate.

Taking one of her mother's purple-veined feet firmly between her hands, Helen began to sponge: the toes, the ball of the foot, the ankle, moving efficiently up the leg. It didn't feel like a body anymore. Helen had long stopped thinking of it that way. It was just part of a process; bit by bit, she would clean. She was on the fingers of the second hand by the time Tim crept into view. For a moment Helen felt knocked off balance. Tim usually avoided the morning ritual. In fact, Helen couldn't remember the last time she'd seen him enter her mother's room. There must be some kind of problem: something lost, something forgotten. Today of all days, he would be wanting to get inside Helen's head, grab a bit of space for himself and mark out his territory. People do like to play games. But there wasn't any room for Tim, not today.

Thankfully, he didn't enter the room, just hung there, peering at the bed from the door frame. He didn't like to disturb; he would have said. But that was rubbish. She knew what the real problem was; he didn't have the stomach for age, real age. She could sympathise with him a little on this. She had resented every birthday since her fifteenth. But then maybe there had been good reason. Fifteen had been when her life had stopped.

The wrinkles, the smell of age, the continual march of time, had seemed crueller to Helen than it did to most women. Because Helen had been forced to stand on the sidelines and watch life slide past.

'Not dead yet?'

It was unnecessary. For an intelligent man, Tim had an unfortunate habit of pointing out the blindingly obvious.

'Not even a good morning?'

'You never speak to her.' He shrank into defence mode.

Let him. Let him squirm.

Helen put the flannel back in the bowl, brushing a stray lock of silver-grey hair from her mother's face. 'We've had over fifty years together, Tim, Mother and I. I think we've said just about everything that needs to be said.'

Helen had a knack for putting people in their place, knowing how to make a grown man feel like a fool without resorting to direct insults.

There was a moment of silence; she would have expected nothing less.

'Have you had my keys?'

'No.'

'I've lost the bloody car keys. I swear, this house...'

There it was – the house was to blame. Everything and anything but Tim. Helen allowed herself a small ironic smile. 'Retrace your steps.'

He moved into the room, just a little. Perhaps it was more of a transfer of weight than a decision to enter. He was about to protest, to tell Helen that 'the retracing of steps' was precisely what he had been doing. He would, no doubt, go on to imply that this house was a nightmare to navigate; too big, too cluttered, too dark. But in the end, he said nothing because she knew all of this. Instead, he watched as Helen placed the small golden bell closer to her mother's hand.

'Can she still get to it?'

Helen marvelled that he could ask this. How could he manage to not notice. Perhaps because it never rang for him.

'Unfortunately, yes.' Helen picked up her bowl and flannel. The job was done. The third tick on her morning's list – *dress herself, chickens, mother*, always in that order. 'She can reach it when it suits her.'

Helen's mind switched instantly to the next item to be ticked off, the one she loved best. The only thing that kept her feeling human: cooking. Having gathered her things, she launched off once again down the corridor knowing that Tim would feel uncomfortable at being left alone with the old lady. Despite the old lady's lack of movement, her presence seemed to demand... something. Tim would have to mumble some excuse to get out of the room. But talking to the old woman was beyond logic, and Tim was a man that liked logic. So he hung there, awkwardly in the door frame.

'Try in the car,' Helen called from the corridor, setting him free.

'Ahh.' He muttered, his voice too loud, as he pulled out of the room nodding, nodding. Pretending – he'd remembered: *Of course – in the car*, but it was all show. The keys would not be there. Why would they be in the car? Most cars had central locking now. Their car had central locking.

Helen would be the first to admit that living out in the sticks gave reality a kind of time warp quality. She was able to pretend that cars didn't have to be locked and that crime was something confined to the TV, not running amok in her home town, not in her village, certainly not on her drive. She stopped for a moment on her journey down the corridor and peered out of the window at the field next door as if accusing it. Only last week, they had dug up the watch. A sad, pitiful example of a Rolex. The leather wristband moulded away.

If that man and his son hadn't been out there with their metal detectors... But they had, and of course, a Rolex-wearing priest had been a novelty all those years ago. He had been a popular man. His disappearance had been noted. It was a small community. The story was, he'd run off. There was talk of gambling and of drink. People had enjoyed speculating about what he might have taken. Surely more than the collection plate? But the priest was a grown man, no cause for concern, and back then, the Surveillance Society hadn't kicked in. Tracing people was not easy.

The father and son detectorist team had turned the muddy watch in to the house. That had never been a given. They could easily have pocketed it, but no. It would seem that there were still honest people in the world, some at least. They handed it over to Tim, as it happened. It was Tim who took it to the police. So, Tim, in effect, had started the ball rolling. The watch had been in the papers, linked with the missing priest. Calls for information and answers were laid out in neat black on white newspaper fonts, and Tim was allowed a little smug satisfaction in proving that crime was, in fact, possible even here. Even in this little pocket of nowhere, strange things happened.

CHAPTER TWO

HELEN

Helen was already installed in the kitchen by the time Tim got down. He was dressed but still on the back foot – looking for those keys. The pots boiled on the stove, chattering fast and furious as local gossips. Helen kept her back to him, her legs planted firmly in a sea of red setters. The dogs would annoy Tim. She shot him a glance when he came through the door, just a quick over-the-shoulder look, but it was enough. She noticed the vein pulsing in his temple – a series of short, sharp beats as if it were about to explode. Repression, Helen knew, was an excellent emotion for getting the blood pumping. But she wasn't entirely sure it was good for the heart? Especially not at Tim's ripe old age. Then again, they were both of an age now where every year, every day, they were simply taking their chances. There was no point in being a baby about these things.

Of course, she knew why he was irritated. She was fully aware of 'the rules'. When they first got the dogs, there had been an agreement – the animals would not come into the house. Dogs were *outdoor animals*, according to Tim; *that's why they were born with coats*. He had actually said that to her, the coat thing. There was always a conclusion backed up by a premise. Philosophers are an irritating breed. So, they had converted the coal shed by the back door into a kennel. It was heated – nothing fancy, but warm enough. The floor had been carpeted. Every few years would see the arrival of a new strip of carpet piled on top of the last. The layers seemed to squash down neatly enough. The colours were always dark and forgiving. The 'Kennel' got more attention than the sitting room. But that wasn't the point. Despite the arrangement, Helen liked to let the dogs in, to indulge them. She wasn't the kind of woman to call them her 'babies'. That thought would never have entered her mind. Tim had claimed once, during some alcohol-drenched dinner party, that in a house without children, women transfer feelings. According to Tim, women could do this to plants, to animals, even to objects. Helen didn't believe in dinner-party theorising. Feelings weren't the kind of thing to be 'transferred'. From all of her experience, Helen concluded that feelings were stickier than blood and rarely flowed freely. But she liked the dogs. There was something to be said for loyalty.

She could feel Tim's disapproval eating through the shirt on her back. It would be worth giving him a little extra, perhaps; a little fuel for his thoughts. Something for him to sink his teeth into. She allowed a chunk of meat to swing from her hand, moving dangerously close to Jasper's jaws: the eldest of the setters. The one that smelt the worst even after he'd been bathed. The one whose jowls were perpetually wet as a sea urchin. He watched the meat in her hand, following its every move as Helen allowed herself just a quick peek in her husband's direction, but Tim avoided her gaze, flapping at the coat pockets of his mac for those blessed keys.

'Making a bit of a party of it, all this food prep?' He coughed his words out as if they were stones.

Jasper, oblivious to the tension, kept those large black eyes fixed on her fingers as that wet, black mouth indulged in a pitiful high-pitched moan.

She dropped the meat into the dog's salivating jaws – a habit she knew Tim found offensive. Yet Tim said nothing. Not one reprimand. Odd, she thought.

'It is a party,' she explained neatly. Though her words sounded a little dry. 'A celebration.'

'More like a murder investigation.'

She let the thought sit for a moment, but only a moment. Tim was getting ahead of himself.

'They found a watch, not a body.'

'And your brother decides to come home?'

'I want him home, Tim. You know that.'

Of course he knew. He just didn't want it rubbing in. Well, ask a leading question...

'Bloody keys.'

'Just...'

'Retrace my steps.' Tim sighed, plundering his old walking coat, his fingers clutching on something cold. His eyes lighting up momentarily with the simple joy of discovery: the keys. 'But I just looked there! I swear I just this second looked there.'

Helen said nothing, only raised one eyebrow in that way she had, which meant simply – *you can't have though, seriously, can you?*

'Smells good.' Tim was now all bonhomie, sticking a spoon into the heavy-based Le Creuset pan and stirring the sauce. 'The return of the prodigal son.'

She lifted the spoon from Tim's fingers as if the whole sauce would be soured by just one turn. Her eyes narrowed in irritation. 'Don't call him that, Tim. Please.'

'Bet your mother'll be pleased to see him. She always did have a soft spot for that brother of yours.'

'Not funny.'

But then he knew that. Helen put the spoon into the sink, refusing the eye contact Tim was so busily trying to hook her into; his face continually moving around the kitchen into just exactly the space she wanted to look.

No way was she going to talk about this now. Why would she? She'd never told Tim what had happened, not all of it: it had always been just some family disaster that, like all family disasters, would be impossible to get to the bottom of for an outsider, and Tim was definitely an outsider. In fact, they were all outsiders: the stupid metal detectorists with the mud-caked watch, the wheedling policemen with their weasel eyes, even her brother, yes maybe even him.

'Must have been some blowout though? And you're sure his coming home has got nothing to do with...'

'No.' Helen sliced through Tim's words. She had no intention of being drawn into this now, not when she had so much to do, possibly not ever. Not with Tim. *Outsider* – she thought to herself. She had the power to decide who was inside and who was out, and as everyone knows – power is a thing you should hold on to at all costs. 'You,' Helen said, dusting the back of the meat in the seasoned flour and regaining her composure, 'are going to be late.'

'What if he's vegetarian?'

She stopped stock-still, knife in hand, the red setters still champing at her heels. All smiles gone, even pretend ones. She put the knife down and pushed the dogs with her legs towards the door.

'Out. Don't be tiresome. Out!' Using her elbow to open the door and her knees to corral the dogs towards the gap, she badgered the animals through the doorway. The dogs whined, resisting each jab in the ribs. Helen didn't like resistance. She didn't have time. She took her meat-sticky hands down on to the setters and pushed the animals; one short sharp shove out of the back door.

'Don't pester.'

The comment might have been aimed at the dogs, or might equally have been meant for Tim. It had a catch-all nature to it, which pleased her. Helen had always liked economy in a statement, and it seemed to do the trick; the conversation dried.

In the awkward moment that followed, Tim grabbed his briefcase and as he did, it sunk through Helen's brain that this halting of the conversation was, after all, a small win. She needed to hold on to those small wins, because she could already feel that familiar wave of despair moving in on her. There was only one thing for sure; today, whatever happened, it would all be wrong. How could it do anything but fail to live up to expectations? She had been planning this day for over forty years, and it seemed to be going tits up before it had even pulled itself off the ground.

She ran her hands under the tap, removing the nest of dog hairs that had stuck so persistently to her palms. There were mechanisms she had in place; counting to ten, thinking of a safe place, thinking of any small successes that her life had offered. These 'mechanisms' could sometimes help to see her through the 'now'. Anything was worth a try. She filled her lungs with one deep breath, stilling her body, recomposing herself. Tim was not an essential part of today's equation. What her brother ate, considering they had survived on nothing but Rice Krispies for years, was not important.

'If he's vegetarian, I have something in the freezer.'

'No doubt. And of course, Carla's easy.'

A small crease crossed Helen's forehead, a question mark forming in her eyes.

'Carla,' Tim reaffirmed. 'Carla Phillips, the American. She's here on sabbatical.'

Still no recognition, and then it dawned on Helen like a roll of vomit bubbling up from her stomach.

'Oh no, Tim. Not this weekend!'

'It's been in the diary for weeks.' He pointed at the offending calendar hanging oh-so innocently on the wall, keeping track of their lives. But that wasn't fair because it wasn't *their* calendar; it was his. He was the only one who had somewhere to be. Her entries were only ever the mundane and necessary – doctors' appointments for Mother, or visits to the vet, or assorted chores that he never questioned, or asked for details on, because they existed in the vast realms of domestic tedium which he tried his hardest to avoid. She felt it was cruel and unfair to bring the calendar in now, as 'witness'. The calendar was his ally, not hers. But dates were made to be cancelled and moved. Wasn't that the whole point of writing them down; so that if there was an iceberg-Titanic crash of events heading your way, you could just tell the ship's captain to put the goddamn thing in reverse? Today was momentous. Today was perhaps the most important day in her life.

'Not now, Tim.' She didn't even bother to take the calendar from the wall and check the date. If there had been some kind of royal bugger-up on the over-planning front, things could surely be moved.

She glanced at his face, the downturned eyes, the chewing of the cheek. *Oh, this*, she thought. *Please not this again; this is not important.*

'Carla's very kindly offered to help me with the book.'

Carla. An affair? Or just the hint of one? Just the edges of it clouding his judgement, driving his pants.

'It's been in the diary for months.'

'Book!' She scoffed, barely audible, but she knew he caught it.

'Yes. That's right, Helen – my book.' He was holding on to

that rag of intellectual property like a child with its sticky fingers wrapped around a rattle. 'In case you've forgotten, it's what pays the bills.'

She said nothing – he could make of her silence what he would. It wasn't so difficult to interpret – resentment, plain and simple and bubbling to boiling point with a little seasoning of hate.

'She'll be going back to the States soon. We can't just drop everything because your long-lost brother decides to pay us a visit.'

'It's his house too.'

She was pressing on a sore point, one that she knew Tim wouldn't let her win. It may have been Helen's house, and her brother's, and the old woman's: the one who lay perpetually dying at the end of the first-floor corridor. Yes, it was theirs, but Tim was the one keeping it all afloat. She could see the gloat in his eyes before he opened his mouth.

'So, he's the guy fixing the roof, mending the guttering... all those choice homeowner delights.'

Helen refused to play. She took an onion and began to chop. 'Sarcasm doesn't suit you.'

'I like a bit of sarcasm; it soothes the soul. The highest form of...'

'Wit,' she cut in.

'So they say.' He smiled. It was the smile of someone who has won. What was she supposed to do?

'Well, wit doesn't suit you either. You're not a funny man, Tim. That is not how I would describe you.' The onion divided smaller and smaller beneath Helen's blade. But there were no tears.

She could feel his jaw opening. He was about to say something else. She couldn't be bothered, didn't have the energy.

'Bring your girl if you must.'

'She's not my girl.' He managed a touch of indignation.

She wondered if he'd been practising amateur dramatics on some of those late nights when he barely got home before lights out.

'She's a lecturer, an academic.'

Helen nodded slowly to herself, one eyebrow raised, the look easy enough to interpret – *Aren't they all?*

He sighed. His hands, she knew, were clutching and re-clutching that case. He wanted this aggravation about as much as she did. He wouldn't want to bring his girl back into an acid bath of emotions. She knew very little about her husband these days, but she knew shrill domestic turbulence would not be the plan. Everyone needed to play their part. Helen had her dogs, her mother, her house and now her brother and a watch: a Rolex. She would throw Tim a magnanimous hour or two's peace with the lovely Carla. Carla was bound to be lovely, at least to look at. They all were: they were young. It was impossible not to be *lovely* when young. Though it was true, some pulled off the combination with more grace than others. Perhaps an hour or two with Tim occupied would, in fact, work in Helen's favour.

'Carla, what was the last one called?'

'Oh, for goodness' sake – don't let's drag all this out again.'

Helen stopped chopping, stopped moving, stood over the elements of the meal that were all waiting so patiently to come together.

'I didn't start it.'

He paused, just briefly, just enough time to assemble a hurt superior stance. Yes, he really could have been taking acting lessons.

'Nice one, Helen. Great way to kick off the weekend. Thanks.'

'Sarcastic bastard,' she muttered as the door closed behind him.

Quiet. What a wonderful sense of peace. She felt her soul expanding into the space Tim had vacated; the shoulders that she hadn't even realised were raised dropped a little when she heard his car pulling away down the drive.

She looked at the food in front of her, pushed the floured meat around with the tip of her knife. If Gareth *was* vegetarian... She slid the meat into the casserole, set a heavy pan on the hob, and began to caramelise the onions. If he was... She would defrost a mushroom stroganoff, just in case. It was always better to be prepared. She wanted everything to appear effortless. They could all have rice. It would work. Silly, she thought, not to know these things, these small insignificant dietary requirements. She knew he wasn't married though. She had managed to ask that when the call came through. She had thought to say, just as he was about to put the receiver down – will you be bringing someone?

'No,' he'd replied, in a voice she hardly recognised, because it was deeper than it had been when he left, well, of course, it would be. That's what forty-odd years of hiding in the shadows will do: forty-odd years of trying to keep yourself the right side of those prison bars. It wasn't just the voice that would end up being dragged body and soul over the gravel of life, and she couldn't help wondering, how much of her brother would be left.

CHAPTER THREE

HELEN

When the phone rang only a week ago, on that grey October, Helen had imagined it would be the doctor. Mother's doctor. It usually was. But the call didn't go the usual way. The caller didn't speak, not at first. Which had been odd and irritating, because Helen had been busy – carrying mother's tray from breakfast – so the intrusion of a silent line had been unwelcome. 'Yes,' she'd barked, expecting to hear some faraway voice mispronouncing her name – a call centre intent on selling her something she didn't need, for an item or policy she didn't have. But nothing, and then just as she was about to ring off, one word, no mispronunciation: her name – 'Helen.' And even though the voice had changed, was so much colder, so much deeper, she knew immediately.

The breakfast tray went clattering to the floor; cup, saucer, tea. Everything tsunamied to the four winds as Helen's knees gave way, and she sank heavily onto the bottom step, her body shaking. Actually shaking as if she had been locked inside a freezer. It was a while before she spoke. Although, perhaps only a minute in total, maybe less. It was difficult to tell when each second had been pulled and stretched and warped. And all the while, she was wrestling her breathing, forcing it to behave. To do what it was supposed to do. Nothing complicated, just that small, surmountable task of carrying a handful of words outside of her body.

'Where have you been?' Stupid really, asking that question. As if it was only yesterday, and he had wandered off down the long gravel drive and somehow got caught up somewhere for an afternoon rather than a lifetime. Did she expect him to sum it all up, there and then?

'I need to come home. We need to talk.'

'Yes.' She watched as dribbles of cold tea chased down the bannister, a casualty of the spill. The tea appeared to be hurrying to take up its position next to Mother's mushed egg, which had secured itself a neat little crack in the floorboard. She needed to concentrate. She had to get back in control.

'Next Friday?' his suggestion.

'Of course.'

'Okay...'

The conversation, the one she had dreamed of having for so long, was over. He was about to put the phone down when she remembered; she could ask...

'Will you be bringing someone?'

'No.'

And she'd felt an overwhelming sense of relief. *Thank God. Thank God*, he will be alone and before there was time to muster a reaction, or ask anything more, he'd gone. But the impact that the voice had created remained in the house, hollow as a crater as Helen continued to sit in the cold empty hall, gripping the handset. Her body crumpled like a dishrag at the bottom of the stairs. As if she might sit there until the following Friday, while the handset buzzed white noise up the stairwell, and the cold seeped over her body. After a while, her knuckles began to turn luminous: that pale-white, bloodless colour that

21

comes from holding on to something just that little bit too tight. It was the dying fingers that brought her back to the present. Deprived of circulation, they began to throb, calling out for action. Yet she continued holding on to the cord, reluctant to cut this umbilical-style tie. Until somewhere, from what seemed like another pocket of time, one of the dogs barked, and she remembered: she could trace the call. She banged the receiver down and hit 1471, catching her breath in schoolgirl excitement at the opportunity of getting close once again to the prize. But the door back into the world of the living was closed – an automated woman delivered the bad news in ice-dry mechanical tones: 'the caller has withheld their number.' Once again, Gareth was lost.

But... Friday week. She held on to this single piece of information like a squirrel with an acorn, taking it out on the intervening days and re-examining it, twisting it this way and that in the sunshine. Worrying about those missing details: what time? For lunch or supper? And would he stay? It was the weekend. Supper could be a stew: something warm and welcoming, something to show off her skills in an understated way. For lunch, she would throw together an omelette, another culinary king which was uncomplicated and unpretentious but smacked of love and home. All would be well.

She had spent the days hoovering and cleaning every inch of the place, noticing cracks and cobwebs with a fresh childlike zeal and excitement. She'd tackled his old bedroom. It had been left untouched since the day he walked out: cleaned, but not lived in. Over the years, she had drawn intense satisfaction from this fact. She could throw open the door and enter the past. But now she realised that this time capsule could appear mawkish. So, she had taken all his clothes out of the wardrobe, piled them into a plastic container with a tight-fitting lid to ward off the damp and stacked them in the attic. She would make no mention of them; there was no need. As soon as the clothes were out of the way, she realised with an overwhelming sense of satisfaction she had done the right thing, that this was the way to go. He was returning; life should be all laid out ahead of them, not snaring them from the past. Forgiveness, wasn't that what they had always been taught? The police might be a problem. The police didn't forgive. But Gareth's secret was safe with Helen, had always been safe with Helen. She could handle the police.

She removed all Gareth's childhood books from his room, apart from one – *The Illustrated Insect Garden* by Eleanor Farthing. He had loved that book, spent hours poring over it. The pictures were beautiful, all European insects catalogued and drawn in inks. But more, there were pencil-etched scrawls and notes between the covers. The handwritten additions were all Gareth's. When she traced her fingers over the lead-etched lines, she could picture him, bent over the book drawing out thin graphite trails, as he sat surrounded by upturned glasses housing beetles or moths or even flies. He was always trapping things. Measuring them up to the details in the book. Writing his own observations as to how the insects lived or died. He had always been a curious child.

Apart from his tennis racket, she took all the toys and stored them with the books. It would all be there if needed. It would show, if questioned, that his presence had been missed. Missed was enough. Missed terribly was enough. The room had to work for *today*, for a successful return. It must pull itself into the twenty-first century – not draw any attention to the fact that on the very day that her brother had walked out, her life had stopped: that Helen and the room had sealed themselves up in a little pocket of history. From the outside perhaps people hadn't noticed. There had been university for Helen and marriage, but

Helen herself was more than aware that nothing had moved forward. The past was the only place she had truly lived.

During the week, Helen had gone to Beales, the department store in Leiston. She had bought a new duvet cover. It wasn't Egyptian cotton, not in Leiston, but John Lewis and Norwich seemed like a world away. Leiston would have to do. If she washed it with fabric conditioner, it would serve the purpose. She did not buy flowers. She hoped Gareth wouldn't bring any. The lost years would not, surely, have dulled that sense of revulsion. Even Tim had got the message early in their relationship and would dutifully pass it along, tactfully warning guests to the house that a bottle of wine was a far better bet. Anyone who attempted flowers soon realised there was no point. Helen took a perverse delight in the fact that they had no vases, not one, and gifts of vases would soon find themselves smashed, or lost, or stored away somewhere to be conveniently forgotten. Any foolhardy guest insisting on entering the house with flowers would inevitably find the blooms stuck in the utility room sink, wrappers on, and not a splash of water over the stems.

But Helen had played 'hostess' long enough to know that it was good to have something, some small treat, to mark a celebration, and in the absence of floral tributes, she bought a new church candle, one that smelt of vanilla and honey. She placed the offering in a cracked-glass storm lantern on Gareth's old desk. She would light it for him in the evening, when he was home, when they were both inside the old house, doors and windows closed. Safe at last from the world.

With the logistics sorted – the house clean, the food prepped, mother on schedule – the day of her brother's arrival stretched ahead of Helen like a spider's web, and her mind would not be still. That uncomfortable knot of questions kept repeating like an undigested lump of bread: where had he been? What did he look like? Why had he never returned? The only thing that never crossed her mind was why he was coming back? Her brain had conveniently skipped the unearthed watch and the newspaper article about the missing priest. Because 'why' he was coming home was surely not relevant – this was his home. He could return anytime.

She rubbed hand cream into her hands, the skin speckled brown from the sun, crinkled under the pressure of her fingers. Wrinkles. Her face, she knew, had fared well enough. For a woman racing through middle age like a Japanese bullet train, she looked okay. But Helen was not oblivious to the cruel fact that her beauty, her good looks, or at least those that were still clinging on, needed the precondition of age in order to be fully appreciated. She was a good-looking woman *for a woman of fifty*, not doing bad for someone *practically pensionable*. The positive adjectives could not function without accompanying explanations. Age is a cruel joke. For most of a woman's life, she will stand outside of the realms of beauty. In truth, there is only ever a very small window, one brilliant flash. Blink and you miss it. Helen had realised a little too late that beauty was a commodity done and dusted far too quickly.

So much of her life had been spent waiting for Gareth. But now that his return was so close, time pulled at Helen's apron strings, elongating every moment until she wanted to scream. She could walk the dogs, but if she was out when he arrived? She wished she had asked for a time, or an approximation. A time would have at least let her live a little around the edges. Then again, there was the strong possibility that he would not return. He might get cold feet. A no-show would be even more unbearable now, because if Gareth failed to materialise, Helen would have to spend the weekend with Tim and his American friend. Tim talking in that pompous way he had, quoting philosophers, summoning them down from the heavens as if they were intimate friends. That was Tim all over, name-dropping the dead.

She caught sight of her reflection in the mirror over the mantelpiece. Gareth would find her very changed. She sighed, glancing around at her surroundings. These, he would at least recognise. It was the same kitchen they had inhabited as children: always a mess because, truly, Mother wasn't interested in the inside of the house. It was the garden that Mother loved. In the summer, there would be no dusting or cleaning. Mother would be out on bended knee in the flower beds; the top of her head bobbing above a Monet-style mosaic of brightly coloured blooms as she attended the season's demands.

At first, Helen barely noticed the bell. But then it rang again, a little harder. Mother's bell, the one by the bedside. Despite herself, Helen was always just a little impressed that the old goat didn't simply lay down and die. What if, Helen thought to herself, as she took a bundle of laundry and headed back up the stairs to Mother's room – what if Helen were to tell her mother that Gareth was returning? A small smile spread across her thin lips; now that might just do the trick. It could all work out very neatly. Though probably, by now, and in the state Mother was in, she might well have forgotten there had been a brother. There were some advantages then to dementia.

In the end, the panic was soon sorted. Mother had dropped a pillow. In truth, it was a relief. There could be any number of summons during the day. A dropped pillow was one of the more

26

pleasant occurrences. Helen turned her mother's legs a little to prevent bedsores, but total prevention was impossible.

'If you don't want bedsores, Mother, you need to stop lying on your arse in bed all day,' Helen told her mother when the old woman winced at Helen's touch. The words were most likely lost on her.

Mother was overstaying her welcome. It wasn't exactly her fault. *But really, Mother*, Helen thought to herself, as she fussed over the sheets, *a woman of your generation should have a little more tact.* People are like fish and cheese; to overstay is bad form.

Helen decided she would make a tarte Tatin, as she rubbed the paper-thin skin on the soles of her mother's feet. There were this season's apples, neatly crated in the shed, and a pastry case in the freezer. A tarte Tatin was simple but stunning in appearance and always a delight. She liked the idea. He would be impressed. She liked the idea that he would be impressed even more than the tart itself. She imagined his smile of delight, and found herself smiling as well. Stupid really. In her mind he was ear to ear grinning. Whereas, in fact, her brother was a person of few smiles.

'You're done,' she said, dropping the foot back onto the bed and rolling the sheet once more over those alabaster legs. But the old woman wanted something else. Even as Helen was leaving the room, her mother was sending one clawed hand out towards the bell.

'Yes?' Helen sighed from the door. The old woman's lips moved, trembled, but the voice remained stuck obstinately in her ribs. 'Yes?' Helen repeated, irritated now because a tarte Tatin meant work, and she didn't want Gareth to discover her working; Helen wanted everything prepped and ready so she could concentrate on Gareth.

Again, her mother's mouth parted, tried to mumble something.

'Good Lord, Mother!' Helen re-entered, taking up position once again at the bedside and putting her ear down towards the old woman's dry-as-a-dead-leaf lips. 'You really must speak up or keep quiet. What?'

'Stta... delphs.'

Of course.

'Stake the delphiniums.' Helen gave the demand a little volume. 'It's October, Mother.' The words came out sharp and bitter. Her mother could be so tiresome. Helen moved the bell slightly out of reach, before walking quickly from the room, passing the diamond windows in the hallway that looked out over the garden, the garden where those glorious flower beds had once been. She glanced over it satisfied, because now it was all blackened and dead. Flowers and shrubs bundled like forgotten corpses.

CHAPTER FOUR

GARETH

H e should have driven. But then Gareth didn't actually own a car, and hire cars worried him – the new paint, the possibility of scrapes, the endless forms. Besides, he liked to know where everything was. Simplicity had become part of his code. So, that was how he wound up in Liverpool Street Station for the first time in more years than he cared to remember, elbow to elbow with a mass of faceless *others* planning their Friday escape from the city. He hadn't realised before that so many people were trying to get out, because for Gareth London had always been a sanctuary: a place to run to. He didn't want to be at the station. He sensed there would be trouble at the end of the line. But there was the watch, a small thing, but like a tumour it had possibilities, possibilities of becoming something so much worse.

There was a woman trying to ram a pushchair through the narrow barrier leading to the platform. She was arguing with the ticket collector. Gareth caught snatches. She had the wrong ticket, *but she couldn't have the wrong ticket, because she had bought it online and she'd entered all the right details! And besides, what difference did it make if she caught this train or the other train, since both trains were going in the same direction?* She glanced around the concourse, appealing for help: hoping to establish some kind of community. She caught his eye, and was about to bring him in, but then stopped – sensing something perhaps? People often did. With his dark features, his unsmiling eyes, Gareth didn't cut the best example of Helpful Witness. Instead of enlisting him, the young woman rattled the stuck buggy in the gate. It eased, and she took the opportunity to pull it back, clearing the passageway so Gareth could pass. He nodded briefly, not bothering to catch her eye before heading quickly down the platform towards the train.

He hoped there was a bar. It couldn't always be guaranteed. He had brought a flask, but a bar would be better. A bar normalised the proceedings, gave people licence to drink – *this is perfectly normal*, a bar said. *Everyone here is drinking. It's the appropriate thing to do in these circumstances.* He pushed onto the train. Others followed down the platform in his wake, a ragtag bundle of humanity. Everyone walking quickly; everyone having some imminent purpose. Even though the train had a full five minutes before it was due to pull out, no one wanted to be left behind. He glanced at his ticket; it looked like he had a seat allocated, but he would find the bar first.

He ordered two bottles of Scotch. Then, as an afterthought, he went for a third. It wasn't as if he had to drink it, although it was unlikely that he wouldn't. It was lucky he had decided not to drive, although... he realised with a sickening thud – that once he got to the house he would, in fact, be a prisoner. Leaving would be complicated without his own wheels. Whisky bottles clutched between fingers, Gareth went off in search of his carriage, his brain turning over possibilities nimble as a gymnast.

30

The train had not pulled out. He didn't need to stay on if he didn't want to. There was a brief shudder. The platform outside began to slide away in a series of jerks. But none of that mattered – he didn't need to get off the train when it arrived. He could slip past the station, ride the thing to Yarmouth. No one would judge if he didn't get off. No one would know. There were options. Only he knew deep down that this wasn't true. All possibilities had been exhausted. Finding himself irritated by humanity, by the inevitability of it all, he poured himself a Scotch. The young thought that life owed them. They didn't realise that the illusion of freedom was just life's little joke, its trap; a trap that their older, jaded selves would have to pick up the tab for. And the young had no idea how much older, how much more jaded it was possible to become. There was a line circulating his brain, a line from a TS Eliot poem. A line that reminded him of "home". What was it? Something about a planted corpse sprouting. Is that what they did, corpses, sprout rather than decay.

CHAPTER FIVE

TIM

S tuffy. It was all so stuffy. The lecture theatre was the smallest on campus, and yet she was drawing the biggest crowds. No surprise perhaps; she was a very attractive young lady. It's always so much nicer to look at something pretty. And she was bright, bright enough, Tim thought as he eased himself in through the door at the very back, late, scanning the room for somewhere to perch, unnoticed.

'Perception.'

She had a good voice, warm and resonant. Not too nasal: Tim had always felt that so many of his *colleagues from across the pond* had a kind of hard-bitten nasal quality to their voices. Not that he would have ever said this openly, some of his closest friends happened to be Americans.

'Perception.'

And those eyes, deep enough to drink you in and let you drown or perhaps let you hang. At the very least dangle from a noose of Helen's making. His wife was a very unforgiving woman, despite the Catholic roots; a religion which was all about forgiveness. But then again, this was a new world they were living in. Perhaps it wasn't quite appropriate – this young

American and Tim. If she had only been just a little older, maybe that would have been okay. Everything had gotten itself so #MeToo, these days. It was difficult to keep up – at what age did the modern woman perceive herself to be fully grown? Capable of making her own decisions? Surely anything over thirty had to be beyond reproach? Though lately Tim had been finding it increasingly difficult to judge just exactly how old a young person was. They all, each and every one, appeared to look just... well – ridiculously wet behind the ears. Like they'd only just got off the bus from high school. Though this couldn't be the case with Carla – it took a while to get a PhD. Thank God for the carbon dating of academia. Carla – the American – could easily be mid-thirties. Easily. And mid-thirties was perfectly acceptable.

He noticed, as she talked, that she had a certain charisma. Charisma, Tim felt, used to be a quality reserved for the male of the species, women were more beguiling. Helen was beguiling. Sometimes. At one point in time. But with the equality of pay, came the redistribution of adjectives. Charisma had always been a difficult quality to pin down. Tim felt, in Carla's case, it must have had something to do with the movement. There was a lot of body movement going on; eyes, lips and surprisingly, arms: she raised her arms as she spoke. Not just from the elbow, the whole thing, as though her ideas were sweeping blades of light cutting through the air. He couldn't help but notice that the arms were shapely, well-toned. You didn't get arms like that from writing in a notebook or typing on a keyboard. Arms like that took a little attention. A gym had to be involved somewhere along the line. As if to emphasise the theatrics, Carla's right wrist was adorned with a simple leather bracelet which kept jingle-jangling as she moved. She hardly needed the projector pumping out images on the wall. Young Carla was quite the solo-artist show.

'Music wherever she goes,' he muttered to himself, and caught someone looking. One of the young postgrads, a girl shooting him one of those shut-the-fuck-up looks that young people seemed to have distilled to an art form. He smiled conspiratorially, but the girl simply scowled and turned her attention back to Carla. Young women had become decidedly bad-tempered over the last decade. It wasn't pretty. But maybe that was what they were after. Then again, everything had changed. Even the academics these days were so casual – no suits, no patches. Okay, so everyone knew that patches were out, but the point remained – casual appeared to be in. Carla was sporting jeans. Tight jeans leaving very little to the imagination. Tim could still remember a different world in which people would ask – *do you think denim is all right?*

'Perception,' she was telling the room.

Carla continued rambling on, providing a pleasant backdrop for Tim's thoughts as he imagined himself taking her clothes off, belt by jeans by shirt. No, he caught himself quickly. Carla was an independent woman. It would, of course, be far more appropriate for her to undress herself. Pleased he had caught himself before the blunder had become too ingrained, he rearranged his thoughts accordingly and sat back to enjoy the half-seen musings that flickered so effortlessly across the inside of his brain.

'Perception is how we see the world?'

Yes, Tim thought briefly, if she stayed for the next semester, she would most definitely need a bigger lecture hall.

Oblivious, she flashed a smile –

'No,' she continued, 'much more. We can do better than that. Perception, how we interpret the world. There is always a viewpoint. There is always someone telling the story. We see with our brains, not with our eyes. Strike that, we see with our minds. But our minds, like stories, like narratives, like shape, are continually wrapping things up. More wrapping here than Santa's place come December.'

Tim couldn't help himself, at the mention of stories he found himself thinking of Helen once again. The brother coming back, that was major. A seismic shift. He'd tried to talk to her about it. Tried to speculate. But she'd seemed even more distant. As though this was a story she had no intention of telling.

A titter of laughter, Carla was running on without him, and that wouldn't do. He took a deep breath, forcing his mind back on track. He would have to listen. Because he was going to need to comment intelligently on the subject matter over the weekend – *perception*, he mused to himself. But found it difficult to concentrate, because there was also the watch. It had been there waiting to be discovered for over forty years. A cheap wristwatch, you could understand, but a Rolex? The police had even said that once they wound the thing up it had started to tick.

CHAPTER SIX

GARETH

L ight strobed through Gareth's closed eyelids. Light, then dark; light, then dark; flickering as surely as if someone were turning the sun off then on, off then on, as the giant autumn orb played hide-and-seek with buildings.

Gareth had been sleeping, basking like a goldfish as he sat, eyes tight closed, in the wide glass windows of the carriage. *Light, then dark; light, then dark.* The heat, the sound, the gentle rocking and of course, the whisky, it had all come together, holding him in a bubble of dreams. A distant memory in which a young boy dragged himself across bare attic floorboards: *light, then dark.* It was Gareth, much younger: *light, then dark.* But it was still Gareth: the unmistakable strawberry birthmark staining the skin on his left hand. How old was he then? He was on his stomach, so height was of no help in an estimation, but going by the short trousers, the haircut, he would set himself at around fourteen. He was in the attic of the old house, scooting across the wide wooden boards on his stomach; a favourite pastime. He could smell the trapped air musty in his nostrils, whilst those gaps in the floor were making it always *light, then dark*, as he pulled himself over the boards, peering down at the rooms beneath. He could cover all of the upstairs rooms like this, and even some of the ground floor ones.

He had been trying to find a voice; he could hear someone speaking. The bedrooms below were empty. He could see into his mother's with the pink quilt drawn tight over her bed, the dressing table surprisingly neat supporting its bottles of potions and creams. The sun was still shining outside. Gareth could tell because the attic was warm, and if the sun was in the garden, Mother would be there too. But still there were voices from somewhere inside the house. He scooted over the hallway, then over Helen's room; draped in abandoned clothes, laying where they had been pulled from her body, mixed with a burial mound of damp towels. Helen's bed was permanently unmade. She had a 'theory' that an unmade bed would keep the dreams in, so it helped you fall back to sleep the following night. He knew this was untrue, because if the bed wasn't made, the cold could find you. The messed sheets would leave you exposed for the night air to chill your bones. But he loved the way Helen always had an answer for everything. Stories were so much more interesting than facts.

On the table in the window below, he could just make out her bottles of home-made perfume, decaying petals wilting in glass jars, illuminated by a shaft of light. But no sign of his sister. Then he heard it – a laugh, a high trill of delight: Helen. She must have been in the kitchen. He scooted to the end of the upstairs attic and readied himself to lower down between the rafters.

The kitchen was a single-storey annex with its own small pocket attic; just a triangle of space, long forgotten since it was virtually useless. There was a hatch from the kitchen, but none of the others had worked out that you could, in fact, reach the kitchen attic through a small, vertical drop from the main building.

That laugh again, ringing out – Helen. It felt like he hadn't seen her for weeks. The mind plays tricks with time when you find yourself marooned in solitude, and of course, he had seen her only that morning, but these sightings were more snapshots, not real contact. There could be no conversation at the moment, not with him up here and her way down far, still living her life, spending her time as she pleased.

At the edge of the main attic he had to be careful. He didn't want to drop too hard. It would make a noise, and besides, the makeshift boards of the kitchen's attic might not hold him. He didn't go down there very often. It was cramped and uncomfortable. He wasn't even sure if this second attic would hold him. Stealth had to be maintained at all times, because if they found him, there would be trouble. He pushed his arms, strong from all his work in the garden, under a rafter and lowered himself gently down. His hand caught on a nail. The flesh tore leaving a red gash, but rather than cry out in pain, Gareth bit into his bicep. Tore into it with his teeth. Under no circumstances could he let them know he was there. Gradually, the pain began to subside. He transferred his mouth to the wound on his hand and sucked until the edges of skin went white. He would have to make sure it didn't get infected, keep it clean. Luckily, he had remembered to bring a bar of soap when he had left the house.

Cautiously, he lowered himself down onto the annex rafters. He could no longer slide on his stomach here; this attic had not been boarded. He was forced to crouch down and move, crablike, from rafter to rafter. One false step, and his foot would betray him; it would come bursting out of the thin plaster and through the kitchen ceiling. He bit his lip; this time to stop from smiling. The thought of Helen and her 'friend' chatting there in the kitchen and suddenly a leg appearing above their heads. A leg that was not even supposed to be in the county! It was supposed to be transporting Gareth through the New Forest on an outward-bound adventure with sixty other legs, belonging to thirty other boys. His shoulders started to shake with amusement. He clapped his hand over his mouth and waited. After so much solitude, anything would set him off. He had to be careful. If she found him there would be no mercy – *mad brother hiding in the attic.* He could hear the jibes already ringing in his ears. He would never live it down.

After what seemed like an age, his ribs stopped convulsing with the swallowed laughter. Gradually, he regained control. This game was too important to lose. He needed to get back to safety. But as he dropped his hand down to his side, ready to go, a brilliant bright jewel of blood fell from his torn skin and slivered between the rafters. He wondered if, were he to die up here, like a rat caught between the boards, they would find his body years later and that mummified drop of blood. '*He died of tetanus,*' they would say, '*just curled up like a rodent and died.*'

'I didn't say I didn't like it.' Helen's bodiless voice came floating up from below, drawing him out of his thoughts. Who could she be talking to? No one ever came to call. They weren't that kind of family. There was never tea, cake and chit-chat. People only ever came on business, and only for Mother. He lowered his head between the wooden crosspieces, placing his eye above a small crack in the plaster.

There she was, Helen, standing in the kitchen, a green silk shawl draped across her hands. It was not something he'd seen before. He knew her clothes. It wasn't that he noticed that kind of thing, more that she didn't have a lot, neither of them did so any new acquisitions always stood out. Their mother had a total scorn for clothes shopping. It was *nouveau* to be too well dressed: *a few carefully chosen pieces should last a lifetime.* But Mother failed to allow for the fact that children grow over the years, whereas clothes stay the same size. The result was a well-worn wardrobe, bordering on the short and the tight side. Helen never seemed to mind. In fact, if she ever did get anything new it always seemed garish as if the item were fighting with her for attention. The shawl that she held across herself now was very bright, very new.

'So.' A man's voice. Gareth squinted, trying to place it. He needed more than just one word. The man was standing out of view, a shadow in the corner of Gareth's vision, like one of those floaters you get in your eye if you stare too closely at the sun. It was only Helen that could be clearly seen. She stood there beside the range, her cheeks pink and flushed, her hair tied back in a loose knot that allowed the sun-drenched locks to cascade, Pre-Raphaelite style, over her shoulders.

'It looks expensive,' she was saying, as she twirled the end of the shawl through her fingers.

The man remained obstinately out of sight. Gareth would have to get a better vantage point. If he installed himself directly above Helen, surely he would be able to see pretty much the exact same thing she was seeing. He began to carefully reposition himself.

'So, you were just walking along and saw this in town, and you thought...?' Helen laughed.

'Exactly.' The man again.

Gareth strained, his ear pressed hard to the floor, but again it was just one word, and delivered so quietly he could barely make it out.

He moved across the rafters. Finding a spot which he guessed was directly above Helen. Once in position, he bent down again and tried to find a sliver of light from the kitchen below.

'And what did Mother say?' Helen again.

Gareth slid his nails down between the wood, moving his

fingers gently, worrying a little space between the planks, before lowering his head to the gap.

'No need to tell your mother is there? This can be our little secret.'

It was the priest. He felt a sickening lurch in his stomach. The past melted away, spiralling like dreams washed down a plughole.

Then from far away, a different time, another voice: 'If you're not going to confess, how will you manage to forgive yourself?'

Gareth's eyes shot open. He was on the train. The strobing light had stopped; they'd left the city buildings behind. Beyond the windows, the open fields spread out before him. But this vision of openness didn't make him feel any better. He liked the buildings. Out here he felt vulnerable; as if there was nowhere to hide. He rubbed his eyes, glancing down for a moment. There was a girl in her school uniform sitting in a row just across the aisle. Public school; a smart blazer, a felt hat, white socks protruding from perfectly polished black shoes. Then he saw it; a trickle of red easing down the inside of the girl's leg. A dark red snake of blood. She was bleeding! There was something wrong; the girl had blood flowering down her calves over her socks into her shoes. He caught his breath, panic welling up inside him. He was going to be sick. The girl glanced in his direction. Stared straight into his eyes, perfectly composed. He stared back at her suddenly confused. Why wasn't she reacting? He dropped his eyes to her socks once more. The blood had gone. It was a scarf; just a red scarf, half hidden behind her body. There was no blood. Not this time.

CHAPTER SEVEN

TIM

Tim felt it would be better if they car-shared. It wasn't necessarily an environmental thing, it just made sense. He would drive. They could rehash Carla's lecture on the road. Any tricky bits, things he couldn't remember, he could play the *driver-concentration card*. Level crossings, traffic lights, junctions; all worked as justified breaks in conversation. He turned his attention back to Carla; she was continuing in the same vein – truth, perception and identities. He'd spent his life unpacking these exact same elements, conjuring up argument and counterargument with surprisingly little movement forward. His phone buzzed, he pulled it out of his pocket. The police. He'd texted them to say Helen's brother had been 'found'. He probably shouldn't have done that. Helen would not be happy. But when the police had worked out that the watch most likely belonged to the priest, they'd quite naturally asked Helen where her brother was. She'd told them she didn't know, which, at the time had been true. But things change.

'If there is an objective truth,' Carla was saying from the podium – objective truth was a possibility which Tim seriously doubted – 'we are continually flouting it. Creating, what I call, narrative identities.'

Oh, he liked that. He jotted the expression down on a piece of paper, wondering if it was hers, or if she'd grabbed it from someone else? It was so difficult to have original ideas. Everything had been said or thought. So now it could only ever be a case of saying the same thing but differently, and probably with more of that *magic* ingredient – humour.

'Identities fuelled by need and want and a desperate attempt to establish a sense of self, for ourselves and for others. This is human truth. Different relationships, different aims, invite different interpretations. Things you deliberately hide from me, or perhaps from your mother, things you are ashamed of, or embarrassed by, you might wear as a badge of honour with your mates.'

Nothing new there, though Tim would have added *wife*; things that you hide from your wife. Not that he was hiding the fact he had contacted the police from his wife. He had just failed to tell her, omitted, or more accurately forgotten. Well, there had been the problem with the keys. Anyway, what did it matter? The police would have found Gareth sooner or later, and probably sooner was better. Tim had done nothing wrong. Gareth though, the brother, Tim knew there was a story there somewhere. You don't walk out for forty years unless you've got something pretty nasty you need to be leaving behind.

In the background, Carla continued to weave in and out of his thoughts. 'So,' she was saying, and the way she pulled out that elliptical vowel, he could tell the lecture was winding up. 'Not *I think therefore I am*, thank you, Mr Descartes, more *I am what I say I am.*'

Done. The clock hands slid into place. The bell rang out clear and strong into the room, and Tim began to clap. He would have liked to say, 'Bravo', but no one said that anymore, so he just clapped and smiled his *bravo* smile. His appreciation was lost anyway, covered by the shuffling of trainers as the multitude of spotted young things pulled their sweaty feet out from under the pews and clustered eagerly towards the exits.

'That was great,' he said.

Carla smiled a small, simple smile, and nodded. She wasn't needy like some. He liked that. She wouldn't go through the lecture blow-by-blow, asking if he felt this was too rhetorical, or that wasn't clear enough. Americans, on the whole, weren't as needy as British postgrads. They had that wonderful air of not caring: a 'founding fathers' belief in standing on their own two feet and creating their world anew. Who gave a toss what the old one was like?

'You came in pretty much at the end.' She smiled, packing away her notes, collating papers into bundles.

'Not at all.' Tim smiled. He'd seen enough. He'd got the idea.

'Three quarters through. The end.'

By God, she was observant. 'Well, it was a great end.'

She nodded, accepting this mild stab at praise as she wound a nest of wires into a neat bundle. 'All okay for this afternoon?'

'Tickety-boo,' he returned.

Carla stopped, and allowed herself a wry smile. 'You don't really say that?'

'All the time. It's very English.' He delivered his line deadpan.

'Professor Martin, I do believe you are teasing me.'

'Okay, just a little.'

She continued packing away.

'Pick you up at four?'

'Great.'

Only as he walked from the lecture hall, did he begin to think that maybe things weren't all exactly A-okay. The brother was a problem. Helen was creating her own little clique; freezing Tim out. The land was not as certain as it had been. He tapped his phone, took one last look at the text thread from the police, just a few lines; a simple *thank you for your co-operation*. Yes, it had been the right thing to do. The police didn't care about emotion, and family ties. You can't just turn up after forty years and expect everything to be the same. The police would get to the bottom of this, pack it away and send that wimp of a brother skulking back to wherever it was he came from.

CHAPTER EIGHT

GARETH

'If you're not going to confess, how will you manage to forgive yourself?' The words came back to haunt him yet again. He ran a nail across the miniature bottle of Scotch, ran it so hard that the nail buckled.

'Do you mind?'

Gareth started, glancing up too quickly, his lips still held in a sneer. He hadn't expected to be interrupted. He didn't want this intrusion. But there was an old woman standing in front of him, her hair grey, her eyes soft and watery.

'Mind, mind what?'

She looked down at the seat opposite, indicating his bag, the one sprawled proprietorially across the seats facing him. He glanced around the carriage. There were plenty of empty seats. He looked back at the old woman.

'Sorry.' Her voice sounded breathy, but determined. 'I like to sit by the door.'

He wondered about moving himself, but the warm sun and the sleep had slowed his body. He needed time to wake up. If she proved too talkative, he'd move himself then. He wasn't the type to worry about hurting anyone's feelings. So she could sit. He moved his bag.

'I don't know why, the door I mean,' the woman blustered. 'I don't know why I like to sit beside it.'

He realised this was probably not going to work. He could pretend to sleep or send bogus texts. He could put his earbuds in. Did he bring his earbuds? He couldn't remember.

'It's not the toilet,' the woman continued. 'Thankfully my bladder is a strong as a camel's.'

Gareth wasn't convinced that camels were renowned for having strong bladders, but since he didn't want to engage, he decided to leave her in ignorance. She would soon get bored, if he didn't feed her with small talk.

It was then that she noticed the wasp caught under Gareth's upturned whisky glass.

He turned the glass the right way up. The insect rose into the air. But it too was drowsy from the sun. It didn't stand a chance. He brought the glass neatly back down on the wasp's body. The sound of wings being crushed crackled under the plastic.

The woman's smiled dropped a little and he waited for the inevitable comment, either relief at the fact that the wasp was gone, or an expression of irritation at his cruelty – *what made him feel he could play God*? But he wasn't ready for what came next.

'Gareth. Gareth Edwards?'

He was about to deny it, but then realised she was staring at his hand, the one with the purple-stained birthmark. He'd been caught.

'I knew your mother,' she explained, no longer smiling, perhaps wishing she hadn't got involved. 'Gardening club.'

'Of course.'

'Is she well?'

'Clinging on, so I understand.'

The woman's face softened. 'Well, I'm sure she'll be pleased to have you...' And then she hesitated, perhaps remembering the circumstances of Gareth's disappearance. It was always impossible to gauge how much other people knew.

'...have me home?' he asked.

She smiled uncomfortably before deciding to look out of the window.

He headed for the bar, away from the conversation, uncomfortable at being recognised. Only an hour out of London and already people were pinning him into place, trapping him with their knowledge, with their gossip, with their beady eyes. As he wandered down the train his body shunted violently from side to side. An unnatural movement. The carriages seemed impossibly long. He passed through one line of seats after the next, faceless people staring up at him as he bumped along. Was he bumping more than everyone else? The drink could do that. His balance was off. By the fourth carriage, he realised he was sweating. His breath was coming in short bursts, and his vision was blurred at the edges. He wanted to splash water on his face, take off his shirt, lean his head out of the window like a dog. He wanted to scream.

He made it past the people to the next concertinaed section, two hurtling bits of metal joined by a hook and a rubber seal. The change of position didn't make him feel better. The noise was louder, filling his ears like raw panic. He stood by the door and pushed down the window. Sweat poured over his face. His shirt clung to his back. His hands shook uncontrollably. It wasn't just last night's alcohol, or this morning's that was causing the meltdown. It was the fact that he was heading into a past that he would have given his right arm to be able to forget.

When the wave of panic subsided, he realised that he had to pull himself together. Rationalise. He could get off at Ipswich. True, they had found the watch. He had seen it in the newspaper. But the incident, the real problem, that was over forty years ago. Surely if they had any more evidence, someone would have come knocking at his door, and no one had. He was safe. They were both safe. He didn't need to go back to the house. He could take a detour: take another line. Go to Cambridge. He didn't need forgiveness, he just needed to forget.

He glanced out of the window and wished he hadn't, because his heart stopped as something black rushed by, flapping away from the thumping wind like a body wrapped in a black shroud. The image flitted across his eyes, so quick, so sure, that he felt his stomach lurch. But he knew there was no need to push the window down and peer out onto the embankment: there would be nothing to see. The demons were all in his head. When your past follows you around it squeezes out the present. That was why Gareth had to go back.

CHAPTER NINE

HELEN

Helen had ticked all the chores off on her fingers: house – tidy; bed – done; food – done. But then she had stopped, stilled like a pillar of salt – what about Helen? Was Helen done? She stared at her reflection as it hovered in the mirror over the mantelpiece. Her beauty was done. Gone. She brought a hand up to retrieve a stray strand of grey hair, valiantly escaping from the knot at the back of her head.

Good Lord, what would he think? He would find her *less*. That was it. She had not lost her looks completely, but all was faded. She was simply so much *less* than she had been; less lovely, less witty, less able to enter a room and make it sparkle. So, what did he want? He had seen the article. He must have heard about the watch. Perhaps the police had made contact. It seemed unlikely. No one knew where he was. They had asked if she knew Gareth's whereabouts when they questioned her about the watch. She had nothing to tell them, honestly, nothing. It was all such a long time ago. The questions, the sudden interest, it was just a storm in a teacup. People were always out with their metal detectors finding things. They did rotations of the fields. They came looking for Roman hoards.

One had been found not so far away. She supposed it was difficult to stop the gold diggers now. The people who discovered the watch had been honest enough. A father-and-son team. Perhaps if the son hadn't been there the father would have slipped the Rolex into his pocket. Or it could have worked the other way. The son without the father might have proved less dependable. But their little jaunt must have been more than simply a treasure hunt. They had said they were after a little father/son bonding. Whatever that was supposed to mean. Helen had no idea. She couldn't remember her own father. Had never met him, so the concept was something she found difficult to appreciate. But the bonding must have proved more motivating than the treasure, because instead of slipping the Rolex into his pocket, the father insisted they bring it to the house. Helen had been upstairs tending to Mother. If she hadn't been out of earshot, then it could have turned out differently. But the father, hoping to set a good example, had handed the watch to Tim. Wide-eyed and gullible Tim, and Tim did so like a puzzle. He said he'd take it to the farmer, but there had been no need. Helen knew who the watch belonged to. There had been a brief fuss. The police had dropped in and taken tea. She had managed to muster up a few slices of cake. It had been two police constables in uniforms. Uniforms were good. Plain clothes might have proved problematic. But the discovery of the watch was not of enough interest to have pulled in the heavyweights. The young PCs, a man and a woman, had been born years after the watch had found itself planted under the mud. Morton and Midrift, Helen seemed to remember. The woman was Midrift, the man with pimples, Morton. She had no intention of seeing them again. There had been a few calls from the press. Pictures of the watch in the local rag, then... Then Gareth had called. Her long-lost brother. So, what did he want?

She shook her head, a stupid question. One that didn't

matter, because at last he was coming home. The house would please him. It had changed a little, but certainly not beyond recognition. It was tidier, more organised. She hoped he wouldn't bring flowers. Surely, he would remember that?

But what does he want? That same question kept ringing through her brain, and now that the logistics of the visit had been muscled under control, she had time to listen to those nagging words that kept rattling like prisoners round and around. And then the answer –

'*You, Helen.*' She could almost hear the words, spoken in that low, gently lilting Irish voice – '*He'll be after you.*'

She took the tablecloth from the drawer. She had often felt that the rituals offered by domesticity were so much more effective in calming a person than the kinds of rituals offered through the church. She did not need Hail Marys and Our Fathers anymore. She was done with that. Give her a washing basket, or a duster, and she could polish away the rot inside her soul, or at least keep it in check, and for now, the house was ordered. She could run the iron over the tablecloth later to remove those clear-cut square lines that always criss-crossed the linen; the ones that reveal exactly how the thing has been folded and sitting in the drawer for an age. Ironing might be the kind of job she would be thankful for if, God forbid, she had nothing to say to him.

She glanced towards the large, heavy chest in the corner. There was time, she thought to herself, to flick quickly back through the past. The chest had stoically continued to sit there, coffin-like, throughout her entire life. It was an ugly, Germanic-looking thing, with its heavy Gothic hinges and dark oak wood. It was one of Tim's pet hates, which somehow endeared it to her. It was true that it was in an awkward place. It didn't quite fit the alcove. But it had been there since before she was born, so she knew instinctively to move around it, even when the room was in darkness.

When they had first married, Tim had managed to stub his toe twice in one week. The thought still made her smile. It had been her grandmother's: a widow's chest. No one had given it to Helen directly, but like everything else in the house, it had washed up as hers by default. Hers to fill with whatever she chose. Reaching into the back of the dresser drawer she retrieved a small ball of wool. Prodding her fingers inside, she drew out the key. Yes, there was time, she thought to herself. A little 'me' time before the games began.

The key fitted into the lock on the chest, as if it was sliding into a slab of butter. It was almost criminal to keep taking the thing out, but then... Tim and his peering eyes and prying brain. Some things were best out of sight, out of mind. Kneeling in front of the heavy wooden box, Helen raised the solid oak lid. Her nostrils filling with the dense air of old wood. One of the red setters, the one called Red (from laziness rather than design), whined and ambled towards her. Pushing his soft silk head against hers.

'You'll have to go back out, you know, when my brother gets here.'

Red gave no reaction.

'I'm not even sure if he likes dogs.'

Red gave a short whine, as if asking *who could not like dogs?* Red setters were not known for their intelligence, the opposite in fact. But their loyalty, Helen knew, was beyond question. The dog could stay in the house for a little while longer. It couldn't hurt.

Reaching into the open chest she pulled out a pair of shoes.

'Green Italian shoes,' she announced aloud to herself, though she had no idea why.

Perhaps in naming things, in labelling them, announcing

them so pragmatically she could remove their power. After all, they were just shoes.

'When he gave them to me, I thought I'd wear them dancing.' She sighed as she stroked the dog gently with her free hand. 'Dancing! Around here!' she scoffed. 'Not surprising they've never been worn.'

She was about to put them down on the floor beside the chest, but then looked deep into Red's eyes, so absurdly hopeful. Hopeful for what, a taste of green leather? Holding the dog's head in one hand she glanced over his features – those sloppy jaws perpetually salivating. She smiled to herself before nuzzling her face into his. Teasing. 'Never been worn, never been chewed either.' But perhaps that was for another time. It seemed cruel to destroy them now, they were still so pretty, and maybe there would be dancing, one day.

The shoes went back into the box.

'Green for envy.' She stopped short. That was what Father Wright used to say. 'That man had a sin for every colour of the rainbow.' She wished her voice didn't sound quite so bitter. Glad there was no one there to hear, she reached into the box once more. This time pulling out a green silk shawl. It slipped like water through her fingers, always cold. She draped it gently over her thin shoulders. 'Can you imagine? Me in my green Italian shoes and my silk shawl.'

Red seemed unimpressed, and despite the fact that the range was on, Helen couldn't help but shiver. She took the shawl off and pressed it back into the chest, as she did her fingers rolled gently over a single string of pearls.

'Pearls for tears.' This time, she didn't even bother lifting them out.

The string had always been broken, a knot by the clasp the only thing holding them together. But since she never wore them, had no intention of ever wearing them, it didn't really matter. Suddenly she was cross with herself. Wear the pearls? How stupid. What a thought. She piled everything back in the box and locked the lid, before nestling her face into Red's deep warm fur.

'I thought he was dead,' she whispered. 'I thought, if he was alive, he would have found me. I didn't think anything would keep him away... so I thought...' She stopped, because deep down she'd known he couldn't be dead. It just didn't work. It didn't fit with human nature; if Gareth was dead, someone would have told her. Dental records, fingerprints, she knew for a fact that you couldn't just die quietly anymore. Quietly get yourself murdered, yes, perhaps, but die quietly? That wasn't how things worked. Someone would have said something. People do love to deliver bad news. She stared at the dog once more, looked deep into his doe-black eyes. 'And now, you my friend, are going to have to leave.'

She turned her attention back to the large widow's chest, removing the key.

'You know far too much,' she teased, getting to her feet, brushing the dog hairs from her skirt, and pushing her hair back into its knot. She was done. This grazing continually through the past was not helpful.

CHAPTER TEN

TIM

Carla had put up a brief fight about the shared-car thing, but in the end Tim managed to get his way. She'd protested – a mock sigh, a few exaggerated eye-rolls. She'd reminded him that she was American and that a car to an American is like a shell to a tortoise. But he'd insisted: this was England, and in England there was global warming, chronic road congestion and besides – the rather old-fashioned view that it was pleasant to travel together and shoot the breeze. He even dug up Socrates and his love of the peripatetic. One of the greatest philosophers of the western world would have approved: journey and talk, a meaningful combination. Clara suggested that poor old Socrates was probably turning in his grave at the blatant jerrymandering of his philosophical thesis, but she gave in, and at last, Tim had her in his car.

Then the realisation hit – what was he going to talk to her about? If he started off on his latest book, the subject might well be growing old and exhausted by the time they reached the house. In which case, the weekend would lie before them like a great black hole, and his 'guest' would be wanting to visit local market towns to buy fudge and postcards for friends. He needed Carla alone in the confines of his office where, on a windy night, the fire burnt brightly, and the whisky shone through crystal glasses like the gemstones of a hypnotist.

He didn't want to get her on the topic of her lecture, or her studies. He could easily hold his own, but he had listened to so many fledgling philosophers over the years, he was keen to leave all stumbling attempts at brilliance festering in the halls of the university. He wanted to enjoy the autumn sunshine and the possibility of youth and excitement. So, he dredged his brain, what was there to talk about? And then he remembered, of course, gossip.

'I forgot to mention,' he managed as casually as someone not trained in the dramatic arts can manage. 'Helen's brother's going to be there as well.'

'Sounds good.' Carla threw the comment away, and Tim realised with a stab of disappointment that she was missing the point. He was about to add the juicy bit when Carla saved him from being typecast as a vindictive blabbermouth, with her simple, innocently casual, 'What's he like?'

'Never met him.'

Now she was interested.

'He walked out when he was fourteen.'

'My God.' She was hooked: an incredulous look on her face, her eyes practically on stalks in that melodramatic way the Americans effect so well.

'Contacted her last week, out of the blue.' Tim paused for effect. 'It's been over forty years.'

'Shit!' She frowned. 'Are you sure it's okay for me to come? I mean, they're going to want some time together.'

'Of course.' He nodded sagely. 'And they will get it, because we are going to be out of their way. We've got a lot of work to do ourselves.'

'The book,' she said seriously, and he had to love her for her innocence.

'Exactly.' He nodded. 'The book. So, all in all, it works out perfectly.'

She seemed satisfied, but he had enjoyed the gossip. It was something he didn't often resort to. He found himself charmed by the engaging reactions it elicited and therefore was reluctant to drop it. 'To be honest,' Tim continued, getting into the swing. 'You will be light relief.' He lowered his voice so she would catch the full import of his words, whilst perhaps surmising that tittle-tattle wasn't Tim's normal mode of conversation. 'The brother had a reputation for being difficult.'

'Oh?'

Even though he was driving Tim could tell that her curiosity had been piqued. Tim knew very little about women. The female mind had always been a mystery, Helen being a prime example. But he did know that women loved nothing more than to discuss 'difficult' people, especially difficult men. It made them feel superior, as if all the world, apart from their own sweet selves, was insane, and it just so happened he had some really juicy facts on brother Gareth.

'Know what he used to do as a child? He used to trap insects.'

'Insects?'

'Helen's mother – when Helen's mother was still talking – said he used to arrange all her glasses upside down, trap moths, flies... even maggots.'

'What?' Carla had that half smile, half laugh on her face, unsure if Tim were teasing or not. After all, he'd already established himself as someone who liked a bit of a joke.

'I kid you not,' he continued. 'Apparently the entire house was like some kind of perverse menagerie; insects staring out at you from every corner.'

He felt her shiver.

'I hope they're gone now, all those bugs.'

'Never fear,' Tim announced mock-heroically, 'Helen is queen of the duster.'

Carla laughed. 'Does she know you call her that?'

'Probably best keep that one between ourselves, lest we incur her wrath, get tidied away forever.'

Carla smiled, before glancing out of the window at the flat fields streaming by and the miles and miles of nothing. 'You are such a tease.'

But he could tell she liked it, the teasing.

'I hear the house is close to the sea?'

'You can walk to the coast.'

'That must be fantastic. I mean in summer.'

Why were they always so enthusiastic, Americans? Everything was fantastic, fabulous, wow! When in life, really, there were far fewer adjectives. It was more facts. Yes, the house was by the sea. This was simply fact. There was very little that was 'fantastic' about it.

'You are so lucky,' she continued.

'Well...' He hesitated; he shouldn't have, but he did, and she was onto it like a shot.

'You don't like the house?'

'It's Helen's family home.' Excuses, excuses, he thought to himself. 'She's always lived there. If I had my way, we'd have a change. A fresh start. And I know this sounds odd...'

'I can do odd,' she offered, which excited him just a little. 'Well?' She tilted her head birdlike to one side, eager for more.

'I always feel as if I'm... I'm an outsider.' Suddenly he felt flat. If he had had more time to compose the sentence, to really think about what he wanted to say, he would not have said exactly what he meant. Because saying exactly what he meant made him appear small and unimportant.

'An outsider? In your own house?'

There! Now she had said it and making it public only served to make it worse. He felt vulnerable as a small boy of eight; standing abandoned in short trousers and a pudding-bowl haircut before heading off to boarding school. He glanced furtively towards her, and realised she was looking at him with intense curiosity. He didn't want to play the sympathy angle, that never worked. Let a girl bed you because she thinks she's doing you a favour and the sex is invariably trite. Let a girl bed you because she thinks she can see into your soul; thinks that she understands your pain and admires your honesty, well that is a recipe for great sex. Therefore, honesty it was!

'It never really feels like that...' He fumbled hesitantly over the truth. 'Like my own home, like our home. The house, it's got too many... ghosts.'

'Ghosts?'

'Not literally, metaphorically. It's like we're simply all holding the reins for someone else.'

Carla nodded sympathetically. 'You should work on getting Helen to leave; push for that new beginning.'

He shrugged his shoulders, feeling world-weary. 'I have tried, on numerous occasions. I don't know. Maybe now the brother's back, maybe that will change things.'

'Gotta be an optimist.'

He nodded and smiled as the road sped by beneath them. As if he was in full agreement and this was the only way forward. But in reality, if she could take off the top of his head and peer into his skull, she would see that Tim was all out of optimism.

CHAPTER ELEVEN

GARETH

There were no taxis outside the station; it was a small branch line. Even the car park was empty. Gareth found the quiet unnerving after the city. The empty tarmac reminding him of a science-fiction film he'd seen as a kid. In the film, the earth was alive and if you lay down too long it would absorb you, because everything was organic; every substance came from the same original melting pot. Which, ultimately, was supposed to mean that good wasn't good and evil wasn't evil. They were just stopping points along an evolutionary line. No one could be held responsible, not personally, because everyone was responsible for simply being part of that same never-ending chain. Gareth didn't agree. The blame had to stop somewhere. He had always been willing to shoulder his share. It was cowardice to shirk responsibility, and although he'd be the first to admit that he had his faults, cowardice wasn't one of them.

There was a sign on the wall advertising a local taxi firm. He pressed the numbers in to his mobile and waited for an answer. It was October, but the sun was still hot, and the tarmac desert was radiating waves of heat. The seasons were all upside down, the leaves on the trees doggedly holding fast. Yet it couldn't go on – within two weeks Gareth knew it would be a different world. The change from autumn to winter could be cruel. People whose lives played out in offices and centrally heated homes were forever being caught out. But not Gareth, he kept up. Living on the streets was an education in itself. He'd learnt lessons that he would never forget. On the streets, you underestimate the weather at your peril. It isn't just a case of getting your feet wet as you dive across the street from coffee concession to work. The sudden cold that hits the country in October always takes a few lives with it. The date was never precise, only the inevitability of its arrival. Gareth could still remember hiding beneath bridges, wrapped in newspaper, watching as icy gusts created vortexes in the street. He would wait for an unsuspecting drunk to happen into the cold blast. Sometimes he wondered if he shouldn't warn them, but no – entertainment was cheap back then.

The cab company answered. A man told him it would be 'Thuh-ty minutes.' 'R's traditionally were a casualty of Suffolk life. Gareth hadn't heard the accent in a long time. These days it was on its last legs. The Suffolk old boys were dying out, and the young had no use for dialect anymore. For a fleeting moment, its gentle lilt seduced him with promises of belonging. But deep down he knew that people like him didn't belong.

He told the cab company he would start walking. They could pick him up on the way. He gave them his route out of the town. He knew it well, even after all this time; straight out of the car park, and down the small high street with its standard collection of shops. Then the shops would break into fields. Long, flat fields, baking in the sun, or soaking up the rain. Either way, when the crops weren't planted the fields would look like a wasteland. It was a five-mile walk from the station. As kids, they'd done it most weeks. There was a bus, but it only ran twice a day and never stuck to schedule. So Helen and Gareth were always walking, long skinny legs striding over the ground. How many steps would they have covered if they had only bothered to count? They had walked on that last day, the day before he left. It was late afternoon. They'd been to London. This was unusual in itself and the mood they were in had made it impossible to do anything as static as wait for a bus. If they had stood in one place for too long, they would have had to talk, and neither of them wanted that.

Despite the warm October sun, the thought of that last journey home still made him cold. They had walked all the way, arrived dishevelled, hot and tired on the doorstep. Mother didn't even bother to stand up to greet them. Didn't even ask how it went. She was kneeling there lost in all that garden of colour; the summer flowers nodding their heads around her, as she wrapped roses in cotton wool. Packing the buds carefully for transportation. There was a show the next day. He couldn't remember which. Over the years he had forgotten all the names. They had walked by her without words, went straight into the house, which had seemed even more bare and empty than usual; shell-like, compared to the bright, luminous garden. He'd run Helen a bath, then gone out to the shed, walking past the roses where his mother had been working. It was early evening by the time he had returned to the garden, and Mother had disappeared. The intricacies of the impending flower show would have been keeping her busy. She was probably prepping in one of the greenhouses. The show had been her excuse for not coming to London, though Gareth felt sure that if there had been no convenient event, she would have found some other unavoidable task, some essential pruning, some essential wholescale fertilisation of the vegetable patch, or urgent snail genocide.

He had run his fingers across the regimented rows of garden tools that hung neatly from their hooks in the garage, before fixing his hands on a large spade. It was an old Bulldog. A good make: its split ash handle ridged from years of use and ingrained with soil where it had been left out overnight or perhaps fallen into a potato trench. The handle was thirty-two inches long; four inches longer than the other spades. His mother was not tall so, by default, the Bulldog had become Gareth's. He felt the length of the handle, warm where it had been stored in the window of the garage. The gentle heat gave the spade the feeling of being alive, and he comforted himself with the thought that he had an accomplice. He wondered if Helen had used it earlier in the summer when she had 'done the deed': when she had dug that trench six feet long. But he didn't want to think about that. He had his own deed to do.

He had assumed that the extra inches of the spade would make the process easier, but the work turned out to be surprisingly hard. You have to be realistic about digging; it's a more physical occupation than most people imagine, and he had set himself quite a task. It was true that he was young and strong; fourteen, with muscles familiar to this exact kind of exercise. But he was tired, emotionally and physically; he had walked all the way back from the station in the hot sun, and as soon as this job was done, he fully intended to retrace his steps and be on the first train out.

Over forty years later, once again Gareth was retracing steps. He was not immune to the sense of symmetry gained by re-entering this world the way he had left it. It seemed right. Curiously, he had always felt there was something spiritual about walking.

He crossed the busy road and headed down a small strip of green lane that would transport him away from the town. The lane had not changed, not in decades or centuries. The light fell, dappled, across the wide girth of path, which ran for around a mile, snaking across open fields before ending in a kind of tunnel of trees where the branches interlaced overhead, and appeared to be squeezing you out onto the other side. He remembered this path from happier times, when he had walked down this exact same space with ice creams clutched in hot sticky hands. By this point in the journey, the vanilla mountains would have already begun to melt. Helen would be licking the cream from her fingers as it dribbled down its cone.

They had done this ten-mile-round trip many times – just for an ice cream! It would have been Helen's idea. Not that he could remember the exact way it would have been worded, but adventures like this, treats away from the home, they were always Helen's ideas. In fairness to Helen, he had been happy enough to fit in. She was only eighteen months older than him, but somehow, she seemed to be a whole lifetime ahead. When they were younger, she would tell him stories about the spirits in the wood, and sometimes on a clear evening they would camp out at the end of the garden. There was an old shed that had fallen down, its four walls stacked neatly by the compost heap, and come summer Helen and Gareth would take three of the old walls and build their own cottage; all open to the wind, just at the edge of the garden where the flower meadow met the woods. They would bring sleeping bags and mounds of hay from the stables which they'd fashion into beds. The hay would always wriggle away from them as they slept, but they didn't care. Helen would set up a wind chime made from old bits of glass that she found washed up on the shore. They'd discovered that if they used a diamond core drill bit, and submerged the glass under water, through gentle pressure they could make a small hole in the glass pieces. There had only been one accident. Gareth had been cut on the side of his face when a fragment shattered. After the accident Helen made him put on goggles; the ones that they were supposed to (but never did) wear for strimming, and some thick rubber gloves that were used in the spring to collect pondweed. Once they got the basics right, there had been no accidents. The colours of the drift-glass were incredible: white, green, amber, red and blue. Helen had said that good drift-glass was more precious than gems, and that someday the world would realise. Then, Helen and Gareth would be ahead of the trend with their multi-million-pound business, selling all the 'stones' they'd collected. They would be rich. Only fate had another future in store for them, something far less sparkling.

When Gareth emerged from the path, squeezed out by the linked arms of trees, there was a taxi parked by the entrance to the tunnel. The driver stood beside it, resting his backside on the warm bonnet – the cab Gareth had ordered. He could have asked to go back to the station. There was always that possibility, but the ball had started rolling now. Events were catching up with him. Besides, maybe he was tired of running.

CHAPTER TWELVE

HELEN

Helen couldn't stay in the house any longer. It was unbearable; the walls were clawing in. Why hadn't Gareth given her a time? Yet again, she was waiting. She could hear the grandfather clock in the hallway marking off the minutes, tick-tock, tick-tock, rhythmic as a wagging finger. She grabbed the dog lead and threw open the back door. Gareth was probably working, whatever that might entail. No doubt he intended to come up after office hours. In which case his arrival would be around seven thirty, provided the trains all ran to schedule. Which they normally didn't. She should have realised all this before. It was still only four o'clock, which meant she had hours to fill. But how could she be certain? Work? What kind of work would he do? She had no idea. What was he even good at? How could she not know these things about her own brother? Her stomach was all knots and acid. She needed to take control. A quick walk might not solve it, but it couldn't harm.

'Mother, I'm going out,' she shouted up the stairs. It was doubtful that Mother understood anything anymore, and as children they had spent years having absolutely no idea where Mother was. She wasn't the kind of mother who parcelled out her time with explanations. But Helen had been to a grammar school. She knew about good manners, and though it had never been explicitly taught in lessons, she was fully aware that it was only polite to inform other living human beings as to where you were going. Mostly. And her mother did still occupy the shape of a human, even if everything else was absent.

Excuses announced, Helen swung the lead out towards the waiting dogs. They snapped in excitement like hungry piranhas, but then she remembered.

'Fuck.' The woman: Tim's girl. She sighed. What a first-class idiot that man was. The girl would be here any minute. She was no doubt motoring down even as the thought was skimming through Helen's brain. She would be sitting in her perky little rented car with her pert breasts and her wide smile. Tim's university *girls* all had pert breasts and wide smiles. And were all, without exception, excited about life, even those studying Sartre. Which seemed just a little incongruous to Helen. Of all the boring-fart philosophers, Sartre was the one with the greatest ability to crawl furthest up Helen's nose. With his *'freedom is what you do with what's been done to you'*. Existentialist claptrap. Sartre just about epitomised what was wrong with just about everyone.

'So basically,' the young, pre-marriage Helen had said to the youthful (at least *youthful* in a relative sense) bachelor, Tim, 'Freedom is whichever path you choose to shovel yourself out of the shit?' Tim had agreed, although, perhaps at that point in the relationship, Tim would have agreed with most things Helen might have said. But what Tim and Mr Sartre failed to understand was that some people were born into a whole shedload of shit; shit that others didn't even know existed. There was no sense of equality as to the size of the shit-pile you inherited. She wished she had realised years ago that, given a sizeable quantity of time, philosophers were the people most likely to tell you the least about life and how to live it. She could have saved herself some of the most tedious and mind-numbingly pointless conversations known to mankind. And now, on top of everything, she was expected to 'entertain'. She really did not need this. But Helen knew she would navigate through, because people of Helen's class if they had one thing in common, it would be that they were stalwarts at making do, and Helen was certainly more adept than most at shovelling her path through the excrement and making it smell okay. It helped to maintain low expectations of life, and low expectations of life was an attitude that had served her better than any philosophical maxims.

She sighed briefly as she began to scan through the logistics of what was fast becoming the major entertainment event of her year. No doubt, any moment her mother would surface from her bed, Lazarus-like, and come walking into the kitchen demanding petits fours. Domestics, Helen thought to herself. Just hold on to those domestics. The first thing would be to check the room was aired for that uninvited American: Carla. It wouldn't take so long.

When Helen opened the door to the guest room, she was relieved to see that it would in fact 'do'. The air smelt of dust-fur, but this was nothing that a little circulation couldn't sort. She threw open a window – so now the room would be cold, but at least fresh.

Helen leaned into the airing cupboard; towels would be needed. She was about to select a large, soft, yellow body towel. She had bought it for herself last Christmas but had somehow never got around to using it. She could fold it on the bottom of the guest bed. It would go well with the blue in the room, but no. She hesitated; she was missing the point. She pressed the towel back into line with the others. Lowering herself down to her knees she opened the bottom half of the cupboard, where she kept the dog towels. Her hands closed on a coarse brown square, the one that she used during the muddy season, just big enough for a body; dog or human. It was immaculately clean, just a little scratchy; dried to a crisp on the line during the last days of summer. 'Perfect,' Helen said softly to herself. Perhaps it might even give the young American a nasty rash. But Helen's smile didn't last long, because she suddenly remembered the rash on the priest's head, the way the skin had buckled red and sore before it had split like a melon.

CHAPTER THIRTEEN

GARETH

From the back seat of the taxi, Gareth watched long-forgotten places work their way across the window. The past ran beside him just the other side of the glass as if hurled onto a conveyor belt. Every corner, every street, every bus stop held a story. But mostly it was the fields which haunted him; massive tracts of land unimpeded by hedgerows. The crops October-torn out of the earth, had left room for carnage. Monster machinery had carved ridges into the thick panels of mud, leaving them cut and curled like rinds of peel. Living in the city for so long, Gareth had forgotten about the mud. But now he realised it had been there all along, waiting. He remembered walks in the fields where his boots had gotten so heavy, he had been forced to take them off and continue barefoot; his white toes sinking into the soil. Helen said barefoot was better. Colder, but better; the mud clods couldn't get a hold and drag you down. Helen had an answer for everything and would probably have had a motive tucked somewhere under her words; the boots must have been slowing him on their walk; she wanted him to speed up.

In the summer the landscape was a different story. Crops

grew chest-high overnight and the mud flattened, hard and inflexible as a grim smile; East Anglia was a thirsty county, and this constant thirst was a problem. When the rains remained obstinate, the watering would begin and watering was a major preoccupation for Mother. Some women worried about bills, or cancer, but for Mother it was hosepipe bans and parched gardens. In order to mitigate, wide green water barrels surrounded the house. Each flank of the building had been laced over the years with a complicated system of pipes and guttering, funnelling precious rainwater into a series of great green plastic tanks.

When Gareth dipped the watering can into one, the water smelt musty; the tanks never emptied out completely. As a child, Gareth had found this notion intimidating; the water at the bottom must have been there for years, way before Gareth's time, way back to when Mother was a child. One summer, the tanks ran low, revealing a thick rank-smelling sludge. Before it had a chance to dry hard, Mother had dug it into the rose garden. Mother liked to dig things into the garden and watch the results. Mother always had a garden recipe she was working with.

Hosepipe ban or no, when the watering season arrived, Helen and Gareth were expected to pull their weight. He couldn't actually remember his mother ever having asked them if they minded doing the rounds. It was more of a duty they had been conscripted into from birth. They could have cut the time in half – focused on different areas of the garden simultaneously, or worked in tandem, or had alternate days off. But they always chose to work together. Helen devised her own rotation method. It had to be implemented twice a day, religiously. It was good not to have to think. Actions were always so much easier when they were automatic. In the morning, before the sun hit, they would fill their watering cans from the tanks flanking the east portion of the house. They would water the kitchen garden first, then head to the vegetable patch. The veg patch was the greediest of all the planting. But hunger and thirst were sentiments they understood. Besides, if they didn't water the vegetables, the net effect would be their own hunger. And an added bonus, in the vegetable garden they could eat straight from the soil. Even many years later, Gareth had never found anything that tasted quite so delicious as the sweet flavour of popped open fresh peas. Running a nail, thick with garden dirt, inside the green tightly-fitting jacket before sliding the peas straight from plant to tongue. He would often stand, sun on his back, watering can in hand, with a carrot dangling its long feathered green tail from his lips.

'Carrot tops,' Helen had called him, fondly. 'We're going to have to get you sent off, or you'll end up a farmer.'

He'd just shrugged. Being a farmer didn't sound so bad. Back then, before that last summer had sunk its teeth into his life forever, Suffolk had seemed like a slice of Heaven; standing, watching Helen spray water from her can in large figure of eights onto the hard soil, it felt like time would always be on their side. It wasn't the best way of watering; the best way was to shoulder-joint-swing the can up and down in vertical lines. But Helen liked the patterns the water made on the dry earth, and sometimes, perversely, he got the feeling that actually Helen liked the way wide-watering encouraged weeds to strike out on their own.

'When you end up a farmer,' she'd teased. 'No one will marry you.'

He'd been eight or nine when she'd given out her proclamation, so the question of marriage hadn't really been on his mind, but the thought seemed to provide Helen with a thick vein of humour. So, Gareth had smiled in agreement. Why not.

'The farmer wants a wife...' she'd sang. 'The farmer wants a

73

wife...' and he'd laughed, happy to bask in the warm light of her attention. Besides, he had the upper hand – he didn't want a wife. He just wanted to stay with Helen, in a place where the bright morning sun would warm his back, and the vegetable patch with its neat, regimented rows of carrots, juicy lettuces and bright bulbous radishes, spoke of abundance. He had wanted to stay there forever.

The meter in the cab ticked through its red squared numbers counting the pennies, adding up the totals, calculating the passage of miles from point to point. It was reading fifteen pounds already, but this was the kind of clock that never stopped. Even when the wheels on the cab ground to a halt there would be one last click-into-place. He could still remember the fear that childhood taxi rides induced; the anxious watch of the count-up. The pressure of the split-second decision; that they might have to shout, '*Stop now*', and scramble quickly from the doors, embarrassed by the fact that there would be no tip. They hadn't done it often; people knew where they lived. Mostly, they walked.

Now, years later when the taxi pulled into the village, Gareth felt a sickening lurch in his stomach. Only the cars had upgraded themselves to mark the passing of time. A blanket grade-two listing had helped lock the village firmly in the past. The habitual line of flint-scaled cottages flanked the road, clustered together as if in support. Huddled so close, Gareth couldn't help but picture them gossiping; chitter-chatter, chitter-chatter. Talking excitedly about this 'new' arrival. All eyes would be on him. There was nothing novel in that. Even the old bird on the train had *witnessed* his return. What were the chances? All these years, all those trains, all the endless stream of people pouring in, pouring out, but in a place like this nothing went unnoticed. Nothing apart from one-on-one secrets. One-on-one, that was the only way a secret could exist.

As far as secrets go, three was not only a crowd, it was a liability.

The village opened out onto a green, a large sloping tongue of grass which ran, as if galloping away, in a clean jail-break sprint from the church. He remembered running down its length, every week, arms outstretched. Escape. But now it didn't seem like that. It had been toying with him all these years, waiting for the time when it would reel him back. In the late afternoon, the shadow of the bell tower stalked out across the cut grass; its stride reaching as always towards their house.

For most of the year, the green in front of the church was left extravagantly bare, but for one week each year, the marquee would go up for the Flower and Produce show. He remembered being around seven or so, and the show in full swing; row upon row of trestle tables laid with white ironed tablecloths, and each table containing some new wonder. There were marrows bigger than his arm, wide and smiling green like the grin of a Cheshire cat. There were single roses, placed in tiny vases and set in a sea of space on the white cotton. There were other tables where blooms exploded out of make-do containers; a milk jug, or a tin bucket, or even once, a bath. Each exhibition was a shout to the local press on the creativity of the village – the proud parents of the *creations* stood behind their treasured offerings, guarding them lovingly until the judges had given their final say, and the press had snapped a few photos. But Gareth had never been interested in the flowers. It was the cakes that caught his eye, and there was an entire corner devoted to baking and crust-amputated sandwiches. Mrs Morrissey, a large lady with thick, American Tan ankles that squeezed, slug-like out of laced Oxford flats, presided over the 'cake corner'. Behind her the tea urn bubbled and steamed, serving only to heighten the image that this was her domain. He remembered once, a tower of iced cupcakes and Helen's determination. Their mother was not the sort of woman who baked. She came from a long line of women who did not, in fact, cook, from a lost era where someone else handled the domestics. It didn't matter who, it only mattered that it wasn't you. They were women with cold hearts, good at orders but lost on the intricacies of an oven. They were women who had failed to catch up: the money had long since been spent, and there was no 'someone' to receive instructions. Mother could do vegetables, but anything sweet seemed to her a pointless distraction from the garden. So, the Flower and Produce show, with its cake grotto (complete with steaming tea urn dragon) had always been one of the highlights of the year for the siblings. They become adept at 'finding' money in the house: down the sofa after the Garden Club had left, in the collection box at church, just before it got handed back. (Helen swore it wasn't technically the property of the church until the church had counted it.) Or the swimming-pool lockers, if they were quick there might be change left in the slots by absent-minded parents. But once, when pickings had been slim, Helen devised a plan. She had given Gareth instructions, briefed him verbally and even acted the whole scenario out in the quiet of the potting shed. He was to feign ignorance on the money front, try to buy one of the large, iced creations with his clutch of pennies. There would be instant refusal; Mrs Morrissey did not strike bargains. But Gareth needed to push it. He had to insist; raise up the coins in his hands towards the dragon, grubby and hot, and she must look at his hands, rather than his face. Because, if her eyeline was directed towards his hands, Mrs Morrissey would not notice the table, or Helen, who would be sliding a cake or two neatly off their plates and into her pockets.

The plan had backfired. The instincts of a dragon should never be underestimated. Gareth had approached in his shorts with his sweaty palms outstretched, and she had looked. But the dragon must have had peripheral vision. In an instant she'd sensed Helen's small white arm. She didn't roar. Instead, fast as a guillotine, her chicken-wing arms shot out and grasped Helen's hand tightly. A single cake was trapped mid-journey, from plate to pocket. Helen stared into the woman's eyes. Gareth watched, unable to move, as the world slowed on its axis for the standoff; Helen's bright green eyes, sharp as buttons, staring down the dragon. The world around them went on, people pushing through the marquee with its sweet smell of trapped, stewed grass, but three of the players, Gareth, Helen and the dragon, had been frozen in time. It was then that Gareth noticed Father Wright, because he, too, was trapped in the same temporal bubble. He'd witnessed the attempt. The situation was looking grave, and Gareth had been on the brink of shouting 'Run!' Because, surely now that the church had become involved, there would be penance to pay. This was stealing. Mother would be informed. Helen would be punished, sent to bed; her face still stinging from Mother's slap with its cold, sharp, diamond ring. The one she continued to wear, despite the lack of any kind of manifestation on the husband front. But Father Wright did something Gareth hadn't anticipated. He moved forward, took the cake from the hands of Helen and the dragon, squabbling like hens over a handful of feed. At no point in time did the priest look at the cake all the while he was engaging with the dragon. All the while he was holding her fiery eyes with his own. All the while he was talking and smiling and charming, as he was slipping payment for the cake into the dragon's tin and backhanding the iced sponge to Helen.

As soon as the cake was clear, Helen shot Gareth a look and they took off. They ran from the marquee, laughing, Helen clutching the spoils tightly in her thin, white hands. They were over-the-moon ecstatic. They hadn't paid! The priest had stepped in offering his own money, but Helen and Gareth, they had got off scot-free. As they raced across the thick tongue of grass, the one that slid down from the church, Helen had pulled chunks of icing from the cake and parcelled them neatly into Gareth's smiling mouth. She'd laughed in delight as though she was Christ feeding the five thousand. The cake would last forever. It would sustain them for years, and they ran from the green across the road towards the long gravel driveway and their farm. Far behind them the plants withered in the heat of the marquee, as the sugar tricked their bellies into feeling full. Later that night he'd woken, an uncomfortable feeling in his gut. He'd stumbled into the kitchen looking for water. His stomach, so full of flour and icing had been churning. He'd opened the back door to the kitchen and vomited into the gutter outside. The noise seemed to echo around the village, yet no one came. He sank down beside the drain, exhausted and wondered how things that taste so good, could end up being quite so rotten.

CHAPTER FOURTEEN

HELEN

The moment Helen stepped back into the house she knew Gareth had arrived. She scouted the kitchen anxiously looking for signs: shoes at the door? A bag? A coat? But there was not one thing extra, only, somehow, a more tangible notion of him; a kind of certain knowledge that his body had passed through this room only minutes before. Gone? Could he have gone already? Would he have come home, taken just one peek, and decided... No. This wasn't worth it. Talking could only make things worse. What was done, could not be undone. Why rock the boat now. It was then that she saw, pride of place on the kitchen table, a glass turned upside down with something small, dark and spindly trapped under its dome. The dog lead dropped from Helen's hand as she walked cautiously towards the table. It was a crane fly, its awkward legs held captive beneath one of her best crystal tumblers. She reached towards the glass and gently, slowly raised one corner.

'It's dead.'

'My God!' she gasped, her hands flying to her face, as tears stung her eyes.

He was sitting in the high-back chair by the range, his face half hidden in the shadows. How long had he been there? All morning? Could he have been there all morning? But no. That was stupid. Why had she gone out? How could she have been so foolish, striding around in the cold outdoors when all the time he was here?

She stretched out her hand, holding it towards the line of his angular chiselled face. Not a boy's face anymore. His features were heavy; his face bristled grey as if scrubbed by a scouring pad with the bleach left in. She wanted to move forward, but her body wouldn't respond. It seemed to have lost the knack of taking orders. Her feet were rooted. She just stood and gaped and felt her features turning to liquid; her nose, her eyes. She was melting, and shaking and lost.

'My God! Gareth.'

Her body began to inch towards him. Once mobility was back there would be no stopping her. There would be an embrace, a kiss, love boundless and unlocked and just like it used to be. But...

'Helen.' His voice came back harsh with the cold notes of a warning; hard and inflexible as a stop sign. She paused with her hand just about to touch his cheek.

It hovered there for what seemed like an age but must have only been a moment. Hovered until Gareth grasped Helen's fingers in his own.

His hands were so hard, so old, so wide. He would take her, would pull her to him... and she waited, waited again while the world turned slow, but to Helen's surprise, Gareth simply shook her hand briefly, a curious half-handshake of acknowledgment, before letting her fingers drop.

'I didn't know what time you were arriving,' she blustered, sniffing, reaching for a tissue, patting at her eyes. Glad she hadn't worn mascara. 'You must think me hopelessly unprepared.'

'Sorry. I didn't know either.'

His voice was so deep now. It was the same voice, just wider; built by stories and events that she had missed.

'It doesn't matter.' Nothing mattered, not now he was here. But her brain teemed with more questions, many questions, too many to ask all at once, so she fell back on the old ones; in particular the one question that had haunted her all these years. *'Where were you? Where?'* but the words, so long rehearsed, dissolved to nothing on her tongue, like water sinking into sand, so remained unanswered.

Awkward, she clutched at a strand of grey hair that had fallen in front of her face. Her nose was running. She was a mess. She couldn't remember the last time she had cried. It felt as if her body was falling to pieces. 'My God, Gareth.'

Then he put his arms around her and held her tightly to his chest.

'Shhh.'

'I thought you were dead.' She sobbed. 'I waited for you for so long.'

'Hush.'

But the years wouldn't be silenced. 'I used to stand in your room, watching the driveway.' An awkward breath caught in her throat. 'Just standing there waiting, and it would all go dark all around me. The colour leaching out of the garden.'

'Helen, hush how.'

But the years had been so painful, so endless the weight of them wouldn't allow her to just move on. 'I waited for you every night. Watched for you. I let it all go dark so that I could see outside better, just in case. So that I could get that first hint of you wandering back up the drive when you returned. I waited there every night for two years. But you didn't come.'

'Shh.' His voice was soft, pressed close to her ear. But the

81

pain, the memory of loss, was so ingrained, that even after all these years, it felt raw.

'Two years, it might seem like nothing now...' Helen laughed bitterly. 'When we've racked up over forty. But it's a long time, believe me. Every night, there I was, surrounded by all your books and your old toys, and... all your clothes.'

He had taken nothing, only what he stood up in.

'You didn't think to write?' The question came out like a slap.

Gareth pulled away, and Helen wished she hadn't been so sharp, because what did all that matter now? It needed to be annexed as part of a different lifetime; that was the only way forward, because here he was standing in her kitchen after all those years. Standing directly in front of her in all his beauty. She had to move past the old wounds before they killed the moment, the here and now, dead.

'I'm sorry,' she said quickly, drying her eyes, sighing as if she was just being silly, had forgotten herself.

'I couldn't write, Helen. You know that.' He drew her face back around to his with his fingers and stared into her eyes. 'I couldn't let them find me.'

She grabbed his hand, holding it tight as if she would never let go again. 'We don't need to do any of this now, Gareth. Let's just draw a line. Yes? You're home and that's all that counts.'

And for a moment it was true, that was all that counted.

CHAPTER FIFTEEN

TIM

'Home,' Tim announced histrionically, pushing through the door into the empty kitchen, and feeling an overwhelming sense of relief that the room was without dogs, without wife and without (what he had come to think of as) the prodigal son.

'My God, this place!' Carla enthused loudly from the hallway behind him, her small, high voice seeming to scratch into the very marrow of the house. The tone sounding so... alien.

'Come through. Come on through,' Tim blustered, pushing the door open a little wider, even though there was already more than enough room for the petite, neatly-modelled Carla to enter. 'Helen's mother,' Tim explained, dropping his voice to a mock whisper, 'she might be sleeping.'

'Wow! This place,' Carla exclaimed again, shooting admiring looks at all the old crud crowding the kitchen.

Odd, Tim thought to himself, how easily impressed people are with anything that is not their own. To Tim, the room suddenly seemed ridiculously large; more museum than home and he wished he'd phoned Helen and asked her to light the fire. For best effect, the fire should be lit so the light could go skittering across the worn flagstones. Then, perhaps, the old beast of a house might begin to warm its bones and look a little more... welcoming.

'It needs some work,' Tim understated, finding a little pleasure in his ability to be pragmatic on the faults of the *grand old place*. But Carla was oblivious, engrossed in the moment and the discovery of this new land, as eager as *Alice*. Her eyes bright with excitement, she turned her attention from the room to the darkening windows and the undiscovered world outside.

'Wow!'

Again, with the wow, and now she was aiming it out onto the festering garden, with its mounds of brambles and toppling arbours. The excitement seemed misplaced to Tim. If she had just discovered Angkor Wat, then perhaps. But the house and gardens were not in the same league. Tim had learnt over the years that Americans have a poor sense of moderation.

Tim hated the garden almost as much as Helen did. But then, that is *responsibility* for you. It has the habit of strangling aesthetic appreciation and murdering spontaneous excitement. If Carla had been the garden's owner, she might well have been more likely to say, 'Fuck!' Instead, she said admiringly,

'How big is the garden?'

'That would be a sore point.' Tim stowed Carla's bag by the door and headed over to the drinks cabinet. 'Two acres of weeds and brambles, delightful.'

Carla nodded, still staring out of the dark window.

'Know what an acre is?' she asked but didn't wait for an answer. 'A unit of land that could be covered in a day by an ox and plough.'

'In which case, that' – Tim nodded his head towards the garden – 'is a thousand acres. It would take years to get your plough through even one bed.'

There was a small rockery just outside the kitchen, its stones hunched inward upon themselves, cowering in the gloom. It showed the imprint of some kind of human intervention; effort had been made at one point in time, but the rest of the garden had been devoured by the overgrown beds. Even in the dimming light of the late afternoon, it was impossible not to see how the land lay.

'Helen's not a big gardener then?' Carla said with not a hint of irony.

'Hates it. An aversion bordering on phobia, or possibly allergy?'

'You're teasing again,' Carla chided.

'On my life. You should see her disgust if she happens to accidentally tune into Gardener's Question Time. My dear wife has a repulsion for all things botanical. She hates the garden, hates flowers. She sometimes fiddles about with the bed just outside the kitchen, the rockery. There are a few...' – he switched his pronunciation – ''erbs, and things.'

She smiled. 'Was that for me? That little bit of Americana there?'

'I speak your lingo,' Tim offered, leaning in towards her slightly. Lessening the distance between them seemed like a good move, in this kitchen where the grandfather clock could just be heard ticking softly in the hallway; time is always against lovers, Tim mused poetically to himself.

'What is a garden without herbs?'

'Exactly, and luckily, Helen likes cooking.'

'I remember you saying, and I've heard people talk.'

He raised his eyebrows.

'The faculty marches on its stomach, and... Helen's got a reputation on the kitchen front. A couple of staff mentioned the *flower* thing as well, so I didn't bring...'

He shook his head in an encouraging manner.

'I thought it must be an allergy?'

'Not exactly. Helen's mother was obsessed with the garden. I guess Helen didn't inherit the gene.'

'It's funny, don't you think? People so often react violently to the likes and dislikes of their parents. But maybe that's just normal? We all want to carve our own world.'

'Possibly, ever since we've been married, Helen's not taken the least bit of interest in it. I told her we should sell some of it off... the garden,' he added as explanation, staring out of the window. And it suddenly occurred to him that it was as if he was proposing to sell a chunk out of the vast, late afternoon, as if they owned the world and this portion of air could be parcelled, packaged and distributed by him and his wife at any point in time. All they needed to do, was agree to sell.

'And she's not interested?' Carla asked, bringing him back to the moment. 'Not open for offers?'

'Nope.' He sighed. 'She won't do a thing. Won't touch it. Won't sell it. Just leaves the whole two acres to rot. I swear one day it'll swallow us up: house, people, cars, everything.'

'A return to nature. Very Rousseau. Where is Helen?'

At the question of his wife's location, Tim suddenly remembered alcohol, and that the sooner the lovely young Carla could have a glass firmly clutched in her hand, and heading towards those pretty red lips, the better.

'She'll be somewhere.' His tone came out flat and disinterested, which was pretty much how he was currently feeling about Helen. 'Can I get you a drink?'

Carla shook her head, raising her lovely slim arms to her face, and pushing her hands through that thick dark hair, letting the bracelet on her wrist jangle softly. 'No, I'm good.'

'I won't argue with that.' Even with his back to her, he could feel her smile.

He pulled open the drinks cabinet and reached inside for the gin. She might not want one, but this was where the weekend started, and he'd earned it. As Carla pointed her toe and ambled off around the kitchen peering into its nooks and crannies, Tim headed to the fridge.

'Hmm... This is...'

Tim turned to find Carla hovering over the large ugly chest.

'Unusual,' she offered.

'Unusual?' He smiled. 'Young lady, you deliver insults with a wonderfully deft touch.'

'No, I just meant...'

'Ugly?' he offered. 'I'd go further. Hideous? Grotesque?' He pretended to slam his toe up against the dark block of wood. 'In a bloody stupid place?'

She laughed.

'Yes' – he nodded slowly – 'all of the above. And yes, I have crippled myself on it many a time. It's a widow's chest.'

Carla's pretty, unlined brow cut into a question mark. 'Meaning?'

Glass in hand, Tim freed an ice cube from its plastic tray and poured the alcohol over. The ice crackled and split, warm against cold, always an interesting combination.

'You sure I can't tempt you?' he asked, holding the glass towards the light where it sparkled.

Again, she shook her head, that pretty hand reaching up in a series of jangles as if to ward off the alcohol.

'She shall have music' circulated around Tim's brain, like the persistent earworm of a trite advertisement, haunting its victim. He glanced back down at the chest, hunched in the corner toad-like.

'Widows,' he began, 'the wealthier ones at least, supposedly had a valuables chest. They stuck all the family silver in, anything of worth, then locked it quick after the man of the house expired. Shoved it in a corner under a few cushions. Hid it before the debtors could get their sticky fingers on the family's goodies.'

'Is it Helen's?'

'Her mother's.'

'Is there anything in it?' Carla pushed her hands gently around the corners of the chest and tried to ease the lid open. She hadn't asked if it was okay to touch, he noticed, but then Americans never did ask. They just assumed that everything was open season unless it was fenced off with security wire, glass shards, and guarded by men in flak jackets.

'Who would know?' He added an air of mystery to his voice.

'Nope. Doesn't budge?' She pushed anyway. Her bracelet jangled, and Tim's earworm took up briefly once again – '*she shall have music*'.

'So it's never opened?' she asked, not taking her eyes from it.

'Not for me.' Tim twirled the ice in his glass, listening as the cubes made that soft high-singing sound that always reminded him of Friday nights. 'Not for anyone. No key,' he stated simply. 'Lost. Been lost...' He paused as if scouring back through his memory, searching out the corners of his archived self for an exact date. He shook his head. 'Way before my time.'

'And how long is that – your time?'

'We've been married...' and he genuinely had to think, because they were not the kind of couple that marked off anniversaries, divided celebrations into 'cutesy' opportunities for, what he tended to think of as moronic present-giving: wood, paper, silver, china – or however it went.

'Almost thirty years.' He hadn't meant for his voice to trail away as it did, into a tone of disappointment. He didn't like how it sounded. Quicky, he raised the glass to his mouth, placing his lips against the cold gin and downing a neat slug.

'What?'

'No, nothing.' He turned away, carried the tonic back to the fridge, the gin back to the drinks cabinet.

'There's something more. I'll pick up on it,' she warned, in her light, teasing tone.

'I'll bet.' He turned to face her. 'They call you Psyche. They say you can unravel a person's soul like a piece of string.'

'They say?' She narrowed her eyes. 'And, who may I ask, are *They*?'

'Students... faculty staff.'

Carla smiled. 'That's quite a quality to have.' She paused for a moment, considering the proposition. 'Hmm. I think I can handle that. I think I like being Psyche – the ancient Greek goddess... gives me an air of gravitas.'

Tim angled his body towards her a little, leaning on the table so that their faces were on a level. 'You are a little like her, it's true.'

Carla laughed. 'Okay, so what is that – upstart American? Because, of course, she wasn't actually a goddess, was she? Just a social-climbing mortal. Wasn't that her story?'

He shrugged. There were no flies on Carla.

'I wasn't thinking of the social climbing, of course, that hadn't crossed my mind. No, I was thinking more of your string of admirers.'

Her involuntary laugh was charming.

'String!' She smiled. 'Oh, come on!'

Tim nodded sagely, always the professor, always the man with all the facts. 'Feminist or no, admirers are a thing you can not deny. But...' He paused, holding her again in his gaze. 'Just like Psyche you're not really playing hard to get, are you? You're just not interested.'

Carla took a deep breath, then paused to hide behind a smile. 'Who's unravelling psyches now?'

Tim took another sip of his drink. He had her now. Flattery

would always do that, if it was played cautiously enough, and provided there was a little chemistry there to begin with.

'They say Psyche inspired the *Beauty and the Beast* story.'

Carla smiled at this new knowledge, pulling her slim hand with its bracelet back over her tightly-clad denim legs.

It was a wonder anyone could fit inside those slim, blue tunnels of material, Tim thought to himself. There certainly wasn't enough room for two. But he barely had time for reflection. He was in hard-sell mode, and the thing he was selling was him.

'Psyche was able to look past outward appearances to see the good in a person's soul.' He shot her a look of absolute sincerity. He knew what he was doing; it was a look he used often.

'I'm glad you came,' he said, brushing her leg simply with the palm of his right hand. It was just a brief touch. It didn't linger or hold. The hand was away before there could be any possible objection. But the contact had been established.

'Glad? That one's obvious.' Her voice was low, barely audible.

'I admire your work,' he stated. 'Your opinion.'

Carla stepped away from the table, away from the range of easy contact. 'You should be careful.'

There was a creak from the stairway. Outside the room, someone was moving.

'Besides, sounds like your wife is in the building.'

He leaned forward a little more. He wanted Carla to be in full control of the facts. 'That, does not dilute my admiration.'

But Carla just smiled and stepped back again, stepped back just in time, as the door flew open.

'I've put Gareth in his old room.' Helen was talking before she entered. There was no hello, no pleasantries. As always, she was launching herself with well-practised gusto into the domestic logistics. Tim often wondered if this habit was used in order to plaster over the cracks in their relationship. There had been a time when she had smiled when he came through the door at the end of the day, now she was more likely to give him a blow-by-blow account of how she had cleaned out the filter in the dishwasher.

'I hope he'll be warm enough,' she continued, still no hello or nod to Carla. It was almost as if Carla were a servant, standing outside the inner sanctum, not worthy of acknowledgement.

'Can you move the radiator in later, Tim?'

'Yes, of course. You know Carla.' Tim took hold of the conversation.

'Carla?' Helen puzzled over the name. 'I'm not sure we've met.'

Helen, Tim noticed, did not take Carla's offered hand, but the young American managed to draw it back so effortlessly that the gesture didn't appear to be a snub.

'Your face seems familiar.' Helen squinted, running her eyes over Carla's features, before shaking her head dismissively as if remembering really was all way too much trouble. 'Maybe it's just one of those faces.'

Carla smiled, not a trace of a bruise from the snub. In fact, Tim noticed, Carla's smile held more than a touch of amusement.

'I'm disappointed,' Carla said lightly, 'I'd been under the impression that the face was unique. All mine. We live and learn.'

Helen stared glassy-eyed, and Tim wondered for an awful moment if she were about to unleash her wrath, but the moment passed. Her eyes softened. Carla, no doubt, was not worth the effort.

'I hope I'm not putting you out?' Carla offered, as Helen

SHIRLEY DAY

grabbed the ironing board from the corner. Helen didn't reply. For a moment the awkward silence was broken only by the clatter of the board being set on its legs.

'So, do tell... what's he like?' Tim asked, genuinely curious.

Helen shrugged, in that irritating way that she had, as if the question was imbecilic.

'Well? Has he changed?'

She slammed the iron down on the board; steam shot through the nozzle reaching up vertically towards the ceiling in a scalding hiss.

'We've all changed, Tim,' she offered pragmatically, laying the linen tablecloth over the board, and flattening its edges with her palms. 'But Gareth's home now.' The iron sighed for her.

Tim nodded, but felt somehow unsatisfied – he wasn't getting the answers he wanted; the ones Carla wanted. The interesting ones. They needed more story. Helen was slipping out of his fingers at every turn.

'Of course he's home, but... for how long, Helen?'

'Shall I go?' Carla's voice oozed absolute tact. 'I should give you two some space.'

Helen put the iron back down on the board rather sharply. This time the steam sprayed out dangerously on all sides as she dragged the hot iron across the white cloth, but Carla's question remained unanswered.

'Your brother?' Tim asked again. 'How long will he be staying?'

'Tim! How would I know? It is his house too,' she bit back.

Tim drained his drink, mumbling bitterly under his breath, 'So I've been told.'

'I'm sorry if I'm intruding,' Carla said gently. But her voice was sounding awkward now. This situation was no longer amusing. It was the kind of thing anyone in their right mind would want to avoid, and between the awkward interactions, the silences seemed to be opening up like black holes.

Grasping the tablecloth up from the board, Helen moved towards the table, nudging Tim slightly from what he had begun to think of as – his corner.

'You're here now, Carla,' Helen said without bothering to look at the young woman, throwing the white sheet up into the air, and letting it float down across the table like a shroud. 'You've got clean towels in your room.'

Tim noticed that Helen seemed to take great relish in this statement. He had no idea why clean towels should prove so satisfying.

Taking her flat palm, Helen ran it gently down the centre of the table, easing away what remained of the ridges. 'Your room is comfortable enough,' she continued, again without looking.

'Oh, I'm sure...' Carla began, but Helen appeared to have no time to spend waiting for the full answer, and cut into Carla's sentence dismissively.

'I understand you two have *work* to do?'

Was there a note of sarcasm? Perhaps he'd imagined it. Helen was brusque at the best of times.

'Work, yes.' Carla nodded innocently.

'For the book,' Tim rushed in.

'Good. Then you will both be occupied.' Helen took a moment to stand back and examine the table. Satisfied, she took the knives from the counter by the sink and began to polish.

'I'll just dump my stuff upstairs,' Carla said, indicating the stairs, jangling her bracelet as she did. 'Might try and grab a walk before it's totally black out there.'

'It's getting late,' Tim protested.

Carla peered out from the window into the darkening gloom. 'I think there's a good thirty minutes before lights out, and I'll take a torch.' Carla turned to Helen. 'You're close to the beach I understand?'

'There's a footpath. It's fifteen minutes, depending on how you walk.' Helen glanced at Carla's shoes: the narrow heel. 'You can take my boots. If they don't fit, wear extra socks.'

'I'm sure they'll be...'

But again, Helen did not wait. 'The boots are by the door.' She indicated the utility room just off the kitchen.

'And a coat. You'll need a thicker coat, no doubt,' Tim added helpfully.

'Have one in my case,' Carla stated simply.

'I could come with you?' Tim offered.

'There's really no need. I don't want to...'

'Impose,' Helen said quietly, her head still bent over the knives as she polished.

'Nonsense,' Tim blustered.

He was going into mother-hen mode, he chided himself – that was always an unattractive disposition in a man. Alpha male, that's what he needed, a little more Alpha. 'The path's not straightforward, and once you lose the light, those mudflats can be pretty treacherous if you don't know your way.'

'Okay. Company would be great if I'm not...'

'No. You're really not. The walk will do him good,' Helen said simply, absolutely. Putting an end to it. It took Tim a moment to catch on. He could have said something. He wasn't sure he liked being talked about in that way, like a dog, but... if he said anything it could all blow up. Besides, he wanted to get out.

Carla grabbed her bag from beside the door. 'I'll just dump my stuff.'

'Upstairs, down the corridor to the right, first door on the left,' Helen issued, without looking.

'Right,' Carla said, closing the door gently behind her.

'Everything okay?' Tim asked.

'Hadn't you better change for your walk?' Helen began to lay the settings, her trained eye putting the cutlery into place as if the tablecloth were dissected into a neat geographical grid.

'I'm fine,' Tim countered. 'What did he say?'

'Nothing.' She shrugged, continuing around the table. 'Nothing was said.'

Tim suddenly felt a wave of irritation. Couldn't Helen understand, didn't she see that this was his house too? It really was. Banks have no truck with emotional house-owning; you don't pay the bills and the mortgage, you don't keep the house. 'Well, how long is he staying?'

'It's not important, Tim, how long he's staying. We lost a lifetime,' she murmured.

'That's a bit melodramatic, don't you think, Helen?'

'But true. The book.' Helen indicated towards the stairs. 'Are you sleeping with her?'

Hurt indignation was always the best counter for such an attack and he was good at it. 'Helen!'

'Well,' she continued, 'are you?'

Tim pulled his wide hands through the grey, thinning hair which was still, thankfully, clinging to his scalp. 'I heard what you said. My God, Helen... She's... she's half my age!'

'I certainly won't argue with that.'

'You can't just accuse someone of...'

'Of what? Something they've done before? Something that's part of their nature? Of what they are? What they've always been. For Christ's sake, Tim. You really are too old. We're all too old. Take a look in the mirror... a long hard look. Don't embarrass yourself.'

They waited in silence. Helen shifting things around the table, Tim feeling deflated. He had had such high hopes for this weekend.

When Carla entered again, she'd changed into a thick snow-white jumper that clung to her body as if she had been sewn into it, and Tim realised that he didn't want to be too old. He didn't feel too old. And he realised something more – he could feel a damn sight younger given the right company.

'Shall we go?' Carla announced brightly.

'Absolutely.'

'Do you need to change?' Carla asked.

But Tim wasn't going to do that, because if he did, he would have to leave Carla with Helen, and once Helen was in one of her moods, Tim was fully convinced that it wasn't safe to leave Helen with anybody.

CHAPTER SIXTEEN

HELEN

'Did I miss something?'

Helen turned to see Gareth. He had washed, she thought, or at least freshened up a little. His features seemed hydrated, less lined. Though perhaps she was just getting used to the fact that his face was wearing more skin than it used to.

'Tim, my husband, and his *"friend"*. They've gone for a walk. Not that they'll see much. It'll be dark soon.' She closed the door to the wood burner. The flames could be seen flickering like thin snakes' tongues through the small glass window. It should take. Her fires always took.

'You still walk?' he asked.

'I have the dogs. I sometimes walk down Green Lane, not all the way into town, but...'

'Remember the ice creams?'

'I've got a freezer now,' she said, and wondered why she'd said it. She had meant that now that she had the freezer there was no longer the need to walk for ice creams, but the words had somehow come out wrong.

'Did Mother recognise you?' she said, changing the subject.

'As Uncle Charlie.'

'She spoke?' Helen was impressed. 'You're privileged. Mother doesn't often speak.'

'Do we even have an Uncle Charlie?'

They were a small family. As far as Helen knew there were no uncles or aunts, not real ones anyway. The seventies and eighties had been a makeshift decade. The nuclear family, in its search for jobs and personal space, had itself been nuked. In the vacuum it created, people promoted friends to key family positions. There had been a sudden proliferation of pseudo aunt and uncle 'upgrading'. An odd habit, Helen thought, and confusing, because it was so difficult to keep up with. As far as true blood relatives were concerned, Helen was pretty sure they had always been alone – a fact she was secretly proud of. The mould had been broken after Helen and Gareth.

'She didn't seem to like Uncle Charlie much,' he added. 'But I didn't bother to correct her.'

'She would have liked you less.'

Gareth gave a snort of amusement, before taking in the room. Giving it that inevitable inventory that she had known he would. She followed his gaze; the bare flagstone floors, the fire now smouldering. The sink units had been privileged – they'd received a small overhaul; the worktops replaced with new wood, which was now old. Yellowed and stained, they looked exactly as the originals had done. He wouldn't have noticed the change. There were no pictures, as was always the case, but the small rustic shelf beside the table now contained cookery books, not gardening manuals. She saw his eyes glance over the spines. The kitchen table was the same. Helen had sat at that very table all her life. In fact, it wasn't really a table; it was the bottom of a dresser and barely up for the job. It had been difficult, as they had grown larger, fitting their legs underneath. There was not enough space between the chair and the tabletop. The wide drawers that ran down what would once have been the front of the dresser, always stuck when you pulled them out. If yanked too hard, the table had the habit of pursuing its assailant, scraping its reluctant feet across the flagstones after whoever had done the pulling.

Gareth must have remembered, she felt, because he pulled the drawer out as if testing it. It didn't exactly glide, but it didn't stick either.

'I had it filed,' she explained. 'Such a simple operation, goodness knows why Mother never sorted it.' But as soon as the words were out of her mouth, Helen realised she didn't want to keep bringing Mother in. Mother was best left upstairs exactly where she was, lost in time.

'How long are you staying?' Helen hoped beyond hope that he would be unable to give her a straight answer.

Gareth took a deep slug of air. 'The weekend. I'm leaving the country.'

Helen's heart seemed to falter. Her knees were suddenly unstable. She leant heavily on the hard Belfast sink, turning away from him so he wouldn't notice the disappointment, the heartbreak.

'America, that's the plan.'

'America!' She was glad that her face was turned away. She felt as if her world was being invaded. First that Carla woman and now this. 'Why America? What are you doing? What business do you have in America?'

He shrugged. 'The usual.'

'Usual?'

But he failed to enlighten her.

'And why America? That's so... so far.'

'The world's smaller than it used to be.'

Helen didn't think so. Not for her. Beyond the house the world seemed vast and unfriendly.

'It's not as far as Australia.'

'True.' Hold on to the little things, the small things, the gifts, she told herself. But no, the thought of him leaving didn't sit well. She was going to have to work on that a little.

'It is still a very long way. You've only just got back,' she stated simply. 'Why the rush?'

But he said nothing and the silence seemed to yawn between them just like all those years. 'I made up your old room. All your things are still around. In the attic or under the bed. Not that your clothes would fit. How tall are you? Goodness!' She laughed. 'I sound like some maiden aunt.' But the laughter didn't last, because it was only laughing at herself, not genuine humour, and there was so much lost, so many pieces that wouldn't fit back together again. And now there wasn't the time. Pragmatism, she thought to herself; use that as your rock. He's here now. 'I thought you would want your old room back. And because this *woman* is staying.'

He looked blank.

'Tim, my husband, his girl, a lecturer. Well, she's staying. Ridiculous, because we don't have people staying, hardly ever. I put her in the guest room. It's still damp.'

She wished she could stop talking. He wasn't interested. How could he be interested in Tim's stupid fuck-up.

'That's fine,' Gareth said, oblivious. 'I mean the room arrangement, not being in the guest room. It's fine.'

'It's a horrible room anyway, always cold.'

'It'll be great, wherever I am.'

Helen nodded. But she didn't want to talk about the house. Why was she droning on about all these things that just did not matter? 'Where did you go?' she asked quietly.

'Long story.'

She turned to catch his eye, but he wasn't looking at her, instead he was scanning her shelves, examining a row of crystal glasses.

'I have time for long stories.'

'This place hasn't changed.' He pulled the drawer out once again, testing, testing.

'It all works now,' she stated simply, 'well, mostly.'

He looked around him, into the gathering gloom. 'You should get a new kitchen.'

'The kitchen's fine.'

'Mother seems frail?'

'Don't be taken in.' Helen placed the kettle beneath the tap. 'Underneath that papery, yellow skin there's a tough old goat still bleating to get out. Do you want tea or coffee? Christ, I don't even know what you drink!' She put the kettle down heavily on the surface as if it weighed far too much. 'How bizarre.'

'Coffee. I drink it black, no sugar.'

'Very cosmopolitan.'

'More economical. I don't like to cause a fuss, and instant's fine.'

'Well, that's a relief. We haven't quite caught up with the times yet.' She smiled, drinking him in. 'Let me look at you again.' She took a step towards him. 'Let me see you.' It was a real man's face now. The boy had gone. It was just the last remnants of young Gareth still peeping out through those cloudy eyes. 'Where did you go? I would have walked past you in the street.' The realisation seemed to take a chunk out of her heart. 'I would have walked straight past you. I wouldn't have known it was you.'

'I would have known you, Helen.'

'And...' She hesitated, not even sure that she wanted the answer to her next question. But yes, she had to know, had to ask. 'And if you had seen me, Gareth, would you have stopped me?'

'Of course.'

He was quick to reassure. She tapped her fingers rhythmically against the draining board, listening to the water in the kettle as it began to sing which seemed to force the question up in her mind – could he be trusted?

'Because, not a word, Gareth. All that time, and I...' Her voice faded.

'Don't.'

She turned on him. 'Have you told anyone?'

There was a pause, a beat too long.

'Gareth?' Her voice sounded too shrill, even in her own ears.

He looked up at her, held her with those unflinching eyes.

'I wonder, I wonder if we don't confess, how will we manage to forgive ourselves?'

The words somehow didn't sound like his. They sounded more like some self-help manual.

'Seriously?' she scoffed. 'People only confess because they're weak. Forgiveness? No one can know. You need to talk to someone about it. You find me.'

She placed the kettle down on the unit so it stopped screaming and turned back to him. Eyeing him carefully as if looking for cracks. He looked as solid as ever. 'Stay off the self-help. Families sort their own problems.' She moved towards him, raising one hand to his shoulder, plucking imaginary fluff from his jumper, an excuse just to touch him. 'All grown up,' she stated, as if they had gone to bed one night as young teens and woken in the morning to this; their bodies swapped for something else, something heavier, and uglier.

'You look tired,' she said, 'but then men are lucky. They can get away with *tired*. You look good.'

'Tired but good,' he repeated, his voice a little warmer she noticed.

There was just a touch of amusement, finally.

'And you?' he asked.

'Not the same, sadly. I've changed, of course: I'm older, less... less lovely. I miss that. The loveliness.'

'What's the alternative?'

For a moment there was silence. They both knew what the alternative to ageing was.

She took the mugs from the cupboard and placed the teabags in the pot. Life goes on in all the little ways, no matter what you do.

'Helen?'

She knew from the tone of his voice what he was about to ask. She had always known that if he did come back he would ask it. She had, however, hoped they could have had some kind of new experience before they started digging up the past. Some moment of joy that would have made everything worthwhile.

'Where is it? What did you do with it?'

She sighed, Tim and his girl would be back soon. They had the weekend. Did everything really have to be condensed into this first meeting? She refused to let that happen. 'Don't let's start this now.'

But Gareth had changed. He wasn't the boy who had left home all those years ago. He pulled her around sharply so that she was facing him.

'I need to know where you put it.'

'Gareth.' She glanced down at his hand manacling her arm. He followed her gaze. Her flesh sat white under his fingers. He was holding her too tight. 'Temper,' she said, letting the word hang for a moment, letting it ring out into the kitchen. Because they both knew that he had a temper. His fingers flicked open like an automatic catch. The arm was released. She rubbed her palm gently across her skin, but not to ease any pain. Curiously, she liked the pain: the sense of pressure, of reality.

'Let's just leave it for the moment, Gareth. Let's...' She reached out towards his left hand, the one with the strawberry-red mark. 'There's enough time. We have the whole weekend.'

She managed to keep the sarcasm from her voice. Was that seriously all he intended to give her? Was that all she was worth? She would have loved to scream, to open her mouth wide, to raise her chin to the ceiling and holler. But Helen did not scream.

'Helen?'

And she would not be drawn. She pressed her index finger neatly across his lips. 'Shh.'

Irritated, he pulled away, turning back towards the old shelf with its line of cookery books. 'This used to be gardening stuff?'

'There's a book on herbs.' Helen shrugged.

'She asked about the garden.'

'Mother? Quite a chat you two had. What did you tell her?'

He'd seen the garden when he arrived. He hadn't walked around it, but even from the small strip from gate to house, he must have seen what had happened. The gravel driveway, once neat and orderly, lined with lavender, was now potholed. The lavender drowned and woody under brambles. The beds, overgrown and choked.

'So, what did you say to Mother?'

'I didn't mention the garden. I could see it wasn't one of your priorities.'

Helen smiled. 'So true, but actually it's all we talk about; splitting the geraniums, deadheading the roses. This morning she had me staking the delphiniums.'

'In October?'

'I don't argue. There are battles it's worth digging in for, but when you're dealing with a woman whose brain is only partially functioning, you pick and choose. We do verbal gardening. Her favourite is to talk of staking delphiniums. When she's really cross with me, she gets me to dig chicken pellets into the vegetable patch.'

Gareth winced visibly. 'Know what? I can still smell them.'

'Once you've smelt that hot fuggy chicken shit aroma, you rarely forget it. Not even with Alzheimer's. She still knows it's punishment and so even now,' Helen continued, 'even though I know there is no vegetable patch or need of chicken shit. Even now, it gets to me.'

'Probably why she does it?'

'You overestimate her ability.' Helen shook her head as if trying to dislodge an unpleasant thought. 'Enough. Let's leave Mother where she is. So, what's your garden like then?'

He raised one eyebrow, a new mannerism surely? One that could only be adopted or taken seriously, if a person had more than a couple of decades under their belt.

'My garden will be communal and filled with large concrete slabs, if I have my way.'

'Sounds perfect.'

She smiled, then turned back to the empty mugs, shaking the instant from the jar, letting a moment of silence descend, with only the grandfather clock from the hallway speaking.

'Remember when we built that rockery, Helen?'

But she didn't want to remember. She didn't want to remember anything about that summer.

'It was just before...'

'Gareth, it was a long time ago.'

'Why did we do that, Helen?' He wasn't going to let it drop.

The grandfather clock continued pounding into the silence, but Helen would not be drawn.

'Helen?' he probed. 'Why did we build the rockery that summer?'

'Oh, come on, Gareth. Give me credit. I told you, no one will find it.'

But he wasn't happy, and her heart sank as she realised – this was why he'd returned. He wasn't coming back for her. He wanted information.

'But they found the watch.'

'So. It was just a watch.'

'If they found that then...'

'No.' She cut it dead. She would tell him nothing. What possible good could it serve?

He nodded, finally getting the picture? She hoped so. She handed him his coffee and poured a tea for herself. 'The police questioned me, but there wasn't any heat in it.'

'Did they ask about me?'

'Yes, they wanted to know who was living here at the time.'

'What did you tell them?'

'I said we were estranged.' The word made her wince. 'I told them we had no idea where you were. Which was true.'

He nodded.

'They're not interested.' She wanted to add that there was no body, but that would just start the conversation up again. 'It was simply routine. They'll have filled the report and forgotten about it. The people who found the watch, the police will no doubt give it back to them. A father and son. They were out metal-detecting would you believe.'

'I read the article in the paper.'

She smiled simply, shrugging her shoulders as if to say – well then, case closed. He took a sip of his coffee.

'You should come out, when I get settled.'

But Helen felt the bitterness rising, she wasn't interested in Gareth's *new life*. Truth be told, she found it insulting. All this talk of new lives, of fresh starts, of going forward, alone away from the house. All those possibilities, they were only ever for someone else, not for Helen. She was going to be abandoned, once again; left to stand sentry over their lives.

'They've been a long time.' There was an awkwardness to Gareth's voice when he eventually spoke. Perhaps he had picked up on the fact that this was all sadly familiar; that there was a pattern here – she was being deserted, and for a moment she couldn't place who he was talking about. Who had been gone? Who mattered enough to bring into her kitchen? Then she remembered: Tim and his girl.

'I don't care about them. I don't care if they drop off the edge of the world.'

'What?'

'Nothing.' But, how could he be concerned with these other people?

'What is it?' he asked. 'Reproach? Is it reproach, Helen? Your mood, your attitude.'

She wondered briefly how they differed, reproach and bitterness?

'No.'

'Then resentment? You don't play the martyr well, Helen.'

'Gareth, stop it.' And she wished she had saved the ironing, or the dressing, or the cutlery. She wished she had something substantial to do. She pulled the glasses from the cupboard and began to fill them with water. 'I'm not playing at martyrs, Gareth.' Martyrdom was always a trait she despised.

'Then why stay? You don't owe Mother anything.'

'You know that I can't leave. If you think about it, if you really think it through, you must realise that. Besides, Mother needs looking after.'

'But here?'

There was a moment's silence before he continued.

'I can pay for a home.'

'So the streets of London really were paved with gold,' she scoffed. 'Next you'll be offering me a facelift and a tummy tuck, just for old times' sake.'

Suddenly he looked old, a deep-set exhaustion pushing his shoulders down and he dropped himself into the chair by the fire. 'I'm just trying to help. And surgery?' He rubbed his face wearily with his hands. 'Don't even joke about it, any sort of clinic. You must know that?'

She moved towards him and gently, hesitantly reached out her hand to touch his hair as if he were a child.

When he spoke again his voice was slow and deliberate. 'I wasn't trying to buy you off.'

She sank down beside the fire, her body resting against his legs, her long, slim arm draping across his knees.

'That's because you can't buy me off, Gareth, it doesn't work like that.'

'No, of course. I just meant that I couldn't look after her, not after what happened.'

'It's the only way. You have to come to terms with people, events. If you don't...' She paused, because she knew what the alternative was, and she had walked so close to its gaping jaws. 'I'm not willing to do that, to give her that power over me. So, I let it go. It's like you, sitting here in my kitchen in all your beauty... sitting here after all those years. I have to let the anger go. If I don't, I'll destroy the moment, taint it, chase it away. Murder the joy out of it.'

'But Mother?'

'No, Gareth.'

'You can't expect me to believe that it's all forgotten?'

Somewhere from the depths of the house came the haunting, high-pitched sound of a bell.

'Mother,' Helen stated simply, sadly. 'She has a bell.'

108

Slowly, she got to her feet. But Gareth reached out for her hand, holding her fingers gently between his own. 'Leave her.'

She smiled sadly.

'Leave her,' he said once again.

But deep down they both knew that wasn't possible.

CHAPTER SEVENTEEN

HELEN

Later that evening, when Helen came back down the stairs she was aware that the house was flexing its internal organs. The radiators were pumping and clattering and the pipes gave out intermittent high-pitched notes as if preparing to sing. People were having baths and showers. One bath, and there would be a single, monotone hum; two meant a chamber recital. Two baths and shower, or possibly even a handbasin, and the house would provide enough background noise for an orchestra. She listened with her trained ear. Tim was most definitely in their en suite shower, and Gareth must be running the bath, the old roll-top that had been sandwiched between the siblings' bedrooms. They would be getting ready for the meal. But there were no sounds of Carla's ablutions. Helen hoped the American was not one of those tedious women who 'forget' to get ready and then insist on keeping the whole party waiting. As hostess, Helen did not have the luxury of a long soak, or a fey attitude. She had food to prep and besides she didn't want to be parted from Gareth for a moment more than was absolutely necessary. She had kept her make-up simple, but chosen carefully: a light-red lipstick, pale powder, a dab of foundation, and the sixties-style black eyeliner that had been her signature as a young woman – classic and simple. She could still draw a neat, straight line over her top eyelid. Though now her fingers had to be held at an awkward angle, dangling above her reading glasses and blocking her vision. It was a tricky manoeuvre, but Helen had always been a person more than willing to accept a challenge. She went for a quick spray of Coco Mademoiselle behind her ears; it was not a scent Gareth would remember from those final years at home, but she was a bit old for Charlie or Rebel, the adolescent smells of her teenage years. She had dressed in an understated, black, Jaeger V-neck and tight, above-the-knee skirt, with thick black tights, and slim-fit Russell & Bromley boots. She looked good, credit where credit was due.

She pushed open the door to the kitchen, and there he was – sitting in the chair in front of the fire. She couldn't see his body at first, but she could see those cheap black shoes. The ones he always wore. Closing the door behind her, Helen decided she would not talk. He had not been invited. There was, in point of fact, never an invitation. He looked older, Helen thought, before turning her face away.

'You've a bit of time then, before the celebrations?' Father Wright said, leaning forward from the chair into the light cast by the fire, a half-smile on his face.

'Everything under control?' He shifted slightly as if settling in for the evening. 'Everyone otherwise engaged.'

She didn't want to indulge him, so she moved to the baking tray and began to lay the crostini out in four neat rows.

'It's nice,' the priest continued. 'When the house is so quiet... the lull before the storm.'

And as if on cue, the wind rattled at the sash windows.

Helen stared out at the night. Looking anxiously into the darkness. 'I should lock the chickens in.' She felt a brief stab of irritation, wishing she'd thought to do it earlier. She would be bound to get muck on her boots or tights. Her hair would get crushed or tangled.

'That wasn't what I meant when I said *storm*,' Father Wright came back. 'And you know it. That wasn't what I meant at all.' The old priest looked towards the door, but she was safe; he rarely ventured out of the kitchen.

He let out a long sigh. 'That brother of yours.' He nodded. 'We both know what he's like. The effect he has.'

Helen said nothing. She could well remember the effect Gareth had. She had been picking up the pieces since the last outburst for a good portion of her life, so she hardly needed reminding. She began to cut the cheese into slices.

'A butterfly flaps its wings,' Wright offered cryptically.

'They'll be down soon.'

'Don't you go worrying your head about that now. Want me gone?'

She didn't reply. The answer was as clear as if she had thrown back her head and shouted at the old man, '*Get the fuck out.*' Not that it would do any good. Not that it ever did. He drew a breath in through the gap in his teeth, a habit he had which allowed him to stall for time. Helen cringed; it always made a short whistling sound. His habits sickened her.

'Don't you worry your head. By the time all your guests get down here I'll be out of your hair. Best if I avoid your man.'

Helen pulled back one of the chairs, a chair that appeared to be waiting so patiently at the dining table, and sat down heavily, leaning her face in her hands.

'Because, I was the one who told your mother she should send him away. Remember?'

Helen said nothing.

'Remember?' he said again.

'I remember,' her voice came, barely audible.

'Course you do. I could see what was happening...

happening right there under her nose. Sometimes you have to be on the outside to see it, to see what's really going on. Don't you think, Helen?'

'It was all a long time ago,' she mumbled.

'Yesterday. For you and me both.' He paused for a moment before sticking out his fat tongue and licking his lips. 'Aye.' He nodded. 'It was a hot summer, that last summer, the one before he left. Remember? The whole country was burning up, parched. But your mother's garden; I don't think I'd ever seen such roses. She was careful, see? Knew when to water, how to prepare the soil. It was the beginning of the summer,' he continued, closing his eyes momentarily, as if he could almost feel the sun on his skin, 'and the heat... the heat still seemed like a novelty. Like a first kiss. Eh, Helen? A first kiss.'

She'd had enough now. She stood and walked to the dishwasher, opened the drawer and began to unpack. But even the clash of crockery failed to stop him. He had set himself firmly onto the tracks of his story and would doggedly follow every inch of it through.

'Nothing was jaded. The vegetables that would shrivel, that would eventually rot, gape open, bloat with flies and maggots, they were still intact. Perfect, sealed flesh, no wounds.'

Why did he keep on, talking, talking, always talking. She pulled out the cutlery drawer; the silverware crashed angrily, steel against steel, as if a battle were happening right there in the drawer, knives against knives, forks against forks, but she could still hear his voice.

'I'd come around that day... as usual... about teatime. Arrived in time for tea. She always did treasure my visits – your mother. We were by the potting shed, and the sun scorching down, sheltering there by the wall. She wanted to pick me some flowers. A beautiful, yellow tea rose, a hybrid, I seem to remember. Didn't even have its own name. But...' and he inhaled. 'Ah the perfume. Yellow. Yellow is for treachery, Helen. That's what I told her. Told your mother that, and then I said to her "ahh but... isn't it pretty with it?"' He smiled to himself, nodding his head gently. Remembering it all like it was yesterday. 'She'd picked a couple of blooms you see, and she said, and I remember her words, because it hit home, under the circumstances. I thought it very astute, and yet, she was not an astute woman, your mother. That was not, I would say, one of her qualities. She said, and I remember so clearly, "the blooms are not what you want, Father. By the time a flower has bloomed it's only days away from decay. We should pick you some buds," she said, your mother. "Because the flower is never so beautiful as when it's in bud." And out of the corner of my eye, all the while as she was speaking, I could see you and your brother lying there at the edge of the garden under the apple tree. He was lying on the ground staring up at the sun, and you.' Father Wright paused, and looked straight at her, holding her there locked in his eyes. 'You were lying beside him, lying on your stomach, your brown legs naked, stretching away like grass snakes, and your hair: long fine strands. You wore it long then... falling free down over your shoulders onto young Gareth, onto his body like silk rope. He was running a flower over your arms, your bare shoulders, up, up, up to your face, making you laugh. But you never pulled away. Never left him. Just hovered there close, as if some portion of your body were glued to his.'

The priest shifted in his chair, an involuntary shiver passing over him. He put the palms of his hands out, nearer the wood burner, attempting to draw a little warmth into his body. 'Well, I thought to myself, time to take matters into my own hands. That's what I thought, Helen. So, I took the opportunity, the quiet of the potting shed, the cool of the shade. I said to your mother, reminded her how the devil finds work for idle hands. How perhaps it would be a good idea for the lad to spend some time away, some formative recreation, a retreat, and wasn't it a coincidence, didn't I just know of a place organised for the summer. A camp solely for boys, run by the Christian Brothers. I thought that would do nicely. That was, so to speak, what was needed. And that was the first time he went away.'

A blast of wind rattled the sash. Outside in the garden, a door banged open and shut on its hinges: the chicken run.

'He's just got back!' she said bitterly. 'I don't want to think about this now.'

The door banged again.

'I don't want this rattling around in my brain.'

The priest nodded and sat back in his chair. 'No,' he said simply. 'It was that summer though. That was when everything started.'

She stood, pushing her chair behind her across the flagstones. 'I'm going to secure the chickens.'

'That would be best,' he offered up. 'You know what chickens are like, either too broody or too flighty. Either way they'll break the shells.'

Helen grabbed her wool coat from the hook by the door.

'Or the fox. That door bangs open even for a moment and he's in there quick as a flash.'

She pulled her coat around her, buttoned two of the large circular buttons to hold it in place, then pushed out of the back door.

'Quick as a flash,' she heard the priest repeating behind her as she stepped out into the wind. Out into the cold and took a deep breath of autumn air, thankful to be out of earshot.

CHAPTER EIGHTEEN

TIM

The grandfather clock in the hall read eight as Tim pulled himself around the newel post and set himself in the right direction for the kitchen. He could tell someone was already down; he could hear someone tapping the table gently as if marking out some inner tune. Probably Helen. She was not in their room. But as he drew towards the door, he saw it was a man hunched over the kitchen table. Tim couldn't help but feel mild irritation. He didn't like people in his kitchen, at least not sat like that, sat as if they had grown like an oak out of the cracks in the stone floor. There was an air of ownership that Tim found particularly distasteful. Gareth, he noticed, was smartly dressed, his hair neatly cut. Tim disliked him already, but that was all right. Hopefully he would not be staying long.

'You must be Gareth,' Tim said, extending his hand.

The eyes were the same intense green as Helen's. The build was more bulldog than Tim's own slim frame. A rugby player, Tim would have said, once upon a time. Though since Gareth had absented himself early from high school, this phase would have probably passed him by.

Gareth didn't bother to stand or look up when Tim entered, but took the proffered hand anyway.

'Tim,' Tim explained, watching as his own arm was raised then lowered.

There was no light of recognition, or even interest in Gareth's eyes.

'Helen's husband?' Tim offered, noticing in the same instance that one of the 'best' crystal whisky glasses was sitting on the linen tablecloth in a small ring of water. This was irritating. But Gareth was a guest. Tim needed to tread carefully.

'You're different from how I imagined,' Tim said.

'Oh.' Gareth's voice was flat.

This was a man, Tim thought, that didn't care much about the opinions of others.

'Yes. You've had quite a build-up. I kind of expected horns and a long forked tail.'

Gareth half-smiled, amused. 'My PR machine seems to have preceded me. In fact, I'm very ordinary.'

Tim doubted that. Who in their right minds would describe themselves as 'ordinary'. He poured himself a shot of the whisky.

'But I suppose it is good to know that I was remembered.'

'Oh yes.' Tim smiled coldly. 'Quite the unseen presence.' He sat down opposite Gareth, positioned himself so he could get a better look.

Somewhere in the room a fly buzzed.

'I expected someone more...' But what had he expected? More what? The image had never been fleshed out. There were no photos. He supposed he had expected more of an elemental force, a dark, brooding, Heathcliff type. 'More...' But he couldn't exactly confess to *Heathcliff*. 'You have the look of her – Helen. There's definitely a family resemblance.'

The fly came to rest on the table. Gareth drained the last mouthful from his glass, and then, to Tim's surprise brought the cup down over the fly, trapping it on the inside.

Of course, Tim thought, he'd been told about this childhood foible. The trapped insects. How very curious.

'What's all that about then?' he asked.

'This?' Gareth held his index finger gently over the glass. 'I like insects,' he explained, his voice a slow weathered drawl. 'Like to trap them under glasses, beakers, anything transparent. It has to be transparent.'

He lowered his face so that it was in line with the glass. 'I like the way they look at me, gaze out at me from under their glass houses.'

'Houses?' Tim repeated. 'You call them houses?'

Gareth nodded his head slowly, still looking intently at the fly.

'Not prisons?'

Gareth shrugged. 'Maybe it's the same thing.'

Tim bent closer to the glass, to get a better look. 'What is it, a fly but...?' The back of the fly was a shiny green colour. 'A bluebottle?'

Tim wrinkled his nose in disgust. It was October. It should be dead by now, but that late summer heat which was clinging to the country by its fingernails had fooled an entire species. 'Gross creatures. Every human tragedy, the only thing that wins in the end is the flies. They gorge themselves on our despair. Come Armageddon and they'll be having a right royal knees-up. It looks bigger under there, more self-important. Ugly bastard.'

'I like spiders best,' Gareth stated simply.

Tim wondered if Gareth was all there. Perhaps Gareth was a bit simple? Or perhaps he was autistic? There was a definite lack of social skills. That kind of thing would have gone undiagnosed when the siblings were growing up. Perhaps this visit would be good. A lot of mysteries could be put to bed. The enigma that had been the brother could be deflated and put to rest. He stood, went to the drinks cabinet, but as he pulled out the whisky he felt the resentment creeping back in. There was not a lot left in the bottle.

'I see you helped yourself?'

'I didn't think you would mind.'

Tim hesitated for a moment. He most definitely did *mind*, but now was not the time.

'You said you like spiders best?' He poured the remaining whisky into his own glass, trying to quell his irritation as he finished it off in one gulp. 'Are spiders technically speaking even insects?'

Gareth smiled to himself. The smile was irritating. Smug, Tim felt.

'Spiders are arachnids. But I observe them in the same way. I'm able to watch. They have eight eyes, but their eyesight's still crap. Bit of a cruel joke that, don't you think?'

Tim shrugged. 'Mother Nature's sense of humour. She's a hard woman to please.' He lifted the glass prison from the fly, turned it quickly and brought it back down on the insect.

'Wedding present,' Tim said, taking the glass away. 'Best kept safe.'

He knocked the body of the fly into the bin, before rinsing the base of the glass and putting it beside the sink for Helen to wash later.

'Ever heard of Macdonald?' Tim asked. 'His triad.' He took another bottle from the cabinet, twisted the cap and poured a generous couple of fingers into his own glass. 'New Zealander. Forensic psychologist. 1950s? 60s... He identified three behavioural characteristics, three indicators for sociopathic behaviour. The one that everyone remembers is cruelty to animals or insects.'

Gareth smiled. 'An armchair psychologist?'

'Me? No, a curious mind. It was merely a comment, not a diagnosis.'

Gareth shrugged, seemingly unfazed by Tim's attempt at *labelling*. 'My behaviour doesn't fit.'

'No?'

Gareth continued. 'It's not cruelty... the insects, the way I treat them. There's nothing sadistic about it. No element of torture. They're just trapped.'

'So you don't kill them?'

'You killed it.' Gareth shot Tim a hard look, a look which made Tim's collar suddenly feel a little too tight.

This was true. Tim had killed the fly. 'I don't like flies on the table.' All understandable. 'I did it quickly, humanely.'

'Humane killing?'

Tim didn't bother dignifying this with an answer.

'Wasps, I kill wasps – they sting,' Gareth offered.

Tim nodded, as if chewing over the information; he could see the flaw. But it was a fly for Christ's sake, and on the table. 'And the other animals in your little glass houses, you let them all out?'

'Normally, if I remember where they are, I let them out.' Gareth shrugged. 'Sometimes I forget. So, they starve. You'd be amazed how long they can survive without food.' He paused for a moment, as if scanning through a myriad of personal images, insect menageries, hundreds of species trapped under a variety of glasses in far-flung locations. 'It's not a conscious decision – to forget them. Just... Just one of those things.' He looked back to Tim, locking him in a stare as if involving him in the conspiracy. 'You know how it is – we all have busy lives.'

CHAPTER NINETEEN

HELEN

The door to the chicken run was banging on its hinges when Helen got there. She checked the catch. Pushed it down then up. The mechanism still worked. It would certainly hold until morning. She entered the run, battling all the while against the wind. Most of the chickens had got themselves into the hut. It was only Natalie Wood, a large Rhode Island Red, who had foolishly wedged herself in between the feed tray and the bail of straw Helen used as a windbreak. Natalie's feathers ruffled in the gusty breeze as she sat stubbornly, all extremities: legs, beak, wings pulled into her fat fluffy body.

'Short-term gain, you foolish bird.' Helen slid her hands underneath the bird's warm bulk, pulling her up from the ground. 'You'll freeze if you don't move and if I get dirt on my clothes, Natalie,' she whispered into the bird's ruffled feathers, 'it will be Sunday lunch for you.' But as Helen moved away from the straw, she saw the small brown egg. 'Ah, so that's the problem. You really are feather-brained, Natalie. Loyalty gets you nowhere.'

She walked quickly to the hut and pushed the bird firmly through the hole in a whirlwind of flapping feathers and squawks before sealing the hatch. She dusted her hands together and examined her clothes. There appeared to be no visible damage. She went back to the small egg and took it gently between her fingers. It was a beautiful breakfast brown. In truth, Natalie was well past her sell-by date. Eggs were rare, maybe that's why she had been reluctant to leave it. But probably not. Helen wondered if hens even had a concept of getting older, of slipping slowly out of the spotlight. She doubted it. The concept of ageing was most likely a curse singled out for humans. Helen slipped the egg into her pocket, locked the door to the run behind her, and headed towards the shed.

It had been an old mushroom shed, so there were no windows and, despite having not been used for purpose for a very long time the smell of fungus in warm earth was unmistakable. There were three rows of mushroom trays running down one wall. Over the years, Helen had used the shed for a multitude of projects. The shelves had been cluttered with all manner of things; fossils, dried flowers. Once even materials for perfume; the three long shed trays lined meticulously with rows of tiny glass containers and empty margarine tubs containing flower petals soaked in water. The shed was the first real parcel of land that Helen had inherited, so it held special significance. For the past ten years or so it had been given over to egg propagation, and Helen knew that this project would probably be the one to see her out.

She stepped in, hitting the light switch on the side of the door and leaving the cruel wind outside. The shed had electricity, a small supply, just enough for a twenty-watt bulb and an incubator. There was no heating for humans, but the shed had been well insulated. Without windows, and with that dark fuggy smell, it had begun to remind Helen of a womb. She supposed this could also be due to the eggs, though the metaphor seemed forced, and not one she appreciated. Tim had described her once as a mother hen, presiding over her kingdom. But Helen wasn't buying this analogy; she was nobody's mother; she had always felt the role was overrated.

She tried to do batches of up to eighty eggs at a time. She'd started a batch off only four days ago, so Natalie's egg wouldn't be able to catch up. It would have to wait on the shelf until joined by others, which, this time of year, could take a few weeks. There was a damp piece of kitchen towel ready and waiting. It would help avoid dehydration. If the egg was stored pointy side down and turned once a day to prevent the yoke sticking to the inside of the shell, there was no reason why it shouldn't hatch. She marked the egg with the green permanent marker that she kept in the shed, drawing a small, neat cross on the shell so she would always know which side was up. There was, of course, no real 'up' for an egg, but the eggs had to be rolled, so she needed a point of reference.

Carefully, she placed the egg back on the shelf, and glanced into the incubator. The eggs were placed in a neat elliptical ring, with one gap, just larger than the size of an egg, at one end. Three times a day, Helen would roll the line forward into the gap, keeping the eggs turned. Four days, she thought to herself. The first batch had been in the incubator for four days, which meant it would be possible to get a glimpse inside. She fished for her phone in her wide coat pockets and switched on the torch, before switching off the lights in the hut. Four days was early to start candling, but it was the best part of the whole process, almost as good as eating. She opened the lid to the incubator and drew out an egg, a wonderful light-brown Buff Orpington. It was most likely one belonging to Julie Andrews. Helen had no idea when the habit of naming chickens after actresses had first started. She had done it as far back as she could remember. She had even had a little notebook that she took with her to the movies so that if she saw an actress she fancied, or a name that piqued her interest, she could write it down and save it for a future hen. There was no internet then, no googling: people had to remember things or write them down.

The roosters too: over the years there had been two Clint Eastwoods, an Orson Welles and recently she'd even had George Clooney for a spell, though that was a sore point. Poor George had got himself in a bit of a mess with a fox. Natalie Wood was actually Natalie Wood the Third, but this numerical appendage seemed unnecessary. Natalie Wood the original, and One and Two were clearly no longer around. There could be no confusion.

Holding the Buff Orpington in her hand she shone the torch into the shell, which went opaque, like a magic lantern show with a shadow theatre inside. It was there! She could see one small dark spot of colour, a crimson dot at the centre of the egg with a spiral of tiny blood-red veins spraying out on all sides. There wasn't much of the chicken about it. At this point, it looked more like a spider, or some new species. A frost creature perhaps? The veins like webs of a snowflake. They all looked the same at this stage. Just like foetuses all look the same. There were tests for humans. Abnormalities could be spotted at an early stage. And yet no amount of fancy machines could spot the big things, like evil. You couldn't tell from a scan if a person would grow up to be the kind of being that would crush other people's lives without even a second thought. Suddenly the phone in her hand began to buzz, the torch momentarily dimmed. She glanced at the screen. A text. Not a number she recognised, but her heart sank when she read the words.

Would like to ask you and your brother some more questions about the watch tomorrow.

Her heart beat louder in her chest. It wasn't the thought of the questions. They could ask questions till kingdom come. No, it was the words 'your brother' which she found worrying. How did they know he was home? And more, as far as she knew, no one had ever asked Gareth 'questions'.

Carefully, she put the egg back into the incubator and closed the lid. Turning up the collar of her coat she stepped out of the shed, bent her head into the wind and hurried back towards the glow of the house, praying the priest was gone. Praying the kitchen was empty. She needed time to think.

CHAPTER TWENTY

HELEN

Helen kicked off her boots in the utility room and unfastened her dark wool coat. Through the crack in the open kitchen doorway, she could see that the priest had gone. That was at least one good thing. She had to stay calm, and the priest's presence rattled her. The police were a problem, but nothing she couldn't handle. Perhaps this was in fact the best scenario. Gareth and Helen would be together, get their story straight. This could all work out.

She slipped her shoulders out of her coat before hanging it on its hook and tonight this small action filled her with warmth. It felt different from all the other times she'd hung that coat in that exact same place because she got to hang it directly beside Gareth's. His was a soft quilted Barbour. She stopped briefly to run her fingers down the sleeve as if stroking his arm. There they were, Helen and Gareth hanging side by side, and without thinking she looped the sleeve of Gareth's coat through her own. Done, she thought, wallowing in a little pool of self-satisfaction. Giving herself a moment to glance in the mirror that hung over the washbasin she straightened her wind-savaged hair. Her brief journey outside hadn't done too much damage, she thought to herself, as she eased errant strands on the sides of her scalp back down with the flat of her palms. It was beginning to frizz. Something it would never have dared to do when she was younger. Her features were, of late, misbehaving. If she pinched the skin on her neck it would remain puckered even after she ceased to hold it. The elastic had gone. When she was younger, her mother had given her a *golden* piece of advice, one of the few pieces of advice Mother had ever bestowed which did not concern horticulture, and it was given at a time when Helen was around thirteen, changing from child to woman. So, Helen often thought of it as the sole nugget of wisdom that the 'oracle' had bestowed in order to help Helen navigate her treacherous journey into adulthood. Her mother had said that, if she was out and her knicker elastic failed, she should let her pants drop to the floor, stand to one side, pick them up, and put them straight into her bag. This was the extent of Mother's worldly advice and had been rendered obsolete by the invention of Lycra. The only elastic that was going anywhere now was Helen's skin, but there was sadly no opportunity to sidestep that and continue on.

Now, it was all about 'making the best'. She examined herself again in the mirror. Her lipstick still held. A small shadow of what could be eyeliner had smudged under her eyes. She erased it gently with a finger. Satisfied, she pushed the door to the kitchen open wide and felt a tsunami of disappointment slap her hard with its savage wake-up call. True, it was tempered slightly, mixed as it was with the delicious aroma of tonight's meal in the oven, but nothing could turn her disappointment around completely. Carla. There she was. Standing at the kitchen units grazing from a plate containing the broken crostinis. That was bad enough. But even worse, Carla was looking so effortlessly young with her elastic skin and American-white teeth.

'Hi, you went out as well?'

'The chickens.' Helen relayed the information without tone. 'I had to lock them in for the night.'

'That wind, it's enough to make any creature fly.'

'Chickens don't fly.'

'Exactly, more of a jump. But see, that's what I meant. With that wind behind them, it opens up all kinds of possibilities.'

'I see,' Helen said dryly as she slid the plate away from her guest. 'I shall use these another time.'

'Oh, sorry.' The young American stretched herself out, as if her pop-up limbs were unfolding after a hard week; her large beatnik bracelet jangling as she moved. Carla was all movement, Helen thought to herself with a touch of irritation, all arms and legs connected and free-flowing.

'I was just starving. It's been such a rough week, full on, and I'm always kind of sluggish come wintertime. I swear human beings are supposed to hibernate October to May. But that beach!'

Was she breathing? Helen wondered. The speech was so quick. Could Carla possibly be circular breathing? Helen had heard that trumpet players did this. In order to keep a continuous outward flow of breath they were able to breathe in through their noses, at the same time as breathing out through their mouths.

'And the marshes! It was so great. Blows away those cobwebs.'

Carla's ceaseless noise was enough to induce a migraine. How, Helen wondered, could she offload this ball of energy?

'I think the men have had baths,' Helen stated simply, 'but there's plenty of water if you'd still like one?'

'Me? No, I'm good.' Carla reached her hands out across the grained wooden worktops, pulling her body into a quick yoga-style flex. 'About your brother.' She paused. 'I hope I won't be in your way?'

'I seriously doubt it,' Helen returned. 'Can I fix you a drink?'

'I would kill for a coffee.'

Helen stopped short and sighed despairingly. This was suppertime. It was gone eight o'clock. 'I meant a drink. Gin and tonic? Vodka?' she offered.

'No, seriously. Coffee's great,' Carla returned, in her water-off-a-duck's-back, thick-skinned way.

Helen on the other hand had no intention of putting the kettle on for hot beverages. There were standards that had to be kept. Even if the whole rest of the world had forgotten. Her house, her rules, aperitifs in the evening, nothing caffeinated until after the meal. Then, maybe coffee, and not one of those ridiculous coffees. Black and cream. That was how it went.

She moved to the fridge and took out the toppings for the crostini: guacamole, tapenade, and a home-made walnut-and-rosemary pesto.

'People don't tend to have coffee before supper.' She was going to have to lay the rules down clearly. 'We tend to have a drink before the evening meal.'

Carla erupted into a short burst of laugher, which sent a seismic reaction bristling down Helen's spine. 'I'm sorry.' She pulled herself together. Intimidated, no doubt, by Helen's blank expression. 'I've put my foot in it, haven't I? I forget, your British etiquette.' And she laughed again. 'It's like walking a knife edge. All the things you should and shouldn't do.' She paused for a moment, in an attempt to bring the situation around. She was, after all, a guest. 'I'm sorry. Let me start again. I didn't mean to offend.' And she shot Helen a charming bright-eyed smile, which might, Helen thought, work on a man, but in the circumstances was seriously misplaced; Helen had already taken offence.

'Why don't we make it a... vodka,' Carla affirmed, smiling

like she'd pronounced the most exciting news since James Watson stumbled into the Eagle and announced he'd discovered the secret of life.

Helen wiped her hands on the tea towel. 'Orange? Or tonic?'

Carla laughed again, her eyes narrowing, feigning an attitude of deep thought. 'Is this a trick question?'

'I am just trying to ascertain what it is that you would like to drink.'

'Normally coffee, but I'll drink whatever makes you happy.'

'Fine,' Helen said, throwing down the tea towel and heading to the fridge. 'Tonic. Gin and... sorry,' she corrected herself, with a tone of mild disapproval over the substitution of vodka, for what should surely have been gin. Vodka was for Russians. Even the Soho trendies of the eighties and nineties had now seen the light. But then, wasn't that symptomatic of this young woman all over – seriously misplaced? That summed her up. 'Vodka and tonic.' Helen popped the ice cubes into the tumbler and laced the glass with a healthy slug of alcohol.

'Ice and lemon?' she asked, as the tonic fizzed.

'However it comes.' Carla shrugged compliantly.

Helen put the lemon into the glass, because THAT was how it came, and handed the glass over.

'Thank you.' Carla closed her slim, tanned fingers around the tumbler. 'You know, supper smells amazing.'

'Risotto for starters. Stew for mains. Tarte Tatin for dessert.'

'Wow, I shall come again.'

Helen was glad that she had her back to the woman. 'Wow' seriously?

'I am starving.'

'Like a farmer,' Helen muttered. The comment went unnoticed.

'Tim has been singing your praises.'

Helen paused, wondering about this 'other' life she had as a two-dimensional character. A life outlined by Tim's verbose observations, fleshed out in anecdotal evidence to his colleagues in the canteen. She wondered if Tim and his colleagues talked about her research. It had been a long while since she had been at the university, but at the time a number of academics had thought her observations on the central paradox in Plato's work were groundbreaking.

'He says you're a great cook,' Carla confided.

So, there it was. Without a second's hesitation or falter, Helen continued to assemble the crostini, as her 'life's work' was reduced to dried bread, rather than profound philosophical thought.

'I've spent a long time in the kitchen,' she said, barely missing a beat. 'You pick things up.' The ice wall between herself and Tim could be swiftly re-erected. The chink removed.

'Do you work?' Carla asked sweetly.

'I look after Mother.'

'Of course. Sorry I forgot. But before?'

She wasn't going to squirm in front of this young woman. Helen had been born in a different age and suddenly her life, what she was, suddenly it was being paraded in front of this girl, this woman who had tumbled all too recently out of her nappies and straight into a thong. Helen's life was not up for critical dissection.

'No. I never worked.'

'Don't you get bored?'

'What a quaint idea. I seem to find plenty of things to fill my time. I did go to university in Norwich, when I left school.'

'Very handy,' the smiling Carla affirmed.

'It meant I was able to stay at home.'

'What were you reading?'

'English and Classics. I got a First.' There, that would shut her up.

But a generic 'fab' was all Helen managed to elicit. No doubt, Helen thought, everyone got Firsts these days. Exams were not what they used to be.

'Tim was running an Aesthetics course. I met him there. It was one of those student-tutor romances. You know the kind of thing.'

'Not first-hand.'

Helen would have liked to slap the young woman at this point. But Helen knew this would have been all wrong. Her hostess skills might have rusted up recently, but the central rule of not slapping guests before an evening meal still held.

'In-house relationships – not really my kind of thing. But it's worked for you,' Carla offered magnanimously.

Superior cow, Helen thought, as she sliced a tomato, but all that came out of her mouth was, 'There's plenty of hot water if you did want that bath.'

Carla shook her head. 'Honestly, I'm good. Can I help?'

Helen covered the tray she had been working on with cling film and pushed it to the back of the units, out of easy reach from 'helping' hands before flipping on the hob, and emptying the pre-chopped onion, celery and rice into the warming oil.

'I don't think so. It's all done.' This was all so unfair. So now she was supposed to be babysitting? Where was Tim?

'This house,' Carla said, launching out into the room, pointing her toes like a little ballerina and following them around the flagstone floor. She had no shoes on, Helen realised with despair.

'It must have been a blast growing up here,' Carla continued, enjoying her journey around the kitchen. Stopping by the toasted crostini, the spare ones without the topping, and beginning to graze once again.

'You'll spoil your supper,' Helen warned.

'Honestly, not a problem, I eat like a horse.'

'I'll bet.' Helen drew her mobile from her bag. She would text Tim. Tell him to get down here.

'So, it was just you and your brother – Gavin?'

Helen's eyes narrowed, as her whole body cringed. 'Gareth, his name is Gareth.'

Undeterred, Carla continued to pick, breaking bits of crostini off with her small slim fingers and packaging them neatly onto her tongue.

'Can I get you a bowl of something?' Helen offered.

The young woman nodded eagerly. 'Crisps would be good.'

'I have olives.'

'Then, olives it is.'

Helen slammed the phone down onto the surface. She'd managed to send Tim a single – ? – he should get the point. She gave the risotto a quick stir, and a little more stock, then went to the fridge for the olives.

Behind her she heard the door open, *thank God*. He'd reacted quickly. No doubt, he would bring it up at supper, all some jolly-bloody-hockey-stick ruse. '*Yes, my wife texted me earlier this evening from the kitchen.*' She turned to chide her husband for his tardiness. But it was Gareth, not Tim, standing there in the doorway, and Helen's anger evaporated.

'You found everything?'

Gareth nodded; his attention was focused on Helen, so he hadn't noticed Carla standing in the corner beside the chest.

'All looks the same.'

'It's cleaner, surely?' Helen said, an amused tone threaded through her words.

Gareth nodded. 'Cleaner', he had to give her that.

'The return of the prodigal son.' Carla moved forward as she spoke, walking towards him, hand outstretched, and Helen couldn't help noticing, as her heart sank, the interest on both sides, and a charge of static in the air; an electrical charge that she was most definitely outside of. Suddenly all seemed very still. Carla's frenetic movements and voice slowed to a single smiling trajectory forward. And at the very edges of her consciousness, Helen could make out a high-pitched jingle, her mother's bell.

'I can hear something?' said Carla. But nobody moved.

The bell rang again, into the silence.

'Can you hear that?' She looked around, trying to locate the source.

There was no escape. Helen took a deep breath and resigned herself to her duty. 'Mother,' she said, which just about summed up the whole problem, then added by way of explanation, 'she has a bell.'

But still nobody moved. Helen did not want to go. She had been there all day waiting in this kitchen, waiting and clock-watching, and cooking, and listening out for that blasted bell, but now that he was here...

The bell rang again. But still Helen did not want to leave these two people who were radiating some kind of energy she hadn't felt for years, some kind of life. But yet again the bell rang. There was no escape.

'Shall I?' Gareth hesitated, about to step back out into the hallway. But of course, this would never work. It had to be Helen.

'No. Supper isn't ready yet. Help yourself to a drink.'

She headed quickly to the door, as the bell rang for a fifth whining time, causing Helen to clench her teeth. 'All right. I'm coming. I'm coming.'

She looked back into the room; it was just Gareth and Carla. Bugger, Helen thought to herself. She'd put the sodding risotto on too. Someone would have to help. It would have to be

Carla, but could Carla be trusted? The bell again. Helen had no choice. She called back into the room, 'Can you stir the risotto?'

Carla looked surprised. 'I guess.'

The young woman pointed her toes, walked over to the pot and grabbed the wooden spoon.

Helen was out of the door heading up the stairs, quickly, aiming to get Mother sorted as efficiently as possible.

'Don't forget to stir,' she called back.

'I'm stirring, I'm stirring.' Carla laughed, pulling the spoon around the pan quicker and quicker.

Helen could hear them talking as she mounted the stairs. They were playing some kind of game – guess my name. Find the gin. One minute life story catch-up. She should have been there. Mother. Helen wanted to hear his 'life story' so badly, all the parts she had missed. It felt like an ache. By the time she got to her mother's bedroom, her mother had fallen back into the usual comatosed state. Whatever she had wanted so desperately had been forgotten. Helen sank down on the bed. Was it true? Had she really done nothing with her life apart from learn how to make fancy fried bread? If she could turn back the clock, set it ticking once again but in a different direction, would she? But that kind of self-pitying regret was ugly nonsense. The kind of thing that got you nowhere. She needed to get back to the risotto before it was ruined and that tart of a girl Carla had stolen Gareth from under her nose. Surely he wouldn't fall for someone like that? But life, she knew, rarely ran along the tracks you set for it.

'All these people in my kitchen.' By the time Helen got back down they were all there. She had waltzed through the door and for a moment they all froze. It was as if they had been caught in the act, the prelude to a brawl or a robbery. The silence was so thick, so immediate it felt choreographed.

'Well, we can go in the front room? If that works better,' Tim offered, as if remembering that he was still the host here. Tim was a weak man for all his academic prowess. But then, that was probably why Helen had married him. He could be pushed into the corner and forgotten about like a houseplant that only needs watering once every few weeks.

'I can get that fire lit.'

And they began to shuffle, or at least Gareth did, and she got the uncomfortable feeling that perhaps he did not want to be in the kitchen with her. Perhaps he felt there was safety in numbers. Safety! What about her safety?

'No stay. Please,' she spoke softly, her eyes not leaving Gareth. Her voice sounding suddenly younger, more nervous, more naked. 'Stay in the kitchen where it's warm.'

'How was Mother?'

'The same,' Helen said. Taking the spoon from Carla's hand and beginning to stir the risotto.

'Is she very sick?' Carla asked.

'Oh yes.' Helen stirred once again.

'How long has she been ill?'

'Always,' Gareth answered.

There was a moment's silence, broken by Helen's laugh. 'Or maybe she's not sick. I wouldn't put it past her.'

'Mothers,' Carla chimed in. 'The cause of all evil. It's a lot to live up to, being a woman. A lot of responsibility – managing to screw it up for the next generation. And how about your father? He still on the scene?'

'Oh please.' Helen sighed. 'We didn't have one.'

'That's a fancy manoeuvre genetically,' Carla said lightly. 'We should be in a freak show.'

'What my sister means,' Gareth took the reins effortlessly, 'is that we never met him. Apparently, he died before I was born.'

'And I don't remember him.'

'And there are no photos?' Carla asked.

'That would seem to be the case. He's a mystery... and...' Helen hesitated. 'We never saw a need for him. We managed without him well enough.'

Gareth shot Helen a look. She wasn't sure what it meant, probably something like... *seriously?*

Luckily, outside the wind began to howl like a wolf, poking its long, wet fingers between the gaps in the window frames, sending a few fingernails of icy air reaching out into the room.

'Do you remember, Gareth? How the wind whistled over the reed beds? We used to say it was voices. We used to pretend it was talking to us. Remember?'

'Oh, what did it say?' Carla piped up.

'It was telling us to do things,' Helen said, her eyes never moving from Gareth.

'Do things?' Tim was curious. 'The wind was telling you to do what kind of things?'

A deep vertical furrow appeared on Helen's forehead, and her eyes hardened with irritation.

'Oh, I don't know, Tim. Things. Just things. Does everything have to be so bloody analytical!' An ugly pause filled the room. Her voice had been too hard, too sharp, far too honest. She took a deep breath and realigned her manners. 'Well I suppose the food is ready. Carla, can you put the crostini on the table? Tim, the wine? We should eat. Please, everyone, sit.'

The sash windows rattled, as if applauding Helen's performance.

'Wow! It really is so wild here.' Carla placed her napkin over her lap and extended a long bare arm out hungrily for the appetisers. 'You know my father would have killed for that garden. Well, the space I mean.'

Helen bristled. Would the woman ever shut up?

'He was a botanist,' Carla continued.

How could the American talk and eat at the same time? Helen watched in amazement, and do it all seemingly without showing the inside of her overlarge mouth. Were Americans put together differently? It couldn't just be circular breathing, Carla had to have some kind of – *no pause for digestion* override. Brave New World, Helen thought, and thanked her stars that she didn't have to engage with it.

'But can you believe it?' Carla continued. 'So, my father's a botanist, and I grew up in the city. We never once lived anywhere with a garden!'

'It must be strange coming back.' Tim pulled Gareth into the hot seat.

'Very... odd.'

Helen hovered, close at hand, walking down the length of the table, armed with a risotto pan, ladling spoonfuls onto plates.

'Why stay away so long?' Tim continued the line of questioning.

Helen eyed Gareth curiously, his face impassive. She knew already there would be no supper-table revelations. Deep secrets needed to be coaxed into the light, given the right environment to bud and flower. True to form he shrugged, leaning over the table for the white wine, having finished whatever he had been drinking before. He didn't ask. Helen noted a flare of irritation sweep across Tim's features. Hadn't Tim got it yet? This was Gareth's home. He could help himself to whatever he pleased.

'It's complicated,' Gareth returned.

Helen felt a small sense of satisfaction: Gareth's answer would irritate Tim. *Complicated* was such a cop-out.

'And how long are you staying?'

'Tim!' Helen's voice barked, with a touch of the guard dog. 'You can't ask that.' The etiquette card was played in full, slapped down on the table. 'You're welcome to stay here for as long as you like, Gareth.'

Helen shot her husband a look, but she needn't have bothered.

'No worries, Tim. It's only for the weekend.'

Out of the corner of her eye, Helen could see Tim bite his cheeks into place, trying to suppress a smile.

'I'm tying things up before the big move,' Gareth continued.

'Oh?' Tim asked. 'Anywhere nice?'

'America. They say it's nice. Sunshine and all that.'

'Depends where you go,' Carla added.

'There's sunshine where I'm headed.' And he shot the young woman a smile. A smile so natural and free, Helen wished it had been aimed in her direction.

'Well, here's to fresh starts.' Tim offered Gareth his wine glass in a toast, thrust it forward in a sign of amnesty. 'I take it this is a fresh start?'

Helen felt her heart break just a little.

'It is.' Gareth nodded.

'You'll have to look me up.' Carla sparkled her eyes in Gareth's direction.

Damn, Helen thought to herself. That bloody woman! 'America's a big place.' Helen may not have studied geography but even she had that fact nailed.

'I teach at Berkeley. Whereabouts are you headed?' Carla continued, as Helen pushed her nails deep into her skin, to stop from screaming. What were all these people doing at her table! Did they know how long she had waited for this day? But the unstoppable Carla ploughed on, oblivious, focusing all attention on Gareth and the excitement of his next move.

'LA.'

'Well believe it or not, we have great transport links. Give me a call, I could help you settle in.'

Gareth nodded. 'I'd like that. Or maybe you could come and visit me?'

Helen suppressed an indignant gasp. She would not be riled. 'We're only two hours from London and it's taken you forty years to get here.' She turned her focus to Carla. 'I wouldn't go holding your breath.'

'Course. Yeah. Got you.' Carla smiled diplomatically. 'And so, Gareth... are you married?'

And not one fork scraped across one plate. Helen actually stopped breathing.

'No.' Gareth looked half-amused as if biting back some secret joke. 'Not really my thing.'

Carla nodded thoughtfully, as if digesting this last nugget.

'I really don't think it's any of our business,' Helen launched in. She didn't want to share him. She didn't want these others learning about her brother as she learned. She wanted to be the only one in the know. They needed to do all of this question and answer routine on their own. But she couldn't help feeling relieved; there was no woman waiting in the wings.

'So, let's drink to...' Tim adopted his best master-of-ceremonies voice.

'Oh please, don't let's start all that *prodigal son* rubbish again.' Helen shifted in her seat, raising her glass. The others followed suit. 'To Gareth and his return.'

Tim and Carla joined glasses. 'To Gareth.'

'And now you're back, you really mustn't go dashing off again.' Helen spread her napkin over her skirt, not wanting to catch his eye in case he came back with a flat refusal. 'I want

140

to hear everything,' she said, genuinely. 'When we've cleared up here, after supper, I want you to tell me every little last detail.'

'Forty years,' Tim reminisced.

'Intriguing.' Carla danced her eyes in Gareth's direction. 'What did you do? Where did you go?'

Helen shot the younger woman a look, but the younger woman was taking no notice. In fact, the younger woman was avoiding eye contact with Helen wherever possible.

'As I said, this is not the time. You don't have to talk about it all now,' Helen announced simply.

But Gareth wiped the corners of his mouth on his napkin and shrugged. 'No, it's fine. At first, I got work in a kitchen.'

'A restaurant.' Helen felt a swell of pride. But when she studied him closely she saw that, for some reason, he seemed amused.

'No. It was a kitchen.'

'Cooking?' Carla asked.

'Washing up,' Gareth corrected, and reached for his wine, which he swilled gently around in its glass.

'You'll never starve in a kitchen.'

'Smart.' Carla nodded. 'And do you still work in catering?'

'Not exactly. I work for a...' He hesitated, lowering his eyes. 'I work for the same organisation. A charity.'

'Oh? What kind of...'

'Too many questions,' Helen cut in. 'Risotto should be eaten hot.'

'Unlike revenge.' Carla toyed with the rice on her fork. 'Revenge is a dish best served cold, isn't that right? If you were coming back for vengeance you must have been storing it in the deep freeze.'

Helen shook her head dismissively. 'What utter...'

'So, are you?' Tim asked brightly, enjoying the metaphor. 'Is that what this visit is about? You "defrosting" your freezer, so to speak?'

'Tim!' If Helen could have stuck gaffer tape over his mouth, she would. 'What is this? He's barely been back...'

'But aren't you curious?' Tim cut over her words. 'Surely you're curious?' He took a large swig of his wine, turned to Gareth and in a couldn't-really-care-a-toss voice, said jovially, 'We thought you were dead.'

'Tim!'

'Well, you can't deny it, Helen. We did think he was dead, and at the time, well, apparently the police thought...'

The police. Helen bristled. But she was getting ahead of herself. This was about Gareth's disappearance not the priest. She needed to keep control. 'The police had to explore all options.' Helen leaned her head into her hands, and sighed, as if preparing an explanation for a particularly dim child. 'It's their job. It was pretty obvious, Gareth, that you'd had a major fight with Mother.'

'Oh?' Carla wanted more.

'Gareth dug up the garden.' Helen didn't see the point in withholding this information.

Carla let out a loud, involuntary gasp. 'You dug up the garden!'

'Every perennial, annual, even some of the smaller shrubs. All dug up and dumped in the pond. You left things in a bit of a mess. They did haul Mother in for questioning.'

'Oh.' Gareth looked up momentarily from his plate. 'How did she cope with that?'

'Furious. Furious because she didn't have time to get the garden straight.' Helen looked back at her meal, circulated her fork, chasing a finger of asparagus that had somehow got unseasonally lost and wound up here, at this 'celebration' dinner, far from home. 'You know what she was like,' Helen

142

said softly, in a manner that clearly meant, *and there's an end to it.*

But Tim was rather enjoying the gossip element of the whole, tawdry affair. 'Curiously enough...' he said, and inserted a pause for maximum effect, 'someone else disappeared at the same time.'

Carla's eyes opened wide. 'Really?'

Helen grabbed the parmesan grater and began grating. 'Tim, honestly! You're beginning to sound like some crass novella. There was no connection. The other incident was weeks earlier.'

'But you knew him?'

Tim really was being very tiresome, Helen thought. 'It's a small village. He left before Gareth. Anyway.'

'Yes, but recently they found the missing guy's watch,' Tim continued on a roll. 'It was in the papers: calls for the man's whereabouts. Gareth, did you see it?'

Helen shot Gareth a look. For a moment the world seemed to turn a little slower.

'No,' he lied. 'No, I hadn't heard.'

'They thought this missing guy,' Tim blustered on, 'well, maybe he'd stolen money, or there was a woman involved.'

Helen wished to God Tim would shut up. 'Who told you all of this? Surely not the police?'

'Aha!' Tim intoned jovially. 'Village gossip.' He smiled, as pleased with himself as a dog that's just learnt to unicycle. 'Just put my ears to the wind.'

Helen shook her head in irritated disbelief. 'Well you shouldn't listen to village gossip. It's invariably garbled, normally spiked with malice, and more often than not put about by village idiots.'

Carla raised one eyebrow. 'Rather than elders?'

'We're pretty short of those, sane ones anyway.'

'So, who was it, this other guy that went missing at the same time?' Carla turned her attention to Gareth. 'Was it a friend?'

'Not at the same time! He didn't go missing at the same time.' Helen's voice came back hard.

'But someone you knew?' Carla continued.

'I really think...' Helen began, but Carla was too curious to quit.

'Look, two people disappear?'

'Coincidence.' Gareth sighed. Raising his palms as if to say, it happens.

'As I said, it was not at the same time, it was a few weeks earlier,' Helen insisted.

Carla looked sceptical. 'Well, that is kind of the same time? Same month.'

Helen felt a wave of red heat shooting through her body. Would this woman ever shut up. 'No, it wasn't the same month. One was June, the other July.'

Carla nodded slowly. 'I think you're splitting hairs there.'

'It was the priest. Father... Father...' Tim stuttered, trying desperately to recall what he'd heard.

'Father Wright.' They said it together. At exactly the same moment, Helen and Gareth opened their mouths and a thin trail of sound rose involuntarily through their bodies, like choreographed cats spitting out furballs.

'That's it!' Tim threw his head back – the victor – as if he had found the name, diving down into the oceans of the past and surfacing, triumphant. 'Friendly with your mother, so they say.'

'A priest?' Carla's voice held trace elements of disgust.

Tim held up his hands in a don't-shoot-me-I'm-only-the-messenger attitude.

'Coincidence,' Gareth stated, firmly.

'My mother?' sneered Helen. 'Gossip and village idiots. As I said. It doesn't bear repeating.' She shot Tim a ray of ice from her cold, green eyes. Tim cringed visibly. But luckily, Gareth made light of the situation. 'Didn't see him on my travels.'

'Does anyone want more parmesan? Or cream?' Helen pushed the rice around her plate, as if the motion would somehow make the food disappear of its own accord. 'I think it's a bit dried out. The trick with risotto is stirring it. You have to stir as it cooks.'

Carla grinned, amused. 'I did. I swear.'

'It's good.' Gareth's praise seemed genuine but was directed at the young American rather than Helen. In return, Carla smiled in that smug, flirty way that only the young can pull off.

'Why thank you. Cookery plagiarism,' she whispered. 'I do it all the time. So much easier than cooking yourself.'

Gareth gave a short, spontaneous laugh. And Helen's heart cracked. She wished that she could have elicited something so wonderfully natural and of 'the now'. All Helen's smiles and laughter were dredged out, tooth and nail, from the past, and there were so many other things lurking there; things that needed to be avoided. So, she hesitated to dip in and out. That brief laugh of Carla's meant new experiences. New memories were being formed. But Helen was standing on the outside.

'Was it a happy childhood?' Carla continued.

'Of course,' Helen came in quickly.

Carla stopped eating and narrowed her eyes. 'Why – of course?'

Helen felt an overwhelming desire to yawn, the American had dipped into pop-psychology mode. 'It was a lovely place to grow up in. We had each other.'

She reached across the table and took Gareth's hand, the one with the strawberry birthmark. 'We had some good times.'

'Some,' Gareth countered, his voice dry.

'But not all?' Carla continued to pry.

'Obviously not all, this is life we're talking about not a box set.' Helen scowled.

'In a sense, beyond a certain point,' Tim launched in, steering the conversation from the personal to the philosophical, 'it doesn't matter if the events were good or bad, it's how we perceive them that's important. Isn't that right, Carla? The important thing is our perception of the events, not the events themselves.'

Carla nodded.

'Crap,' said Helen, and the conversation died.

'That's not entirely fair, Helen,' Gareth said, picking his words carefully. Shooting her a warning look. 'So, Carla, how do you know...' Gareth stumbled momentarily, searching for the name. 'Tim?'

'We work together, at the university.'

'Sociologist?' Gareth asked.

Because, no doubt, Helen thought to herself, the verbose crap swilling around the kitchen table seemed to align itself neatly with a fabricated-yesterday discipline such as sociology.

'No, philosopher and social anthropologist.' The title tripped, well-practised, from Carla's lips. 'I'm just here for a year. Almost done now.'

'Philosopher.' Gareth smirked. 'Big title. So, are you going to save the world or the soul?'

'I don't make a distinction.' She smiled.

Helen didn't bother to stifle her yawn. 'I thought that was all philosophers ever did, divide things up. Words and meaning dissected into obscurity. Cut, cut, cut, with your tiny little scalpels till you're all too bored or verbally impotent to take any kind of action.'

Carla gave a thoughtful look, took a slug of her wine, and wiped the wet liquid from her lips whilst simultaneously appearing to wipe on a smile. 'I'm not that kind of philosopher. You have to choose when to stop cutting.'

'Saving humanity through words and thought,' Gareth announced, enjoying the extravagance of the statement.

'You make me sound like a superhero. I could wear a shirt.' She raised one hand, drawing it over her chest as if writing a logo across her body. 'A big S. I'd like that.' Her smile slipped for a moment, and the more serious Carla, the one with the PhD, returned. She was digging her teeth into the problem. 'Maybe understanding comes before saving. It's a good place to start. Do you have a better one?'

Gareth nodded briefly, assimilating the twists and turns of thought. 'Even with all that shifting perspective stuff?'

With a sickening lurch, Helen remembered the text from the police.

'Only makes it more important,' Carla droned on.

'And you live close to Berkeley?' Gareth asked, so innocently, so lightly, as a knife twisted in Helen's heart.

There could be questions tomorrow, not like this: stupid curiosity. Helen pushed back her chair. 'I think we've finished here. Everyone done?' she announced, and Tim's jaw fell open in surprise – his plate still not clear. He was obviously not done. Carla also had three quarters of her food left.

'I'm still...' she interjected, but was cut dead.

'You shouldn't talk so much. It's rude. We shall be here all night at this rate.'

'But...' Tim mumbled.

'I think I may have over-catered.' Helen bounced up from the table and switched off the oven. 'We can have the stew tomorrow.'

'I'm just...' Tim tried to diffuse Helen's sudden, over-efficient outburst, knowing from experience that they were being *tidied away*.

'But we've only just...'

'I'm afraid I went overboard. The risotto was certainly more than enough, and I can bring you the cheese through to the study.'

There was a brief pause. No one moved. 'I thought you and Carla had a book to write?'

'Well, we do,' Tim agreed. 'But I'd planned on making a start tomorrow.'

'Oh, for goodness' sake, Tim. You do procrastinate. You and Carla want to save the world, you should be getting on with it.'

'Helen, I really...' He had his *this-is-unreasonable* expression writ large over his face, but she didn't care. She wanted them out.

'No time like the present. You only have the weekend.'

Carla was looking from Tim to Helen, Helen to Tim, like a ball boy on a Wimbledon court trying to estimate where the ball would drop. Luckily it only took her a moment to realise that the ball was well and truly in Helen's court. The game had been won, and in order for Tim to be saved from final humiliation Carla must concede.

'That's fine,' she said simply.

'But the cheese,' Tim protested, and Carla's cringe was visible.

'As I said, I will bring the cheese through.' Helen enunciated each word, making it all perfectly clear.

'But tomorrow...' Tim's heels were going in.

'Carla is here today,' Helen returned. 'Stop stagnating, Tim. You have the whole evening.'

'Look, I'm fine with that,' Carla said, taking the metaphorical ball that was trapped in the net and angling for a quick exit off the court.

'Okay.' Tim shrugged. 'To the study then.'

'I lit the fire.' Helen was already clearing the plates.

'Can I help?' Carla asked, as Tim moved towards the door, shoulders slumped.

'No, please. You two just run along.'

Carla stood and picked up her half-eaten risotto bowl.

'Don't put the hot dishes on the desk,' Helen added, handing Carla a mat. 'It'll mark.'

'Right,' Carla said, sheepishly now, Helen thought to herself, taking a little satisfaction in this small triumph.

'This way then,' Tim called like a scout leader from the hallway.

But there was not time for Helen to truly wallow in this small win. As she watched them leaving, her fingers ran over the phone in her pocket. The police would be here tomorrow. Helen needed to get the story fixed.

CHAPTER TWENTY-ONE

HELEN

With Tim and Carla dispatched, Helen felt her shoulders lower. The evening had been a disaster. She had rehearsed this reunion for years, played it out again and again in her head. She blamed Tim and that awful woman.

'That's what *she* used to say.' Gareth's voice cut through her thoughts.

'What?'

Helen turned towards him, confused.

'You, sending Tim and Carla off like that. Mother, she used to say – "you two just run along then".'

Helen couldn't help but wince at the comparison. 'Don't be unkind, Gareth.'

'I wasn't.'

She paused for a moment, took a deep breath. Of course he wasn't being deliberately unkind. He was no doubt tired after his long journey. This had all been too much. Allowances must be made. She took the plates to the sink. 'Can I get you anything more to eat?'

He shook his head.

'There's far too much here.' She stared in dismay at the

cheeseboard and tart. 'I don't know what possessed me. To be honest, I think I was showing off.'

Gareth poured himself another glass of wine.

'You drink a lot.'

'I thought this was a celebration,' he said ironically. 'What's the book about?'

Helen looked blank.

'The one Tim's writing?'

'Oh, I don't know.' Helen opened the dishwasher and began to pack. 'Some overblown crap that'll never get read.'

She paused, straightened up, ran her fingers through her hair. 'I'm sorry about that woman.'

Gareth shrugged. 'I like her.'

'Is she pretty?'

'What do you think?'

'A little obvious. A little too flat-chested. Appalling bone structure. Cheap,' Helen pronounced, satisfied, as if having stumbled over the core problem. 'Kind of cheap-looking.'

Gareth laughed, amused despite himself.

A new memory, Helen thought to herself. We are forming new memories. The thought contained such beauty that she found it almost painful, as if her heart which had been trapped in ice, had suddenly started to thaw. But it wasn't safe. They needed to prepare for tomorrow, for the police and their questions, even though she desperately didn't want that, because to prepare for tomorrow they needed to talk about that summer, and that man.

Gareth leant back against the units, staring at his sister as she tidied, taking the unused casserole from the oven.

'I didn't know if you were vegetarian or not.' She stuck a fork into the mushroom stroganoff. 'Can't use it again. I defrosted it. I'd been waiting so long, I suppose I just excelled myself.'

'Doesn't matter.'

'The stew will keep. We can have it tomorrow. I could liquidise the mushrooms for Mother. She could have them cold.'

'It doesn't matter,' he said again, but she knew this anyway, so she carried on scraping the plates.

'So, they questioned Mother?'

Her heart sank, this was the least of their worries now. But it was a good start, it would help keep their story straight.

'They interviewed her when you left. She was mortified, as you can imagine.' Helen allowed herself the small pleasure of briefly enjoying her mother's discomfort, even after all these years.

'What did she say?'

'What could she say? She didn't know anything. She wasn't exactly renowned for her observational skills. She could spot aphids from twenty metres, but...' Helen slowed, stumbling for the right words.

'You shouldn't excuse her. I don't know why you stay.'

Helen closed her eyes, trying to muster all the fractured pieces that were *Helen*, the daughter, the wife, the sister – trying to assemble them all in one place so that she might find the strength to take control and move forward. She smiled sadly, put her hand on his shoulder and said quietly, 'I put it behind me. It was a long time ago.'

'Even the train?'

Gareth, she realised, didn't want calm. He didn't really want *coping strategies for moving forward*. Gareth had come to Suffolk to reopen old wounds, and she couldn't have him do that.

'I don't remember the train,' she stated simply. 'I was very young. Gareth...' She paused, knowing this was going to be difficult. 'I got a text from the police, they're coming to the house tomorrow. They have a few questions about the watch.'

'The watch?'

'Well, of course they mean the priest. We need to be on the same page. Have you told anyone?'

He looked away.

'Gareth?'

'No. You?'

She shook her head. 'We need to keep the story simple. Father Wright took some money from Mother's safe. He visited us, the money was missing, he went missing. Simple.'

'That's what she told them? Mother?'

'Yes. I kept the money. Fed it back into the housekeeping. She didn't notice. It was only eight hundred pounds.'

'Enough to encourage a person to steal, to run away when they were wearing a watch which must have been worth double that?'

'Maybe, but it's not our job to speculate. The police can do that. We need to fire fight. The less we give them, the more difficult it is for anyone to find holes. We don't know anything about the watch.'

'Funny thing is I don't.'

'We were children. Children don't notice things like that. The watch is unfortunate, but it doesn't change the story.'

Gareth drew one hand through his hair, his action weary, his shoulders slumped. 'But what about for us? What about what we remember?'

'That doesn't matter. That's gone. We can't tell them any of that.'

'It's not gone, Helen. And now the police are involved. How did they know I was back?'

She shook her head. 'I don't know. Maybe they don't, for sure. Maybe it's just a lucky guess.'

He sighed. 'Okay. But what about the real story. I need to know.'

She didn't say anything for a moment, just walked to the sink, thrusting her hands into the warm water and starting to wash a few of the larger pots that were stacked there. She wouldn't face him. Not for this.

'The train,' he said simply.

'What? I don't know. It all went okay. I don't remember anything.'

His voice, when he spoke again, was hushed but angry. 'I don't believe you, Helen. You were bleeding!'

She plunged her hands deeper into the warm suds, shaking her head. 'I don't remember bleeding.'

Most kids had memories of trips to London, visits to the Natural History Museum, the dinosaur, a burger in the station. That's the sort of memory you can add to your collection. Their visit to London hadn't been like that. She wouldn't go over this now. They needed to be closing the past off, not opening it out.

'What if there had been a problem?' he said quietly.

But Helen would not be drawn. 'There wasn't.'

The large pot washed, she took the sponge from the sink, determined to get the kitchen straight. 'As I said before...' She talked as she wiped, collecting crumbs together, chasing them with the sponge to the edge of the table and catching them in her hand. 'It was a long time ago.'

'Not for me. The memories won't lay still. I can still see it all: the journey down, the clinic, the smell of bleach. And that smug bastard in the surgery. "Friend of the family". That nurse, the way she looked at us.'

Helen stopped moving, frozen to the spot.

'I've forgotten,' she said in a low whisper.

'You must remember the train?' His voice was torn with emotion. 'They'd botched it. The abortion. God knows how. Do you know?'

She shook her head, feeling the tears prick the edges of her eyes.

'Gareth, we don't need to do this. It's done.'

But he wasn't stopping. 'I wrapped it in a piece of my shirt. It wasn't the whole thing, just a bit, just some bloody bit of flesh. I thought...' The words caught in his throat. 'When I remember back... when I remember it, I think of it pulsing, beating in my hands. But it couldn't be?'

'No.' Helen shook her head again, this time trying to reassure him. She knelt down by his side and took his hand in hers. 'No.'

'I took my shirt off, wrapped it up, threw it out of the window onto the embankment.' He stopped and looked straight into her eyes. 'You cried so hard. Then that woman in the carriage, she gave you a sweet. Don't you remember?'

Helen shook her head.

'A butterscotch and you started gagging.'

'I hate butterscotch,' she said, her voice barely audible. 'I was very young.'

'And when we got home, we walked all the way from the station. She didn't even meet us. We walked up the driveway hot and sweaty and there she was, Mother, in the garden, that beautiful garden. Kneeling there in all that colour, wrapping rosebuds in cotton wool for some...' he hesitated, '... some show.'

Helen held her gaze to the floor, at the bright patterns cast on the flagstones from the fire. 'I have to take some responsibility as well for what happened. It wasn't just her.'

'You were a child.'

Helen reached out her hand gently and placed it on his lap.

'I was older than you. She wasn't a bad woman, Gareth. Not really. When you look at it properly, I mean really think about it, it wasn't actual cruelty, just neglect.'

Gareth pushed Helen's hand away and moved over to the

155

fire, as if hoping that it might be able to warm something inside him that was so cold it was struggling to survive. 'I took you into the house. She didn't even come to greet us. So, I took you into the house, with the dried blood caked on your white school socks. We'd worn our school uniforms, our school uniforms to a clinic that performed abortions because there was nothing else clean.' He raised his eyes heavenward in disbelief. 'Walking into that place in our school stuff! Then at home, I ran you a bath and...'

Helen smiled gently, remembering. 'Got me a bowl of Rice Krispies.'

Gareth glanced down at his sister, still kneeling on the hard stone floor. 'So you remember that?'

Helen shrugged. 'It was always Rice Krispies or Frosties. We lived on cereal. It's a wonder we didn't get rickets.' She paused momentarily, as if waiting for her thoughts to catch up. 'They're fortified now.'

Gareth looked blank.

'Cereals. They're fortified. Sensible women all over the country eat them all hours of the day. We were just ahead of our time.'

'There were always carrots and lettuce.'

'No dressing.' She raised her eyes. 'Did she think we were rabbits?' She stopped suddenly, saddened again. 'Sorry, that was unfortunate.'

A small brown-and-yellow spider crawled across the table. Gareth drained his glass before placing it firmly over the creature. Helen smiled.

'You still do that?' she asked, getting off her knees and standing beside him.

'It's a Lace Web, come inside out of the cold.'

'That's what the spider's called?'

He nodded.

'It's a pretty name.'

'They bite.' Gareth tapped the tumbler a couple of times.

'I won't stroke it then. I'll have to buy some more glasses.'

'I told you. I'm not staying.' He got to his feet, pushing back his chair. But he didn't get far. It was as though the floor were made of treacle. He simply turned away, and leaned on the mantelpiece, gazing into the fire. 'I hated her.' He sighed. 'Wrapping roses in cotton wool. Where is he, Helen? The priest.'

And as he said the words, Helen felt that creeping nausea that she always felt when she thought too hard about Father Wright. A sinking feeling that he was there watching, waiting, in the shadows behind her. But she was a grown woman now. She was no longer under his spell.

She shook her head slowly. 'It doesn't matter.'

'I want to know.'

'Why?' she asked, fixing Gareth with a hard stare. 'What difference does it make? And for the questions tomorrow, for the police, the less you know, the better.' Her gaze softened. 'Gareth, you shouldn't blame yourself. I don't blame you. He was wrong. You were only trying to protect me...'

'There's just...' He stopped himself, unsure of his words, unsure of how to proceed with a subject he had tried so hard to bury. 'It's as though there's a piece missing.'

'Leave it.' She moved towards him, reaching forward but scared to touch. 'Gareth, I have missed you.'

'I didn't mean to kill him.'

There it was, out. The last time he had said these very words was over forty years ago, in this same kitchen. It was as if they were on some eternal loop, unable to make any real progress forward.

'It doesn't matter. All this doesn't matter. It was a long time ago.'

'Then why, Helen,' he blurted, 'does it feel like yesterday?'

'You misjudged the punch. You were stronger than you thought.'

He shook his head.

'And now, all these things coming out... About the church.' Her voice was bitter. 'About the priests.'

'If we had gone to the police with it, maybe everything would have been...' He paused, the words dying unspoken on his tongue. When he spoke again his voice was barely there. 'Different.'

'You think?' She couldn't conceal the bitterness.

'Maybe... maybe we had a responsibility too...'

Helen pulled away. She went to the sink and stared out into the garden, into the dark.

'We! It had to be my choice. Mine.'

She expected him to say something, some reassurance. Instead, there was silence. Time away had made him braver. She had to remember, keep hold of, being the victim. 'Besides,' she said, staring out into the night, 'they wouldn't have done anything.' Her voice sounded weary now, almost pragmatic. 'They didn't. They never did. Back then children were children, some sub-species. That's why all these cases are coming out now. The age of silence is over. You were protecting me.'

A burst of laughter could be heard from the other room, Tim and Carla, lost in some philosopher's joke. Some kind of life, some kind of present. Helen looked angrily towards the door.

'God, I wish you could still do that – protect me. He's on one a term. Can't keep his cock in his pants. Never could.'

Gareth looked shocked. 'Carla?' He shook his head. 'I don't think so, Helen.'

Another burst of laugher echoed from the hallway.

'If not now, then soon. Or so he hopes,' she said, her manner dry and cold. 'He's getting older, losing his touch. He used to have quite a touch. He's not much to look at now.' She sensed Gareth's eyes on her back. 'Well, he's not, but... He used to be a brilliant man, exciting. That always reels them in, with their tiny skirts and their open faces. All wide eyes and awe.' She paused, looked down at her fingernails. Her hands always surprised her, the age spots and wrinkles that were beginning to look more like scales than skin. She should have worn Marigolds more often, but it was all too late for that now.

'But he hasn't published in years. Nothing worth reading. Anytime he starts writing, you can be sure he's getting restless. Carla, she's not the first "book".'

'Why did you marry him then?'

Helen shook her head. 'I was a young woman. I found his world exciting. Different.' She paused. 'You should have written. You should have let me know where you were, just that you were all right. They wouldn't have found the body. I told you. I got rid of it. I promised. You were safe. Mother would have calmed down. The flowers would have grown back.'

'But they didn't'

Helen looked puzzled. 'What?'

'The flowers. She never replanted the garden, did she?'

Another burst of laughter floated across the hallway.

Tim's voice could be heard loud and teasing from the other room.

'Cheese! We want cheese!'

They both looked towards the door.

'And then you married Tim.'

She moved to the cheeseboard and placed a small knife beside the cheddar.

'I was older.'

She took two cheese plates from the dresser, wiping them quickly over with a tea towel.

'But you see my point. Why would you do that? Why fall into the same kind of relationship?'

'Not the same.'

'Hungry little mice in here.' Tim's voice again. 'Gouda you to remember us.'

Helen sighed. She picked up the cheeseboard but did not move towards the door.

'It was all I knew, and you, you'd gone. And I missed you. My whole world fell to pieces when you left. But...' She let her gaze drift towards the floor where the firelight danced over the flagstones. 'You knew that. Father Wright might have broken me, but you leaving... that destroyed me. Tomorrow...' She shot him a hard look. 'When the police come.' Why hadn't they given her a time? Why was she always waiting? 'Just stick to the story.'

'Brie, quick!' Tim's voice again, and then laughter. Always, somebody else's laughter.

CHAPTER TWENTY-TWO

GARETH

The wind had chased away the clouds, so that the night sky lay over the house bright and clear. The lack of light pollution meant the stars were out and brilliant. After living in London for so long, Gareth had forgotten what stars looked like. They weren't at all like the isolated satellites that hung above Richmond. More like sparkling pinpricks of chicken seed scattered across a vast, curving dome.

He had waited until three in the morning. No, that was wrong, he had set the alarm for three, not that he remembered actually doing it. The conversation with Helen had broken up, he guessed, at around twelve. He hadn't laid eyes on Carla or Tim after they'd left the table. He'd heard the mouse impressions, and the 'jokes'. Helen had delivered the cheese. He had asked again about the body, but he was pretty sure Helen had refused to give up any details. It was difficult to be certain since the alcohol ensured that the end of the evening had been swallowed up by the pothole of forgetfulness. That didn't matter though. He had other ways of navigating, not infallible, but systems that he often put in place. If Helen had told him where the body was, if there were no secrets left to be unpicked,

Gareth would not have woken up when he did. He wouldn't have set the alarm. The fact that the alarm had been set was a sure sign that Helen was remaining mute. She had been right that the less he knew, as far as the police were concerned, the better. But she was missing the point. Maybe she could afford to do that. She'd been wronged, seduced. But Gareth had killed a man. He wasn't the victim here. He was the perpetrator.

'If you're not going to confess, how will you manage to forgive yourself?' Always that voice in his head. He wasn't sure forgiveness was a possibility, but given the same situation in reverse, some other poor soul tortured by their past, what would he advise? Certainly not sitting on the crime until it ate away at a person from the inside; until there was nothing left of the human being that he might have been.

Gareth had been drinking since the train. So that was around ten hours. He had a habit of drinking too much, binges rather than a regular occurrence. Sometimes he just needed to lose himself. The ten-hour slow stint was probably better than the alternative: getting totally smashed as soon as he'd set foot in the house. Because, when he got smashed too quickly, the time that he lost could be from anywhere, not just from the end of the evening. Memories became patchy and unreliable. That's how he would describe it, lost time. The doctor had a different diagnosis: a blackout. But Gareth preferred his description, because these 'blackouts' didn't mean that he'd keel over. He could, in fact, appear to be functioning perfectly normally. He could hold a conversation. He could go in to work. He could ride a bike or drive a car – provided he didn't get caught. The only thing he couldn't do was remember. So, what a blackout actually meant was that his body was going around without him. When his blood alcohol content was too high, he stopped making long-term memories. His mind was just throwing away everything he did, which had its own attractions – he was living only in the immediate.

When he woke at three, because the alarm was going off, his first instinct was to whack it over the head, turn over, and get some more sleep. But the way that the moon was shining in through the window unnerved him. There were about ten overturned glasses now, all facing down, each trapping a different variety of creature underneath. But that didn't worry him. All that was normal. The thing he found so unsettling was being back in the room he'd had as a child. As if overnight he'd been transported through time. Then he remembered; the journey, the train, his mother washed up in her bedroom, the kitchen supper, and the alarm at three indicating that he had a job to do.

There was an empty pint glass next to the bed, drained of water. He guessed he must have downed it. Despite this, his mouth still felt like someone had died in it and been cremated. But at least the Gareth of last night had been forward planning. The Gareth of last night had also set the alarm clock, clever bastard, so that the Gareth of this morning could find that damn body.

He swung his legs out of the bed. The contents of his stomach – mainly liquid – sloshed around like a cork on a high sea. He had to take a moment to steady himself. Then the Gareth of this morning popped a headache pill that the Gareth of the previous evening had thoughtfully left by the empty glass of water.

He'd taken a torch from the kitchen. He'd opened all the drawers in a futile search. Then, just as he was about to give up, he remembered the fuse box. They always kept a torch there as kids. In Gareth's childhood world there were power cuts and dodgy electrical wiring. To his surprise, when he opened the battered old electrics box the torch, or at least one of its descendants, was still hidden there.

The dogs could have been a problem. He was not keen on dogs and if the buggers had started barking he would have been right up shit street. But he'd found a Tupperware container of stew, put that in the kennel as he'd walked by, and suddenly he and the dogs were old friends. He was pleased to be out in the garden. It was wide and flat, and Helen had pretty much ruined the whole bloody affair single-handed. Okay, so he had started the process all those years ago, but in her own sweet way Helen had certainly given it more than a helping hand. He avoided the mushroom shed. He always hated that place. It was dark and damp and too obvious. She wouldn't hide a body in there. She said the police had searched the property, looking for him. Of course, they weren't looking for the priest. The priest had stolen money and ran off. It was the young Gareth that they were concerned about. But it was the same difference. If they'd searched the place for one body, they would have found the other one. But they had made no such discovery.

It had to be the rockery. They had built it that last summer. They built it before the priest died, but the soil was already 'disturbed' so it would have been easier to move it again.

He went to the garage. It was a mess. He had to force the door open. Inside was life's detritus; fridges, chests of drawers, buckets and a long rusted lawnmower. If the body was in here it would take an age to find it, but then it wasn't like this when he'd left. Mother was in charge when Gareth had walked out. This area supported the garden. Its demise would have given her a heart attack. The house could go to rat shit, but anything garden-related had to be as organised as an army barracks. He pushed the door in as far as it would go and squeezed through the gap.

Most of the stuff was just as Mother had left it; seed packets, catalogues, cracked terracotta pots. He wasn't interested in any of that. He headed straight for the back wall, for the heavy garden tools. Sure enough, they were still there. Not hanging up though now – propped against the wall or fallen to the floor. He bent down and rifled through the pile. His heart almost sank when he touched the ash handle: the old Bulldog spade. It was still there. He pulled it out from the pile. The other forks and shovels went clattering across the floor, but no one would be able to hear, not this far from the house. He smiled to himself as he gripped the ash handle, as if meeting a long-lost friend – it would still do the job.

CHAPTER TWENTY-THREE

CARLA

Carla didn't put the lights on; she didn't want to wake the house. She had pulled the flush, because the bathroom was an en suite. But the pipes made such a goddamn racket she wished she'd left the pee to fester.

It was when she got back in bed that she realised her water glass was empty. One thing she knew about the UK – you never, ever drink from an upstairs tap in a crappy old house. The whole plumbing system is most probably lead. On top of that, the water on the first floor is usually fed by a tank in the attic. A tank that's been sitting there for what could easily be a hundred years. Almost. Her father had been in the habit of hiring houses in different countries for the summer. The fact that they lived in an apartment with no garden meant that, come July, he was itching to get out. They'd done mostly American states, and a couple of English counties. Yorkshire or Lancashire, she couldn't remember which, and there had been some place in Scotland too. She remembered the rain and being bitten a lot by flying insects. Long story short, she'd got the gist of the country house rules; anything earlier than the 1950s and the same rules applied; don't drink the water from an upstairs tap.

So that was how she found herself creeping down the corridors in her short jersey nightdress; not wanting to switch on lights, disturb dogs, bump into lecherous professors or for that matter their fire-breathing wives. Wives who were most likely even now, even at this moment, lying in wait at the foot of the newly rediscovered brother's bed. Yup, that was one to avoid.

Empty glass in hand, she made her way to the kitchen. There was a faint glow from the smouldering fire, not really enough to see by. But if she switched the lights on the dogs might bark, and if the dogs barked the wife might come blundering in with the family shotgun. Did they have shotguns here? She was guessing Helen most definitely did. Besides, the wiring in this place was a goddamn mystery. It could take her decades to find the right switch. So, she stumbled forward towards the sink. Then something moved and she felt a cold sliver of fear flood over her body.

She opened her mouth in a scream, but a large hand clamped tight over her lips, as a length of wet slimy material bumped against her naked leg. Mouth out of action, she was about to go for the balls, when she heard Gareth's voice.

'Shh, you'll wake the house.'

The hand came away.

'Shit!' she exclaimed.

'Sorry.'

'Shit. My God!' Her heart pounded in her chest fit to explode. 'What are you doing here? You gave me...!'

Gareth hit the lights.

He was standing in the kitchen, fully dressed in jeans and a coat, but the jeans were caked in dirt, and in his hands he carried an old strip of material, more mud than cloth.

'Sorry. Didn't mean to startle you. You okay?'

Carla nodded, then started to laugh.

'My God, you scared the shit out of me.'

'Sorry.'

'I didn't want to wake anyone,' she mock-whispered.

Gareth stared out of the room into the dark hallway. All was quiet. He held his finger to his lips as he closed the door through to the house.

'Seriously, you seriously scared the shit out of me. I was after water.' She held up her glass, as if offering evidence.

'Sorry,' he said again.

'I couldn't find the light.'

Gareth nodded, walked to the bin, opened it and rammed the material in.

'What is that?'

'Oh, just some rubbish from the garden.'

'You were gardening? Now?' She glanced out of the window. It was pitch black out there.

Gareth's mouth twisted into a wry smile. 'Looks a bit odd?'

She raised an eyebrow in reply.

'The garden's a state, thought I'd go make a start.'

'Right.' She drew out the word, wary of the tease.

'Get a few bulbs in. They'll be flowers come Christmas.'

Now she was smiling, sceptical, but smiling. 'Okay.'

'Sorry,' he said again.

'Sure.'

He pulled off his coat and draped it over the back of the chair. His hands, she noticed, were covered in mud, as if he'd been out for an evening's entertainment with a group of moles.

'You finished the book?'

She looked blank.

'You and what's his name.'

She shot him a pretend hard look. 'Tim.'

'Tim.' He smiled.

'But you knew that.'

'I did. You and Tim, huddled in the study working on a book.'

'Oh, that.' She smiled, remembering. 'Hardly huddled. But yeah, sure. Knocked the book up between the risotto and the cheese. I'm quick like that.'

'You know, Helen thinks you're after her husband?' he said, a barely perceptible thread of amusement lurking behind his words.

'Please. Helen needs to get out more.' Carla paused and gave him a hard stare, which had just a hint of flirtation. 'And you, what do you think?'

She felt a pang of disappointment that he didn't pick up the flirt now it appeared to be running so nicely. Instead, he walked to the tap and began to wash the dirt from his hands. The sink running brown beneath his fingers.

'I think that she's mistaken.'

'Oh.' Carla drew a little closer.

He had his back to her, but she could see his face reflected in the dark window. He was a good-looking man. Sure, he was old. But he was carrying it well. The muscles of his arms still toned. His face was angular and he had a good strong jaw.

'Mistaken?' she asked. 'And why would that be?'

'You're right, Helen needs to get out more.'

He turned off the tap, grabbed a tea towel, and turned to face her as he began to rub his hands dry. Carla waited for a moment, expecting him to say something more, but nothing came. The grandfather clock in the hall ticked. The night was disappearing.

'I should get my water and go to bed,' she said.

He looked up from drying his hands, put the towel down by the sink and leaned back against the kitchen units.

'Problem is,' she hesitated, 'you've got me intrigued. What were you really doing out there?'

169

He said nothing, just took the glass from her hand, filled it, then handed it back.

'There really are mysteries here, aren't there?'

'Oh?'

'Midnight strolls, talking reed beds, chests that don't open.'

Gareth looked puzzled.

Carla pointed behind her, to the ugly widow's chest that appeared to be sulking in the corner.

'It doesn't open?' He seemed genuinely curious.

'Lost key.'

Gareth nodded. 'And you like mysteries?'

'Ahh... ha.' Carla smiled, her eyes starting to sparkle. 'Depends.'

'On?'

'Depends on who's involved.'

Pointing her bare toes, she moved just a step closer.

'For example, you. I'm interested in you.'

'I'm very flattered.' He smiled. 'But... I'm... Well...'

'Not available?'

He smiled. 'That's right.'

'So there is someone?'

'No. No one. It's... my job.'

'Busy?'

He nodded. 'Work doesn't really fit with it.'

'Charity work?'

'That kind of ballpark.'

There was a brief pause while she weighed this up. Wondering if she should lean on the conversation a little more, or was it perhaps best to let it drop. But what was the point in leaning? He obviously had no intention of spilling the beans.

'You're enigmatic,' she continued. 'I like that.'

'Not always a good thing. My advice? Always choose a friend who's an open book. Sadly, that's not me.'

'But open books are a little bland, don't you think? Personally, I prefer curiosities.'

He smiled, but she sensed a touch of sadness behind those green eyes.

Suddenly she shivered.

'It's cold,' he said. 'We should get back to bed.'

Carla looked towards the fire in the throes of its last death rattle. 'Like I'm going to sleep now. Could we maybe sit by the fire for a bit? You should drink more water if you don't want to wake up with a hangover. Keep hydrated. Another log in that burner and I think you could coax it back to life.'

Gareth looked thoughtful. She thought he was going to say no. That the evening would close, that the mysteries would remain locked away like the chest. But to her surprise he nodded and grabbed himself a glass.

Carla looked to the fire, with its single large armchair. 'Jeeze, it's cold in here.'

'Warmer than it used to be. We never had central heating growing up and the wood burner does a good job.' Gareth took the metal handle from beside the fire, opened the small window on the burner, and pushed some of the dry logs that were stacked in a neat pile by the hearth into the belly of the stove. He didn't close the door but watched as the flames began to devour the wood.

'You want to sit beside it?'

'Always the gentleman.'

She sank into the armchair as he grabbed himself a kitchen chair from the table. Making sure, she noticed, not to drag it across the floor.

'You don't have a throw?'

He glanced out into the utility room, grabbed Helen's coat from the hook and threw it towards Carla slow enough for an easy catch.

'Thank you.'

She adjusted the coat over her knees. 'There, sorted. And your chaperone, sleeping?'

'I'm happy to leave her if you are.'

'More than happy.' She pushed her hands towards the fire, drinking in its warmth.

'Better?' he asked.

'Thank you.' Carla leant forward into the light. It was better. The evening had been a little too bizarre even for Carla's eclectic tastes. 'She's quite intense, your sister, territorial. I mean about you. She's all Rottweiler.'

Gareth laughed. 'She's certainly no Labrador, and territorial?' He sucked in his cheeks. 'Yeah.'

'Is it good to be back?'

'Good?' He thought for a moment. 'No. But you're an unexpected bonus.'

'Oh?' She couldn't help but smile.

'I think you're helping to diffuse things.'

'Were you at the same dinner party?'

He laughed.

'No seriously, I'll take the compliment. Thank you. Always happy to help.' They stared into the fire, into the caves made by the dying embers. 'Do you mind if I ask you...' She pulled back, studying his face in the firelight. 'What happened here? What made you leave?'

Gareth shook his head. 'The usual teenage angst.'

'People don't just run off. Kids have problems, sure, but...' She studied him even closer. 'I'll get it out of you. Eventually.'

'To be honest, I'd like nothing more than to get it all out. I've been carrying this for way too long.'

'What? Gareth? Carrying what?'

But suddenly he seemed far away. His eyes fixed on the flagstones with their dancing light show. And Carla stopped trying to lead the conversation. There was no point. She let him keep his silence, turning to watch the light as well. It was so pretty, almost hypnotic. There was an ant crawling across the floor, walking in a perfect straight line as if it were on an invisible ant highway cutting across the kitchen. Gareth broke the moment. Picking up her abandoned water glass, he drained the last dregs, before turning the glass over, leaning forward and trapping the ant underneath.

'Gareth?'

'Sorry, it's a... bad habit.'

'Why trap an ant under a glass?'

There was a moment's silence. Then he smiled. Not the smile of a psychotic. The smile was open, honest, childlike almost.

'I like ants.'

'Okay?' Carla asked, letting her voice undulate with a question mark, like this wasn't really much of an explanation. 'So, you trap them?'

'Why not? And you? Do you like insects?'

'They're okay. I like bees.'

'Everybody likes bees. That's not really counted.'

She laughed. 'Good point. But... so why ants? Why would you like ants?'

'A million things.'

'Just a million?' she joked. 'Okay, convince me. Some ant facts. Not a million, a few will do just fine.' She pulled her legs underneath her body, like an acolyte keen to follow his every word. 'I am here to be won.'

'Best fact?'

'Please, nothing mediocre.'

Gareth nodded thoughtfully. 'The Queen, she mates only once. One brief period of copulation before setting up her colony. Sex once in a lifetime.'

'Bit sad,' Carla said pulling her bottom lip into a pout. 'Just the once?'

'She can keep the sperm viable for up to fifteen years.'

'Fifteen years!' Carla exclaimed. 'You sure about that?'

'Certain. Harvester ants can live up to twenty years.'

'That seems...'

'Like a neat fact?'

She nodded. 'But you said there were millions. Got any more up that dirty old sleeve of yours?'

He glanced self-consciously at his mud-caked sleeve.

'Ants,' she said helpfully. 'Sorry, I didn't mean to sidetrack you.'

He nodded. 'Okay. Try this. If the Queen dies, the whole colony dies. They form a kind of suicide march. Work and work till they expire. They don't sleep, just work. I spent a whole summer once, watching ants.'

Carla laughed. 'You wouldn't get away with that now. Your face would be glued to some monitor. You'd be watching some kind of matrix, hero, interactive, virtual crap. No time for insects.'

'It was a different world.' Gareth took a deep breath, and his eyes seemed to flicker a little.

She got the feeling he was running his mind back over the familiar landscape of his childhood. But he didn't look happy, more like a person being forced to endure some distasteful content as it spilled out at them.

'What?' she asked softly.

'There was much more...' he narrowed his eyes, searching for the right word, 'I guess freedom.'

'Can't be bad.'

But he didn't reply.

'Gareth?'

'At the time I thought it was perfect.'

'You know what? I always distrust that word. *Perfect*, it's only ever surface tidy. Perfect means something is obsessed about. Other things, they're just neglected. So, I'm suspicious of *perfect*.'

'But you'll go with freedom?'

Carla assumed a mock-thoughtful attitude for a moment, before nodding graciously. 'I think so.'

'Yeah, well there was certainly a hell of a lot of freedom. We did exactly what we wanted to do. Woke when we felt like it. Went to bed when we got tired. Didn't always go to school... But, okay, so, "perfect"? The garden was perfect. But the house we lived in – squalor. Upper-middle-class squalor: leaking roofs, holes in our shoes, cracked dishes, plates piled high in the sink. Mother was too posh for washing up. Didn't even occur to her.'

'Too posh for dishwashing!' Carla exclaimed wistfully. 'God, I could do with some of that.'

He smiled gently. 'You're great the way you are.'

'Well thank you, but... middle-class squalor.' She toyed with the term. 'I'm not sure we have that in the States.'

'It's a British speciality – squalor, blended with a large helping of smug superiority.'

She laughed. 'So you watched ants?'

'One whole summer. I remember thinking, when I was watching this one ant colony, I remember wondering – because there was no way of telling – if the Queen was alive or dead, not without breaking into the hive. Which would have spoilt the fun. So, I remember thinking to myself – were they working? Or were they dying? And how would anyone know? There they were, a continuous line of ants crawling from some cracked paving stone towards this fallen branch. I could have moved it closer. I could have saved them a lot of trouble. But I didn't.'

'Oh? And why wouldn't you?'

'They'd still walk for the same amount of time.' He

shrugged. 'Even if the food source was closer. If it was closer, they'd just do more circuits. And I thought that maybe a long walk in the sunshine – the sun was shining, it was a warm day – I thought maybe a long walk would be preferable to being under the paving slab where there was no sex, no sleep, just darkness.'

'So, you were how old?' Carla asked, trying to picture the boy in the sun with his ant highway.

'I don't know, maybe ten, eleven?'

'And Helen, was she interested?'

Gareth smiled. 'No. That's probably why I remember it so clearly. It was one of the first times I'd been without Helen. We were inseparable. But that time she was trying to make perfume: collecting petals, putting them in jars. She's eighteen months older than me, but always seemed so grown up. She was at that age when girls become conscious of how they look. She'd read an article when she was visiting the dentist. It was one of those magazines.'

'Women's magazines?'

Gareth nodded. 'Sometimes I'd steal one from the surgery for her. Get off the school bus early with a mysterious pain in my gum.'

Carla laughed. 'In your gum!'

'Pain in the gum, it's non-specific, so, not demanding treatment.'

'You did that for magazines?'

'Had it all worked out – I'd get off the bus early and drop in at the dentist on my way home. Pick her up a few copies, nothing to do with plants, anything to do with fashion, gossip. One magazine, it was for teenagers, weekly or monthly I can't remember. But it had this regular article about using natural remedies in make-up – flowers and things. Helen had turned one of the mushroom sheds into a kind of perfume lab. Played in it for years. There were empty margarine tubs filled with stagnant water. Everything lined up, all neat and organised.'

Carla raised an eyebrow, playfully. 'I'd expect nothing less.'

'Every morning she'd walk down the line of tubs with one of those big metal watering cans, pouring a little more rainwater into this or that tub. All the tubs neatly labelled. All at different stages of fermentation. I can jot down the recipe if you like?'

'Quite an offer.' Carla smiled, ironically. 'So, these perfumes, they were good?'

A look of quiet resignation descended over Gareth's features. 'Everything smelt of mushrooms.'

'Oh my God!' Carla laughed. 'Poor Helen.'

'Occasionally she'd come out of the shed, mole-like, clutching one of her tubs, watering can in hand. She'd find me in the garden. Push the tub under my nose and ask what I thought.'

'And you told her?' Carla's eyes narrowed. She knew the answer already.

'I found it difficult to comment. I told her I thought it was pretty, because that's what I thought she wanted to hear. I always tried to tell Helen what she wanted to hear, even when I didn't understand.'

'Maybe, at some point in time, someone should have stood up to her? Perhaps it would have done her good.'

Gareth shrugged. 'I was a kid. She wasn't much older, but she was the one who fed me, checked my school uniform, looked out for me. She wasn't like... She wasn't hard like she is now,' he said sadly. 'Neither of us were. So, why not let her have her perfume?'

'So, you helped make it?'

'Boys don't make perfume.' He shot Carla a wry smile. 'Not back then anyway. So that was why I had so much time on my hands.'

'For the ants?'

'Exactly. Helen was preoccupied. The "lab" was the only time she showed any interest in botany. Normally, she had nothing but scorn for Mother and her garden, the whole horticulture thing.'

'So?'

Gareth looked blank.

'What happened to the ants?'

He shrugged. 'Oh, I don't know. Helen got bored. Realised she wasn't going to get a commission from Mr Fabergé. Sought me out, watering can in hand. Found me crouching by the paving slab, watching. Loitering there in the sunshine.'

'And she watched too?'

He shook his head. 'No. She poured water over them. Washed all the ants back down the crack.'

'Really?'

'They were just ants,' Gareth stated blankly.

But Carla frowned, struggling with the idea. 'That's not the way the story should have ended.'

'Stories don't always end the way you want them to. Sometimes someone has to get thrown under the bus.'

Suddenly she felt cold again.

Gareth continued staring into the fire, as if trying to draw its life into him. But now he looked rigid, barely alive Carla felt. Like he was just going through the motions. When he spoke again his voice was quieter.

'I was just pleased she'd come out of the shed. It was a long time ago.'

He lifted the glass from the ant.

'Run!' she whispered.

Gareth laughed softly as the ant did exactly as it was told. 'Lucky bugger.'

The fire in the kitchen was beginning to die, and a few brave birds had begun to sing the morning in, despite the darkness.

'We should go to bed,' Gareth said reluctantly. Getting to his feet and offering her his hand which she took, not noticing as the coat slipped from her lap.

CHAPTER TWENTY-FOUR

HELEN

It was seven when she woke. Seven was late for Helen, but then she had slept badly. Tim had spent the night making a noise not dissimilar to a car with a flat tyre: snoring, with wet flapping lips. She sniffed the air. She could detect no trace of semen, which meant, no doubt, that last night had been a disappointment for him. She rolled over in bed, so that her body lay facing her husband, dragging the blankets with her. Taking the thumb and first finger of her left hand, she attached them to Tim's nose, as it stood upright, pointing at the ceiling, not a care in the world, and pinched hard for a few seconds. Pinched hard enough to remind Tim's body that it did in fact have a nose, but not hard enough for him to wake. As with most things in life, Helen conceded to herself, it was a fine balance. The thought of him bumbling around, under her feet, for a whole two hours longer than was absolutely necessary was unbearable. If he went back to sleep, she could at least scrounge a little peace out of the morning.

Perhaps Gareth would be up too. Tim spluttered uncontrollably for just a moment, his body fighting to regain the correct breathing/sleeping mechanism, and she released the pinch. His breathing reset, the snore gone. Whale-like, he rolled over, and the bed rocked like poor Jonah's rowing boat.

Belting her dressing gown, Helen walked down the corridor to Mother's room. Here lay another complication that she did not wish to wake. Her life was filled, Helen realised, with attending to people she did not actually like, and she wondered if this was the case for most human beings.

She walked down the long, empty corridor towards Gareth's room. The door was shut. She pressed her ear to it. There were no sounds. He may not even be in there, she thought to herself. He may, she thought, have left late last night. He knew where the car keys were: same place as always. He could easily have taken them, got into the car and gone. But would he leave without all those unanswered questions tied up? She could tell they were burning a hole in his brain. In the end, he would have to leave without those precious answers, but no doubt he wouldn't realise that. Everyone thinks they're going to win until they lose. Then from inside the room, she heard the headboard bang against the wall in the wake of a body movement. Just one bang, then silence. She placed her hand gently on the bare oak door, as if she could feel Gareth's presence through the wood. He was home, and she so desperately wanted to wake him, to run in and pull off his blankets. To plead with him to come and help with the chickens or sprint headlong through piles of autumn leaves just as they had done as children. She hadn't thought about the leaves in years. Those golden autumn play-fights. How they would start off raking the downfall into neat piles, which they would always end up throwing. How they would bury themselves underneath amber-coloured leaf mountains, laughing as the papery scales crackled like fireworks around them. But that was a long time ago. The time for play had gone. She would not wake him. She struck off down the corridor wondering, as she walked, why adults didn't do these things anymore. The fun things. Why, when you turned twenty, did you stop having leaf-fights or building sandcastles purely for the pleasure of jumping on them? Of course, Helen knew that there were lots of insufferable adults who continued to function through these activities with their kids, or for their Instagram, Facebook, Twitter accounts – whatever the latest social media trend was. But when did a person actually stop doing it solely for their own personal pleasure?

She came down the stairway and went first into Tim's study. There were no signs of passion. The chairs had been brought to the corner of the desk. The sofa, which was velvet and filled with duck feathers, had only one large dent on it, about the size of Tim's backside. So, it would appear that Carla had remained on guard and had sat on one of the hard, cross-backed chairs by the writing desk. The plate of cheese was now empty and abandoned beside Tim's manuscript; unable to find its way to the dishwasher alone.

She picked the manuscript up. It was around sixty pages long and spiral-bound, which Helen thought was an unnecessary pretension for a first draft. A twin-lock fastener would have been perfectly adequate. She flicked through the white pages. The typeface was nice, not Tim's habitual Garamond, but what she assumed must be Caslon. It was a little less flamboyant. Beyond that, she had no comment. She put the bundled pages down and carried the cheese plate to the kitchen and the dishwasher, which would need to be emptied first.

But she didn't head straight for the washer. Gareth's coat was draped across the back of a chair. A wave of bittersweet sadness washed across her body. To have signs of his existence trailed carelessly around the house was everything she had dreamed of during those empty years. She walked towards the coat, took it into her hands and buried her face in the soft, black fabric; breathing him in. Her eyes welling up. It wasn't crying, just an involuntary response. As if she were wearing herself inside out, and all reactions were instinctive. She sighed. Then suddenly realised: the coat had been on the hook last night. She had touched it briefly when she came in from the chickens. She had, in fact, lightly knotted his coat to hers, linking the arms. So, how had his coat shaken off its partner and come wandering into the kitchen?

She pulled at her top lip uncomfortably. Gareth must have come back down after lights out. They had gone up together, separated on the landing at the top of the stairs where she had given him a brief hug. She had heard Carla and Tim, still in the study, laughing and smug, snorting up the cheese and their inane jokes. Gareth had most definitely gone into his room, because she had watched. She had waited at the top of the stairs by the top post as he walked down the length of the corridor. She had seen him open the door. He had given her a brief sad smile before he'd disappeared inside, and the door had closed. She remembered it all in precise detail.

She'd heard Tim and Carla come up around one o'clock, and then she'd stopped listening. But somewhere between one in the morning and seven, Gareth must have gone for a stroll. The sleeves of the coat, she noticed, were a little muddy. Not that this was a problem; she could sponge them easily enough. But the mud was still partially wet.

Still puzzling over Gareth's late night stroll, Helen took the coat and headed to the utility room. If the mud dried, she would brush it off, then sponge it later when most of the residue had gone. But the logistical domestics soon evaporated from Helen's mind; her coat was not on its hook. Someone had moved it. She hung Gareth's Barbour back in the exact same position it had been taken from the previous day and scouted around for her own coat: not on the hooks. She glanced back into the kitchen. It was on the floor beside the armchair. Curious, she picked up the coat. The sleeves were not wet. She held it up to the light. A few dog hairs. More than normal? she wondered. She was unsure, and it seemed to have lost its shape as if it had been left lying on the floor for days. But then it was getting old. Yet, just as she was about to put it back on the hook, she got a waft of perfume. Not her own. Musk. Someone who wore a musk-based scent had been wearing her coat. She sniffed again. Definitely musk, and a hint of sandalwood. She crinkled her nose in disgust. If there was one thing she hated more than rose and lavender, it was musk. It reminded her of deer. It reminded her of rutting animals. Bitterly, she threw the coat down beside the washing machine on her *dry-clean-only* pile. It had to be Carla.

Helen headed for the kettle. She took it from its stand and placed it under the tap. The garden was still in darkness. *So,* she wondered, as she drew the water into the large open spout, *what exactly was Gareth's game?* She sighed, moved to the fridge, swung the door open, and noticed that the stew had gone.

Helen placed one hand to her forehead, squeezing tight as if the pressure would release a thought process that might harbour some reasonable explanation. But what in the world that could be, she had no idea. Gareth and Carla had got out of bed, come down to the kitchen, and decided to have a midnight picnic of stew sitting on her coat? With a stab of heartache, Helen remembered the little summer cottage they had created as children, the walls of the old shed open to the wind and rain, and the glass wind chimes finding music in the air. A cold shiver passed over her body. All of that was gone, she thought to herself. That whole life had been punctured. She had been forced to make a different set of wheels to carry her forward into a new life, and she had done okay. She was still rolling forward, at any rate. 'Damn that bloody woman,' she muttered.

She headed to the wood burner, there were things to be done, the kitchen must appear welcoming when he came down.

All this was essential; she had to ensure that the house felt like a home, his home. She would try to coax the fire back into life. If she just held on to the familiar domestic frameworks, she could weather this unpredicted blip on the radar, this Carla. An unexpected love interest would be easier to control here, in the confines of the home, and that at least was something to be thankful for. If he ever did manage to get to the States, it would all, very quickly, be out of her influence. Bending to the fire, she realised it was still warm. They had obviously sat on Helen's coat in front of the fire. But was it sitting? The thought bit into her heart like acid. She reached for the handle to the wood burner and opened the door. She threw another log in the grate, closed the stove and pushed herself up.

'Oh yes. They've been busy, your man and that woman.' It was the priest. He was standing at the back door as though he'd just been for a quick stroll around the garden.

'Pretty little thing, that one,' Father Wright continued.

Helen said nothing. Instead she straightened her back and made a beeline for the kettle, which had begun to scream. Outside, it was starting to get light in the garden, and as she passed in front of the thin glass windowpane, she realised where the mud on Gareth's coat had come from; the rockery had been turned over.

Father Wright stood behind her, framed in the reflection looking over her shoulder at the mess.

'He's very motivated, that brother of yours, when he sets his heart on a thing,' Wright said, staring out onto the garden, seemingly impressed by the chaos. 'Motivated, that's how I'd describe him, eh, Helen?'

Looking down she realised that her hands had become luminous white where she was gripping the sink with such a force that the blood had ceased to flow.

'Gets the job done, I'd say.'

Flexing her fingers, Helen poured the boiling water over the teabag and squashed it against the side, while Father Wright took up her vacated position at the window, staring out over the rockery.

'Pulled that whole top layer off. Must have taken him a good hour, maybe two.'

She carried the teabag over to the bin. She would not be drawn into conversation. But on opening the bin, she gasped as if taking a physical blow to the stomach. There, just above a mesh of unwanted salad leaves and risotto dregs, was a muddy strip of cloth – her old school uniform. She picked it out of the bin, straightening the edges, brushing off the caked mud with the flat of her hand.

'So, what was it then, Helen? Eh? Some kind of shrine to lost innocence? Don't flatter yourself.' The old priest nodded his head slowly. 'He'll find what he's looking for, you know. He won't give up. He knows something's wrong. That's the thing, isn't it, Helen? Everything's drawing to a close, spinning closer and closer and tighter and tighter. And who's at the centre then, Helen? Eh? Answer me that? Who is it standing there holding all those threads?'

'Morning. Anyone else awake?' It was Tim.

Helen realised that her hands were shaking. She pushed them down into the bin, forcing the school uniform deep into the soft recesses of old food and the week's unwanted. She pressed down so hard she could feel the sludge rising up past her wrists, she pressed and pressed, until the shaking stopped.

'No,' she said, pulling her hands back up, checking them momentarily, before heading to the sink. 'You're down first.' The priest had gone.

Tim took his regular place at the kitchen table. Always the same seat. Why did they do that? Why was it always the same seats?

'Pleasant evening?'

Tim nodded. He opened his mouth, about to query some of the more awkward bits of the *celebratory* meal. But this was not the way Helen wanted the interaction to go. The situation needed to be managed.

'She's pretty, Carla,' Helen said casually, as she put the kettle on once again to boil, even though it didn't need it.

Tim shrugged. 'They're all pretty.'

Helen nodded magnanimously. 'Some are prettier than others though. She's pretty.'

'I'm saying nothing,' Tim mumbled. 'Don't want my head bitten off.'

She stopped making the tea, her spoon still in the cup, and turned to take him in. 'I'm sorry, Tim. I didn't mean to do that; have a go at you. I didn't mean...' She paused as if finding it difficult to locate the words. 'Those things I said. I'm sorry. The way I barked at you both.'

He nodded his head sadly, not in total forgiveness. But it wasn't an outright dismissal either.

'It's just all these women,' she said sadly.

'It's not "all these women".'

'But Carla?' Helen insisted.

'She's just a fellow academic.' He shrugged the comment off lightly.

He was good at that. He'd had years of practice.

'Oh, Tim, come on!' Helen implored. 'She idolises you.'

And the old fool couldn't help himself; he smiled modestly.

'I...' he stuttered, with a glint of pride in his eyes.

'I can see it in the way she looks at you. The way she hangs off your every word.'

Helen took a moment to breathe, letting the thought of this adoration engorge Tim's head just that little bit more. 'The book must be good,' she said, in a hushed, excited whisper.

And he was like a child again, puffing out his chest in pride – *look at my crappy old potato painting, or my tooth that's just come out, or my shit that's sitting there in the potty*. It was true, some children had to have even their own excrement applauded. That would have been Tim, and that kind of *need*, that kind of expectation, didn't go away.

'It's going well.' He nodded.

He was in danger of bursting the buttons on his shirt if his chest swelled any wider.

'I'm so glad.' She walked towards him and stood at the other side of the table, staring into his eyes. 'I always knew you were brilliant.'

His mouth opened just a little, as if about to protest.

'Shh,' she said, holding her fingers up gently as if to stop his needless defence. 'Don't be modest. It's true. I knew you had that streak in you. That...' She searched for the right word. 'That possibility of brilliance. And...' – she dropped her eyeline apologetically – 'maybe I haven't always been able to show it, how I feel.' She raised her eyes again, locking them firmly with Tim's. 'I had a quick look at it this morning.'

'The manuscript?'

She nodded eagerly. 'The draft in your study. I hope you don't mind?'

He shook his head; he didn't. She knew he wouldn't. It was all fuel to the ego.

'But it's not finished.'

'No,' she said excitedly. 'But it's good. I think you're onto something.'

'It's not my idea. I mean...' Tim blustered, but she cut through his words.

'Maybe not, but it's fascinating.'

She placed her hands gently on his shoulders. 'Do you

remember when we first met, that study of yours? All those wet afternoons? It never stopped raining that term.'

She paused for a moment, gently rubbing her hands over his shirt, kneading the flesh below. 'Is it like that with her? All that closeness, that intimacy?'

Tim reached up for Helen's hands, a gentle act of reassurance. 'Helen,' he said softly, 'nothing's going on.'

She sighed gently. 'Maybe not yet. But you can see that she wants you.'

Helen lowered her face so that it was beside his. She could feel the warmth radiating from his skin. 'It excites me, Tim,' she whispered. 'The thought of you with her, the thought of you touching her.'

'But we're just...' He was trying to protest, trying to push her off. But Helen's slim hands could draw magic out of the air, and she mixed the magic into his skin.

'The thought of her pretty white flesh,' Helen continued, softly, softly. 'Pressed against yours, naked. Her skin, so perfect, you can almost see through it. See her blood pulsing in her veins. See all that life. Feel it.'

He was closing his eyes, leaning back in the chair. His breathing dropped to a low instinctive lull. 'Her breasts, so perfect,' Helen continued, her voice soporific and slow. 'Like the garden of Eden all over again. Remember?' she whispered. 'Remember how it was, Tim, for us, all those illicit afternoons?'

'Helen,' he moaned. He stood, pulling her into his arms.

She nestled her head into his wide chest. 'You should take her out. Take her for a walk down by the coast. Get a room. You could get one at the pub. You know, the place on the quay; the one that has the log fires in the bedrooms?'

His hands travelled hungrily over Helen's body. 'Then you report back to me, all the details: blow by blow, step by step, touch by touch. All the elements of seduction, lay them out for me.'

He held Helen at arm's length for just a moment, drinking her in, no longer interested in the young American. 'But...' he protested.

'Shh.' Helen placed her long slim fingers to his lips. 'I don't mind. In fact, I'd find it a pleasure. Do you understand that, Tim?'

'My God.' He was almost growling now: a deep, low rumble as he pulled her closer. 'I'd forgotten how beautiful you were.'

'Foolish of you to forget.'

He leaned in towards her, his lips hungry for contact, but skilfully she managed to slip away.

'Not now, Tim. Come back after you've had her. And the bracelet,' she said, almost as an afterthought. 'You know that thing she wears? After you've had her, bring me the bracelet and I'll wear it for you. But you must take her. I give you permission.'

Tim exhaled. 'You're sure? Because...'

Helen shook her head. 'I'm sure.' She raised her face to his, let him kiss her for just a moment, then pulled away.

'Don't let her go,' she whispered.

'God, you drive me mad.' Every inch of his being appeared wound like a spring.

'Good.' She laughed.

'There's time before they wake up.'

'No. You need to be fresh for her.' Helen smiled playfully. 'You need to be hungry.'

'Okay,' he agreed. 'I'll just... I'll get the room. I'll drive down there.'

Helen nodded. 'They open at eight.'

'Right.' He moved towards the door.

'Tim?' she called, and he turned with such a look of hope

and excitement on his face, she felt almost cruel. 'The car keys,' she said simply.

He laughed. Took the keys from the hook by the door. 'Tell her I'll be back.'

'And don't forget the bracelet,' Helen called after him.

He blew her a kiss. 'It's yours.' And he was gone in a cloud of testosterone-induced excitement.

'Nicely done, Helen,' said the priest. She turned to see him sitting in the armchair beside the fire. She was about to tell him to go fuck himself, but managed to pull herself back, get a grip. Because if she started speaking to the man now, he would never leave her alone. She knew the rules. Speaking to yourself is madness, and however real Father Wright might appear, Helen knew for a fact that he didn't exist, not anymore.

CHAPTER TWENTY-FIVE

HELEN

It was cold when Helen tramped out of the house for her regular visit to the chickens. She had decided not to wear the coat. She was, in fact, unsure if the coat would survive the winter; fraternising with the musk-and-sandalwood-smelling Carla had been a bad move. Instead of pulling on the coat, Helen had tied her bathrobe tighter, put her wellington boot-liners in her boots, and secured a scarf around her neck. It was not a flattering look, but the chickens, despite having connections with Hollywood, never complained about the way she dressed.

A brief stop at the dog kennel was enough to inform Helen as to the fate of the stew. The Tupperware container had been licked clean. Red poked his long nose through the wire.

'Later,' she said simply, conjuring a handful of dog biscuits from her bathrobe, and pushing them through the mesh.

As she walked over the badly cut grass towards the run, she glanced back over her shoulder. She always had the sensation that the house was crouching behind her; that when she walked forward, it picked up its red-brick foundations and skulked after her in the shadows. If she turned, it would stop. If she turned around too quickly, however, she had the unnerving feeling that it might fall on top of her. There was a light on in one of the upstairs rooms. A faint, rectangular glow seeping out into the morning gloom: Gareth's room. She felt a hollow, empty sensation in the pit of her stomach, as if her internal organs were standing on the edge of a cliff and about to jump. It was such a small, innocuous glimmer of warm, orange light. Why couldn't it stay there forever?

She arrived at the chicken run and let herself in, locking it behind her. She undid the door to the hut and peered inside. These were her breeding stock. They were huddled sleepily beneath their feathers, Natalie Wood rubbing shoulders with Julia Roberts. Helen checked the feed and water, then reached back into the hutch. She pushed the chickens to one side, grasping the eggs from under them, and placing her spoils in the wide pockets of her robe. Out of seven hens, she managed three eggs; it was the start of winter.

Safe out of the cold in the mushroom shed, she marked the three new eggs with her green permanent marker; the same cross that would be used to orientate the egg once it entered the incubator. She turned Natalie's egg first, before placing the other recent acquisitions, pointy side down, on the damp kitchen towel.

Then she opened the incubator and began to turn the eggs, rolling them around the elliptical circuit into the vacant space in front; each time an egg was rolled forward, another space would open up behind. She picked up one egg to do a spot check. She switched out the lights and shone the torch on her phone at the shell. It had been five days. It was the same story as the day before: one tiny dark spot spewing out a net of red thread veins. Often five days would be enough to see the heart beating. But today there was nothing. She wondered if someone shone a torch at her own ribcage, would they see her heart? She had thought it had turned to stone, yet now that Gareth had returned, now at last she seemed to sense it finally stirring.

~

Back in the kitchen, Helen put the heavy pan down on the hob. She split the rashers of bacon that were holding together as if they'd been glued and laid them out in parallel lines across the base of the pan. She put fresh water into the coffee maker and switched on the light to heat the element. The bacon began to sizzle. She leant across the sink and opened the window. There was an extractor fan that Tim had insisted on, but it made such a racket. It was true that in opening the window, she let out the heat from the boiler. But the birdsong won hands down over the grind of the extractor fan. Besides, she would only open it a crack.

'Bacon, God, how I love bacon.' Carla was standing in the doorway, dressed in a fresh T-shirt and jeans, straight from the shower. She could not have looked fresher if she had been created from scratch this morning.

Helen took a deep breath, before turning to her guest, not smiling but managing at least a thin veneer of *attentive*. 'Good morning. You slept well I trust?'

'Great. Anyone else down?'

'Tim, I think he's off organising an activity for you.'

'Activity.' She laughed. 'And your brother?'

Helen felt the bile rising in her throat. 'Not yet. Gareth will arrive when he feels like it.'

'Not a morning person?'

'Not an anytime person. He's always been a moody bugger,' Helen said lightly. 'So, I suppose you want some then?'

Carla looked confused.

'Bacon?'

194

Food has the ability to calm all factions, Helen thought. Wars should be conducted over dinner tables, not battlefields, and the best chef should always win.

'Wouldn't say no.' Carla nodded enthusiastically at the possibility of a few fried strips of pig. 'I'm ravenous.'

'Goes without saying.' Helen remembered the coat on the floor, the previous night's kitchen sex. How she hated this woman. She would have so loved to slap her, hard. Instead, she calmed herself, took a deep breath and went in for a different kind of kill.

'Look, Carla, I need to be honest with you.' She crossed to the doorway, and pulled it firmly closed.

'Oh?'

'You need to watch Gareth. I mean,' Helen corrected herself, 'you need to be careful.'

Carla looked confused. 'Careful?'

Helen took a deep breath, as if summoning up courage. 'Look, I don't like to have to do this.'

She leaned back against the counter. 'He doesn't...' Helen paused momentarily, as if searching for the right word, '... function like other people, my brother. Don't let him take you in.'

Carla shifted her weight uncomfortably, spreading out her bare feet into what Helen seemed to remember would be second position for a ballerina? Toes pointed outwards, feet flat. It could be an affectation, but it was also, she realised, the kind of position that could withhold a quick shove backwards. Helen liked the young woman a little bit more for this. Wary was a better way to live your life than blind optimism.

'He doesn't function?' Carla asked. 'What does that even...'

'He's different. Different. Doesn't have the same moral code.'

'Wow. Okay.' There was a brief pause for thought. 'You know what he does now? His work?'

'No.' Helen had to stop herself from snapping. What did his career matter? There were more important things.

'Yes, a mystery,' Carla mused. 'But he said it was some kind of a charity, and charity surely, that's caring.'

'I think the *some kind of*, is the crucial part of the description. I wouldn't go giving him money.'

'He hasn't asked.'

There was something a little bit too sharp about Carla's words. Disappointingly, Helen realised, Carla was one of those insufferable young women who insist on making up their own minds.

'But, he is a bit of a curiosity.'

Helen could work with this.

'Curiosity! He left. Walked out. You call that a "a bit of a curiosity".'

'But why?'

'Oh, wouldn't that be easy?' Helen took a deep breath, trying to compose herself. After all, it hadn't been Helen that had stormed out. She had been the calm rational one – the sibling that stayed. 'There are no answers with Gareth,' she said, 'only riddles. Look, this is difficult. I don't want to have to say anything against him. He is my brother. But listen to me, Carla, he will crush you. He might not mean to destroy you. I am sure that would not be on his mind, but that's what he does. What he does time and time again.' She was surprised at how satisfying it felt, dumping it all. But then her nostrils twitched, bringing her back to the here and now with a bump. She glanced at the bacon, no longer sizzling. The edges looking charred as dead bodies. 'Damn, this is burnt.' She pulled the pan from the heat.

'It's okay, please, it doesn't matter,' Carla said lightly, more interested in the conversation than the demands of her stomach.

196

Helen sighed. 'He pulls people in because of that air of mystery, that element of pain. He smoulders, my brother. It's just the way he is, and of course, that's attractive. But get too close and it hurts. We all wound up damaged, Carla. All the women who got close: me, Mother, all of us. He hurt us all then dropped us.'

Carla was listening. Intently.

'He's like a puzzle, and you desperately want to fit all the pieces back together; to make it lie flat. But it won't. It won't sit straight. The pieces don't fit. You'll never get to the centre of who he is. You'll just get lost. Go in and you won't get back out again.'

'How do you know?' Carla asked. Quiet, but determined.

'I've been caught. Do you think I'm not broken? Why do you think I'm still here, washed up, discarded like some long-forgotten toy?'

'Yes, but how do you know what he's like now? That was years ago, over forty years ago. A different lifetime.'

'Not a lifetime!' Helen's face wrinkled in disgust. 'That would all be too convenient. You can't shrug the past off. It doesn't work like that. The past is part of us. It always has been. It's shaped who we are: both of us, all of us.'

Carla's phone buzzed. She glanced at it, thankfully.

'Oh, it's Tim.' Helen could hear the relief in the young woman's voice. 'He says don't bother about breakfast.' She glanced towards the burnt bacon. 'We'll grab some when we're... He's outside in the car. I'll just get my...' She walked, a little self-consciously, towards the utility cupboard and grabbed her coat. 'Sorry.'

And she was gone.

Helen emptied the pan, rinsed the graphite-dark insides and started again. Hands shaking, she pushed the window open a little more. How dare that woman come in here with her fresh-as-a-daisy outlook on life and start measuring it up against all the crap that Helen had to pull herself through. How dare she. This was not how this reunion was supposed to go. Why had Tim brought that stupid girl to the house. Idiot.

Just as she leaned back in from the window, the door to the kitchen opened, and a sleepy Gareth entered sniffing the air.

'You burnt the bacon?'

She pulled on a smile. 'I was distracted. Stupid.' She glanced down at the pan, moved the rashers with the spatula. 'This second lot is fine.'

He rubbed his eyes and threw himself down at the table.

'Here.' She placed a glass of water and a headache tablet in front of him, then went back to her bacon.

'Is Carla down?' He drank the water and swallowed the pill.

How irritating, Helen thought, that his first question should be about the American.

'Sleeping, I think.' She flipped the rashers and pressed the lever on the toaster, so that the muffins balancing above the frame disappeared into the bowels of the machine. 'I saw your handiwork.'

Gareth squinted his eyes, not getting her point.

'The rockery,' she continued. 'Bit extreme, don't you think?'

He shrugged.

'What were you expecting to find?' she asked, crossing her arms in front of her.

'Oh, come on, Helen.' He pulled one large hand through his short-cropped locks.

'No, honestly. What were you expecting to find?'

But he said nothing.

'And even if you did,' she hissed, her voice much lower despite the fact that the house was empty, 'what purpose would it serve now?'

Again, he said nothing.

She sighed angrily. 'Do you honestly think I'd bury it there?'

'I don't know, Helen.' His voice sounded weary. 'I don't know what to think.'

She drew him off a coffee, placing it on the table beside his right hand.

'Black, no sugar,' she announced.

He took a sip as she continued to glare at him, arms refolded. The toaster had popped up, but she was not in the buttering mood. 'I just don't understand what you're trying to prove.'

'No? Maybe it's not about you understanding. Maybe I just need to know.' He slowed his delivery down, so that there was no fear of her missing the fundamental point. 'I need to know where he is. I see him everywhere. In everything. And now there's the watch.'

'Seriously. Forget the watch. It means nothing.'

'Not to the police, obviously.' He turned the spoon in his coffee as the silence gathered around them.

'We talked about that.' Helen's voice sounded curt, final.

'What time are they coming?'

'They didn't say. Just today. Probably. I don't know. It doesn't matter. We have our story.'

'Story,' he mumbled, barely audible. 'But maybe that's not good enough anymore. Maybe I need to know.'

'You honestly think *knowing* would make it any better? He'll still be there... following you around, watching. You can't wash something like that out. You're not a child anymore, Gareth.'

He didn't reply.

'You know what I do to get rid of him? I imagine him off on some cruise around the Mediterranean. On one of those great, grotesque, shiny white boats, smiling like a smug, overfed bastard over his dog collar. Just smiling into the sunset. Try that little scenario if you like,' she said bitterly. 'See how that fits.'

'What's in the chest?' he asked, and for a moment she was caught off guard.

He indicated towards the great ugly thing positioned stubbornly in one corner. Helen let out a loud, spontaneous laugh.

'You think he's in the chest?'

Gareth's skin flushed under her ridicule. 'No,' he said sharply. 'I asked you what was in the chest.'

'He gave me presents. He gave me things,' she said sadly. 'Presents, things he thought I wanted.'

Silence.

'He always left something, some piece of crap in return for my...' She hesitated. 'Favours.'

'Please. Euphemisms don't suit you, Helen.'

'Okay. He gave me presents in return for sex.' There it was. 'He gave me presents because it made me complicit. I'd been rewarded.'

Gareth had lost that pink flush. Instead, he was now turning a luminous shade of pale. She wondered if he would vomit. Perhaps.

'Paid off,' he muttered.

'That's about the size of it. Or maybe more, I was engaged in the transaction. The presents made me appear to be a willing party. Life, Gareth, it's about making the best of all the crap we don't understand. That's what people do, people who survive. We cobble together all the shit dumped on us and hope we can extract something that...' She paused, finding the sudden confessional exhausting. 'Something that makes sense, that feels just about liveable.'

Gareth pushed his chair back and went to the chest. He tried to open the lid, but it was stuck fast.

He looked lost, confused. 'So you kept them, these presents?' He sank down on the curved barrel top.

'I have no idea why. To be honest, it's taken me a long time to figure it all out.'

'Did you ever tell Mother?'

She shot him a sarcastic look. 'Well that would have gone down well.'

'You should have told her.'

'Oh? And which part? What do you honestly think she would have done? And what about you? Was your solution any better? I was sixteen.'

'Fifteen,' he corrected.

'A few months off sixteen. Did it really matter what I did? But you, Gareth, what you did... You...'

They both jumped when the door knocked. Three sharp confident raps. Then silence, a silence so deep, so tense, in which they both just stared at each other as if fixed in time.

'The police,' Helen said. 'They've come.'

CHAPTER TWENTY-SIX

TICK TOCK

'So what would you call this then, *wetland*?' Carla said, striding out across a labyrinth of muddy paths. Her boots were Helen's, and too big, but this did not appear to be slowing her down.

'That's right,' Tim gasped, trying to sound enthusiastic. But it was difficult when you were knackered and had unwittingly found yourself on an outward-bound expedition with Dora the Explorer. None of this was going as expected.

'How far have we walked?' she asked with not one breath out of place, as he came up beside her.

He took his phone out of his anorak pocket. She had downloaded an app in the car park: *WalKing*. She seemed to be under the impression that the app would be 'a whole heap of laughs'. Now *WalKing* was standing over them like a boot camp sergeant major, commenting sarcastically on their progress.

He looked at the screen. Along with a lot of information he did not understand, it was telling him to – *work that body, buddy*. If the app's slogans were supposed to be motivational, they were seriously missing their mark. He pushed the device back into his pocket, and tried to catch up on his breathing.

'Three miles,' he announced, rounding up to the most impressive digit. 'But oh dear.' He stared up into the clouds. 'That looks like rain. Think we should be heading back now. There's a lovely pub...'

'Oh come on, Tim. This is fun. Doesn't the app give us a gold star if we do ten K?'

And she was off again, tramping on ahead along a boggy path edged with reeds. He stared up at the sky. Black clouds. If it rained, he would have to put up his hood. It was one of those emergency hoods they sew into anoraks. Its front edges were trimmed with some kind of elasticated cord so that it clung to the skull, making even the most distinguished of men look like an overgrown baby. If the hood went up, his chances of the inn with its fire and fuck would be out of the window.

'Coffee or tea?' Helen ushered the police into the front room.

'Coffee would be good,' the plain-clothes detective said. Morton or Midrift was also there. Helen wasn't sure which one. She had lumped the names together. It was the policewoman who was still playing tag and appearing even more tight-lipped than on their first meeting. Helen seemed to remember that was Midrift. She could probably ignore the PC without serious consequence. But this latest offering in his camel mac and dark-green trousers had a DS in front of his name. Jackson. DS Jackson. He was in his late forties with a face like shammy leather. Everything about Jackson's appearance suggested that this most 'routine' enquiry had somehow become more 'of interest'.

'Coffee. Yes, of course. Could I just ask, DS Jackson?' Helen hesitated in the doorway. 'I have already told you everything that I know. What is this about?'

'Your brother. We wanted to question your brother.' DS Jackson positioned himself in the chair at the far end of the room, but didn't take his eyes off Helen as if he was soaking her in.

'My brother?'

'Yes.' He shifted in the chair, but not awkwardly, more as if he was settling himself down firmly in order to develop a large root system that would hold him fast. 'We understand he's returned home.'

She let the pause hang there for a moment. She would not be intimidated, not on her own turf.

'That's right,' she said. 'Last night. Can I ask, how you knew?'

'Your husband kept us in the loop.'

She felt a tidal wave of anger sear through her body. Bloody Tim.

～

Tim was so tired of this game. He wanted to go back. He'd be far too knackered to perform if Carla didn't slow down. He noticed a sanderling picking its way across the marshes, its stout bill pushed out in front, as its little legs frantically bicycled along the mudflats, giving the bird the appearance of running after its nose. Tim knew that feeling. 'It's an incredible landscape, archaeologically speaking.' He puffed. 'They found the remnants of a Saxon boat once. Just the shell. All the ribs. The bone structure.' He paused, trying to catch his breath, looking out over the marshes. 'Look. Look.' He tried to inject a little excitement into his voice. 'A heron.' He called, in an attempt to slow her down. 'See!'

She looked. He wasn't sure if she had seen. If he had been standing nearer, he could have taken her arm, kept her close as he pointed the bird out. Her face held in line with his. But she was too far away. He realised with a sickening jolt that he was running out of time.

～

'So what brought you home?' DS Jackson stirred his coffee.

'I...' Helen shifted awkwardly in the corner. DS Jackson noticed.

'Please don't let us keep you, Mrs Martin. It's your brother we wanted to talk to.'

'I don't mind. It's no trouble.' Helen tried to erect a smile as DS Jackson turned his attention back to Gareth.

'Mother. I came back because she's getting older. I felt it was time.'

'And why did you leave? Initially? You were fifteen I think?'

'Fourteen,' Gareth corrected.

'No one came to find you?'

'The police tried,' Helen blustered. 'You must have records? Mother and I tried too.'

'I...' Gareth cleared his throat. 'I didn't want to be found. Family troubles. Differences. I felt I had to get away.'

～

A flock of birds flew up from the marshes, covering a quarter of the sky before resettling in a different spot.

'Look, Tim, look. They've come down on the flat there, see?' Carla held one lovely young arm out in front of her as she pointed. 'I think we should get closer,' she announced eagerly.

'Actually...'

But she wasn't listening. 'I think we can get right up near them if we head out this way.'

There was a narrow path sticking up between tussocks of marsh grass. It looked slippery. One false step and they'd be in the mud. But he had to stop thinking like an old person.

'Right,' he said decisively. 'Grab my arm.'

'It is so peaceful here. And that sky!' She looked up into the wide sky, stretching on for eternity.

'Graham Swift,' Tim tried to keep his voice level, in control, 'said there was no hiding from God here. It's so flat; no corners, no hills, nowhere to get away.'

'No hiding from God,' she repeated, laughing, opening her arms out wide either side of her body, as if offering herself up.

~

'If you're not going to confess, how will you manage to forgive yourself?'

The grandfather clock in the hallway ticked. Gareth shifted uncomfortably in his seat, wishing that phrase would stop coming back to haunt him.

'And Father Wright?' DS Jackson asked. 'You remember him leaving?'

This would have been the time, Gareth thought, to confess. The interview was beginning to remind him of another interview, in a different room, far away. A safe place. It was when they had initially put him forward for the job in the States. He'd said he didn't know. Didn't feel he was up to it. Penrose, Gareth's mentor, had never known his backstory. Gareth had never told anyone the events of that last summer. But Penrose had always known there was something holding Gareth back. Something eating away at him from the inside.

'If you're not going to confess,' Penrose had said, 'how will you manage to forgive yourself?'

That was when Gareth had decided it was time to go home.

'Mr Edwards?' DS Jackson's voice broke through Gareth's thoughts. 'Father Wright. Can you tell us where he went?'

~

Suddenly there was an almighty crack. A bolt of lightning split the sky as if the heavens really had been torn open, and it started to rain.

'Come on!' Carla exclaimed. 'Race you back; one, two.' She paused playfully. 'Three.' And then she was off, tearing away over the mudflats, past the reed beds, and onto the narrow muddy path.

'Fuck,' Tim said out loud, before shouting out to the wide East Anglian, Godless sky, 'Fuck! Fuck! Fuck!'

~

If you're not going to confess, how will you manage to forgive yourself?

The rain beat on the windows. The clock in the hallway ticked.

'The priest...' DS Jackson continued. 'Can you tell us where he is?'

A flash of lightning illuminated the room, scouring the corners of their shadows.

'No. I'm sorry,' Gareth said truthfully. 'I have no idea where you would find Father Wright.'

CHAPTER TWENTY-SEVEN

HELEN

Helen decided to butterfly the lamb. Gareth had been sulking in his room for most of the morning, and a good part of the afternoon. She'd seen him from the kitchen windows at around twelve, picking through what was left of the flower beds. But he hadn't sought her out, so she'd left him. The police interview had gone well. She was mildly irritated that Gareth was continuing to poke around. Surely he must realise now that the less he knew the better.

She was going to keep everything simple tonight: lamb, roast vegetables and the tart. Cheese was easy enough. If she took the board out of the fridge a couple of hours before they ate, they could please themselves if they wanted it. There would be a lot of food for just two people, but the lamb could be served cold tomorrow, as could the tart. Nothing would go to waste.

When she heard the front door open, she felt an incredible sense of peace wash over her – it was Gareth. He must have done a complete 360-degree search of the house and wound up back where he'd started. She heard the footsteps across the hallway, wiped her hands on a tea towel and found a smile. But, when the door opened, her heart fell through her chest down to

208

her feet. It was not her brother. It was Carla, standing there rosy and bright, with wind-pinched cheeks. Looking even lovelier than she had at breakfast.

'Wow, that smells *so* good.' The young woman entered the kitchen as if pulled by her nose.

Helen tried to regain her composure. It took her a second to tidy the ruin of her smile and replace it with something functional. When her voice came out of her mouth it sounded dry, but as ready for public appearance as if packaged in a Swiss finishing school. 'I hadn't expected you back for supper.'

Carla's features ran briefly through a mixture of confused emotions. She was a bright girl, and would have realised that Helen's *seemingly* innocent comment, delivered in a *seemingly* innocent manner, might have a landmine hidden beneath.

'Oh, I'm sorry,' she stumbled. 'I didn't realise.'

'No.' Helen took another two plates from the dresser, as the young American squirmed.

'I didn't mean to put you out.'

The sentiment, Helen realised, was genuine. The woman was at least apologetic. But just because the sentiment was genuine did not make the intrusion acceptable. 'Seems to me you've used the *not putting us out* line once already this weekend. I thought you were going to stay out with Tim?'

Carla paused before answering, and Helen felt like she was being sized up. 'No,' Carla said simply. 'That didn't really work.'

Helen turned back to the salad she'd been preparing, a bright carnival of leaves that arrived in a neat air-filled pack from Waitrose. She popped the bag and emptied it into a plain white bowl. 'Luckily, there's enough food. And the house,' she shrugged, 'well it should be big enough for all of us. One would hope.'

'I should think so,' Carla came back, enthusiastically. 'All these rooms. How many bedrooms are there?' Then she hesitated. 'Sorry, is that question rude? Am I allowed to ask questions pertaining to size?'

Helen took the olive oil and a small bottle of raspberry vinegar down from the shelf. 'Only when the size is impressive.' She poured the familiar one-to-three ratio of oil to vinegar into a small glass jar with a tight lid for shaking. 'Seven,' she said. 'Well, seven first-floor bedrooms. Though most aren't used.'

Carla nodded to herself, as if chewing over the thought. 'I am suitably impressed.'

Helen put the dressing beside the salad bowl. She wouldn't combine them yet; it was too early. The dressing should be added just before the eating, or the leaves would start to rot.

'It's not as big as it looks, the house,' Helen said casually. 'Although,' she remembered, 'one summer, Gareth hid out in the attic for six weeks. No one knew he was there.'

'Six weeks!' Carla's jaw dropped open. 'And no one noticed?'

Helen shrugged. She hadn't actually realised this was such a big deal. 'It was a different era,' she explained simply.

'Do you know what I love about England?' Carla smiled.

'I couldn't even hazard a guess.'

'I find the English so straight.'

Helen nodded, pleased with the assessment, but Carla hadn't finished.

'I mean on the surface you're all so...' She paused, as though aware that she might be treading on sacred ground. 'I hope I'm not offending you?'

Helen shook her head lightly, in a water-off-a-duck's-back attitude. So, Carla continued, 'You're all so very straight, so proper.'

'Proper.' Pleased with the proclamation, Helen ran it over her tongue.

'Yes,' Carla agreed. 'But underneath... underneath you're all as quirky as hell.'

Helen's lips shrank into a thin line, as if she held a lemon between them. She managed only a short, sharp, 'Indeed.'

Then, from upstairs, the bell. Helen brushed her hands across her skirt, pleased for once to be able to make a quick exit. 'Saved by the bell,' she said, ironically, and walked towards the kitchen door.

'You don't have a job for me then?' Carla called after her host.

'I'll think of something,' Helen shouted back down the stairs.

As she walked towards Mother's room she amused herself with *jobs* that might be found. Long jobs that would take Carla far, far away.

When she got to Mother the old woman's lips were parched and dry. Helen poured fresh water from the jug and held a glass to the old woman's face.

Nothing was turning out as expected. She wished she could reset the whole sorry thing. It would perhaps have been better if he hadn't come home. If she had held him forever young and adoring in her mind.

When she came back into the hallway, she was just in time to hear footsteps outside on the gravel drive. One tread was heavy – a man's, harmonised with the lighter step of a woman.

Thank God, she thought. Tim will have taken Carla out again. She had been right to make the young woman squirm. Carla wasn't wanted. The evening would work. She would have Gareth alone. But when Helen arrived in the kitchen it felt emptier somehow.

'Oh good,' Tim called brightly from the hallway. 'Hoped I'd catch you. Gareth said he was going to take a jaunt down to the pub, grab some cigarettes.'

'Filthy habit,' she managed, in her disappointment.

'Exactly, but I asked him to pick up a bottle of Scotch as well.'

'He went with Carla?' She tried to keep her voice flat, devoid of emotion.

'Yes. She's probably after more steps.'

Helen looked blank.

'Oh, you know what they're like with exercise. Walk all over you if you let them.' He laughed.

CHAPTER TWENTY-EIGHT

TIM

The grandfather clock continued to count. Tim stared anxiously at its face. It read eight o'clock. They had been sitting at the table, in a dark brooding silence, for half an hour. Helen was in one of her moods. Behind him, in the oven, the lamb continued to shrivel.

'We should start,' he said decisively.

'No. We wait.'

The clock ticked. Tim shifted awkwardly in his chair.

'I didn't think you'd mind me telling the police your brother was back.'

She chose not to answer. He chose not to take her silence to heart.

'They could have got caught up.'

Helen tapped her fingers gently on the tabletop in time with the beat from the clock. 'I'm used to waiting.' She paused. 'You see what he's like?' she hissed, barely able to contain her irritation.

They sat in silence for a few minutes more.

'Our young American friend – you didn't fuck her then?'

Helen asked, as easily as if she'd been asking him if he'd like carrots with his peas.

'Helen!'

She sighed in irritation. 'Oh, for Christ's sake, Tim. Don't be such a prude.' She flattened her hand decisively on the wooden tabletop. 'I need a cigarette.'

'You said earlier it's a filthy habit. We've stopped.'

Helen shot him a look full of acid, and he withered.

She went to the dresser, reached up for a narrow tin case and searched inside for the slim, white paper rolls.

'I'm guessing you don't want one,' she said, lifting a cigarette out, 'because you've *stopped*.'

He didn't reply. She opened the back door. The air came into the kitchen like a cold curtain of ice. Helen lit up. 'Nothing?'

'What?' he said, confused.

'Our young American – not even a furtive grope?'

Tim looked away, embarrassed. 'I don't know, Helen. Maybe I'm too old for all of this.' He glanced back towards the door and his wife. 'Are you sure you saw something?' He ran his hands through his grey thinning hair. 'She doesn't even look at me in that way.'

'You're too weak. You don't know how to exploit opportunities.' She sucked the sweet nicotine into her lungs, before exhaling a soft plume of purple-tinged smoke into the garden.

'I handed you everything on a plate, said I didn't mind, even suggested a venue. You were given a licence to lay, and you still couldn't pull it off.'

'She just doesn't...'

'Of course she doesn't. You needed to get her away from him.' She stared angrily into the night. 'You don't know what he's like.'

Tim shrugged. 'He seems all right.' The clock ticked. 'Maybe he's changed?'

Helen stared scornfully at her husband. 'You don't know him.'

'Look,' he said, his voice slow, calm, 'what happened this morning, I haven't seen you like that for years.'

'You didn't keep your end of the bargain.'

'Helen, why don't you come with me now? There's time.'

She turned away, facing back out into the night.

'Look, I'll buy you a bracelet.'

'For God's sake, Tim, grow up. It's not about the bracelet.'

He let the grandfather clock fill the space again for a few moments, then said calmly, 'I think we should eat.'

'We wait.'

CHAPTER TWENTY-NINE

CARLA

Carla glanced quickly in her compact mirror, removing a smudge of eyeliner that had got trapped beneath her eye. It hadn't been a long walk to the pub, forty minutes maybe. But her make-up had been done with the thought of a kitchen supper, not a forty-minute escape through the Suffolk wilds. At the bar, Gareth was ordering drinks. The table was already showing one round of empties. Shots, they had both seemed to need something quick. She glanced nervously at her watch. They were going to be really late, but then it was his sister. The ball was in his court, and come to think of it, she wasn't sure she could do another cosy family meal. Carla was fast coming to the conclusion that there was a lot to be said for TV dinners. She put the mirror back into her bag and glanced surreptitiously at her phone. There was no signal. This whole place was beginning to feel a bit like the land that time forgot, and maybe that wasn't a bad thing. Maybe some places got lost for a reason. She comforted herself with the fact that people still had legs; if Helen and Tim wanted the two escapees badly enough, someone could walk or drive down to the village.

Gareth put the drinks down in front of her. A white wine

for her, but he was still on shots: a whisky. No mixer. She'd never seen a neat Scotch quite that large before.

He smiled briefly, then took a swig.

'Where did you go with Ted?' he asked.

She smiled. 'Ted? Seriously? Tim, took me some place out on the estuary? By the marshes.'

He nodded.

'Are you okay?'

'No. I feel like I'm standing on sand,' he said wearily. 'You know how the sea eats away at the shoreline, how it crumbles the ground from under your toes till there's nothing beneath you, just a sludgy mess where the ground once was.'

None of this was surprising to Carla. The atmosphere in the house was bordering on toxic. Half of her, no, most of her couldn't wait to get back in the car and head towards Norwich. But there was something about him, something hurt that made her keep wanting to reach out. She leant forward and let her hand rest gently over his.

'You need to step to the side,' she said softly. 'If the ground's not firm. Take a deep breath. Step to the side and try again.'

'We went through a lot, Helen and I.'

Carla nodded. 'The past can be a tricky place.'

'She got pregnant when she was fifteen.'

Carla put down her drink a little too hard. She hadn't expected this.

'Who was the father?' Then it dawned on her, the colour drained from her face. 'Was it you?'

'No! Shit. No, she's my sister.' He took a long, hard swig of his drink. 'It was the priest.'

'The one that went missing?'

Gareth nodded. 'That last summer, Father Wright signed me up for some camp in Dorset. I didn't want to go. I was good at letter-writing, especially forging signatures. Helen and I, we'd had a lot of practice. So, I just wrote to the camp, said I wouldn't be there, family reasons, can't even remember what now. Then I signed it from Mother. The morning I was supposed to leave I went out the front door, waved goodbye, then doubled back. Went in the back door. I hid up in the attic.'

Carla looked guiltily down into her glass. 'Helen told me you hid in the house once for six weeks.'

Gareth smiled bitterly. 'Actually, yes. I overheard. When you were talking tonight in the kitchen. I was in the hallway. Know what the odd thing is? I didn't realise before, but Helen knew all along that I'd been in the house when I was supposed to be at camp.'

'I'm not sure I'm getting this?'

'That summer, when I was in the house. I always thought no one knew; I'd got away with it. I didn't tell Helen cos... It felt kind of odd. Like I was a voyeur.'

Carla looked puzzled. 'Voyeur?'

'You see, I caught glimpses of something I wasn't supposed to see through the cracks in the floorboards.'

'Oh shit.' It was all hitting home now. 'The priest and your sister?'

'Yeah. But you see – if Helen knew I was there in the house, watching. It gives the whole thing a different slant.'

'Fuck. It was all staged?'

Gareth nodded slowly. 'I was Helen's audience.'

'And the priest? What happ–' But she didn't finish her sentence. 'Fuck. He's dead?' she whispered.

'Probably. I hit him. Hard. Then he disappeared, and recently...'

'He might have run off. Maybe he thought the game was up.'

But Gareth wasn't listening. 'There was the watch. You

see... I can't move on until this gets cleared up. I need to unpick it all, try and understand what happened.'

'And the America thing. Was that true? Are you going?'

'I was. I thought. I hoped I could leave it all behind. But you see, Carla, I can't move forward till I find out the truth. Whatever it is, it needs to be out on the table. Without the truth I don't even know who I am.'

'My God.' Carla sat back in her chair. 'There's that garden. The bit outside the kitchen?'

'No. We built that before the priest disappeared. Anyway, I looked.'

'No, I didn't mean he was under the rockery. Not that. Have you ever looked at it, I mean closely? It's like some kind of witch's medicine cabinet: monkshood, deadly nightshade, foxgloves. The plants in the garden, they're not just plants, Gareth, they're poison. Your sister's herbs, most of them are deadly.'

CHAPTER THIRTY

TIM

Helen had finished her cigarette. The door to the garden was closed, which was at least one blessing, Tim thought to himself; it had been cold enough to freeze his balls off. But it was still icy: Helen had returned to the table and was sitting opposite him, in silence. He felt like one of those dolls in a doll's house; everything set out and waiting, waiting, waiting. Besides the fact that this was all a crock of shit after a long week of work, a failed attempt at seduction, and a series of (quite frankly) confusing come-ons from his (perhaps) psychotic wife, Tim was hungry.

'We should eat,' he announced.

'We wait,' Helen replied curtly, without moving a muscle in her body. Hands placed on the table, either side of her empty plate. 'Where's your willpower, Tim? It's only food. We wait.'

'But I'm hungry,' he explained, reasonably enough, he felt. 'They'll probably get something down there. They're most likely still at the pub.'

'Is that all you think about, your stomach? Aren't you worried about her?'

Tim shrugged. 'I don't know, she's...'

'You saw what he did to my rockery? Tore it up.'

'He did that before, isn't that right? That story about him dumping all the plants in the pond.' Tim went picking over all the evidence, trying to make some kind of sense of it; like Hansel following the specks of white stones out of the wood. But it didn't make sense. He kept coming up at the same point he'd set off from. 'So, what is that all about, Helen? The plant thing?'

She declined to answer.

'Helen?' But still nothing. His patience was wearing thin. 'Helen,' he repeated.

'All right,' she replied slowly, taking a deep breath as if steeling herself to lay everything bare. 'I had to go and see a doctor... in London. Mother did nothing; too busy with her garden. So, Gareth took me. We went by train. The whole thing was...' She hesitated. 'It was one of those experiences...' Her voice trailed away momentarily. 'If I could have had a lobotomy instead, I would have gone for that. But sadly, that wasn't on offer.'

'What was it, Helen? What was wrong?' he asked quietly.

But she didn't reply. Just lowered her head, and gazed at her hands, the knuckles white where her nails were pushing further and further into the table.

'Is...' he hesitated, '...is that why you can't have children?'

'Oh, for goodness' sake, Tim,' she snapped. 'Do I look like the sort of woman who wants children?'

He glanced away, awkwardly, feeling as if he'd been bitten.

'When we got back,' Helen continued, 'Mother didn't even come to greet us. Didn't even ask me how it went. Not one word. She was too busy packing for some flower show. That night, as we were sleeping, Gareth dug up all her borders. Then,' her voice sounded completely flat, as if cauterised of all emotion, 'he disappeared.'

221

'Why the visit to the doctor?'

But there was no reply. Tim took a deep breath, then tried again. 'Helen, what did you do in London?'

'Oh, for goodness' sake, Tim. Do grow up. You don't seriously want me to spell it out, do you?'

He continued staring at her across the table. 'I think I need to hear it.'

'It was an abortion. I had an abortion at fifteen.'

'Who was...?'

But she cut him dead. 'The father? Guess, Tim. Why don't you guess? You know it's there in your head – the thought.'

'Gareth?'

'And why not?'

'My God.' He could hardly catch his breath. 'He raped you?'

'Oh, wouldn't that be just so convenient? Then you could stake his head on the gatepost, avenge my honour. No, Tim, he didn't rape me. It was all me. All my idea.'

His face twisted into a grimace of disgust. 'My God, Helen. That's depraved.'

'But didn't you know that about me, Tim?' she hissed. 'Wasn't that one of the things that excited you about me in the first place – the fact that I was, just that little bit, depraved? My poor little Tim.'

He stood abruptly, pushing his chair back, sending it clattering to the floor as he placed his hands on the table for support. It felt as if his whole world, everything that it had been built upon, had been ripped from under his feet.

'You...'

'I disgust you?' Helen moved her chair back and got to her feet. She stood opposite him, the table between them. 'Please,' she offered helpfully. 'Please let me at least do that for you. I seduced him. Just like I seduced you all those years ago in your study, with my wide eyes and my perfect flesh. You've been useful, Tim. Financially, you've been very useful, and I wouldn't say that I haven't enjoyed you occasionally. But you see he's back now. After forty years I've got him home.'

'I feel sick,' Tim clutched his stomach.

'Oh, for goodness' sake, don't be such a drama queen.'

'But this morning?'

'Please, Tim, do grow up.'

But he was shaking, his entire body jittering with emotion. 'I'm going. I can't stay in this house.'

'Good. Can't you see I've had enough.'

'You? You've had enough?'

'You've served your purpose.'

'My God. Helen, you're mad. You're crazy. I'm serious. I don't want this.'

'You think I do. Go. Just go.' She picked up the bread knife from the board by the sink and hurled it across the kitchen.

He watched it clatter to the floor at his feet.

'It's too much,' he said quietly, but firmly. Then left.

CHAPTER THIRTY-ONE

HELEN

After the sound of Tim's car had drained into the night, Helen stood for a moment in the silence. Letting the house absorb the events, until the sound of the grandfather clock seemed to merge into something else. A rhythmic beat. Clapping. She could hear clapping, slow clapping – the sarcastic kind.

'Small conquest really, Helen.'

She didn't need to turn around to know that the priest was back. The hairs on her neck stood on end, and, despite the fire, the kitchen had grown a little colder.

'But he was always easily controlled, that husband of yours,' the soft lilting voice continued. 'Gareth now, and that young girl? That's a different story. You'll have to work harder on that little problem.'

She shook her head, as if trying to dislodge the priest, but the priest would not be quiet.

'You didn't seriously expect it to be easy, did you? Come on. Things are different now, Helen. Gareth's all grown up. And you, well you're in the autumn of your years. Be honest now, you'd be hard pushed these days to get a man to change a tyre for you, let alone keep your secrets.'

She hoped that now he had delivered his 'piece', the apparition would disappear, but instead it went over to its favourite chair: the armchair by the fireplace, not the original. The first thing she had done, when she was promoted to *lady of the house*, was to get rid of the old chair. But it was still the priest's favourite haunt. She would burn the new one, she resolved. Maybe next week, when she did the leaves, that damned chair would be on top.

But, for now, he sat staring into the fire, rubbing his cold dead palms in its warmth.

'You know he's going to piece it all together,' Father Wright said slowly. 'Him and that girl, they're going to want to know more, I reckon.'

She could feel Father Wright's eyes boring into her back. She could hear the smug smile in his words. 'I'd say that times have caught up with us at last, Helen. Wouldn't you agree? You're going to have to do something pretty drastic to get control again.' He nodded to himself, staring back into the fire. 'A call for drastic action I would think, that's what it is. Go on, Helen, try your hand. Let's see what you can come up with.'

CHAPTER THIRTY-TWO

HELEN

Helen picked her way across the garden. The mounds of damp grass that had been abandoned after a poor, half-hearted attempt at mowing had been transformed into lumps of ice overnight. They made walking difficult. And she was late this morning. It was already eight, so it should have been light, but a thick petrol-grey bank of cloud was hanging grudgingly over the sky. She knew she didn't have much time. Today, Gareth would be attempting to leave, yet again. She needed to be on hand to stop that, but she also had things to do, and she was late for the chickens. She walked a little faster, the cold seeping through the rubber of her boots. She had forgotten her boot liners, because Carla had taken them when she went on the marshes and hadn't put them back into the boots. At the thought of the young woman, Helen felt bile rise in her throat. The day was getting away from her in all the wrong directions. She knew she was going to have to pull it back around and wrestle the damn thing into shape, but then she was good at that. There had been no call from Tim, though she hadn't really expected one. All contact now, she assumed, would be conducted through a third party. The lawyers would be involved. Truth be told, she couldn't remember the last time Tim had told her he loved her. She hadn't personally said it since she'd managed to get him down the aisle. But Tim had remained under the misapprehension that they shared something 'special' for an unfeasibly long time.

She arrived at the coop. In all the excitement, she had not locked the chickens in the previous night. Natalie, foolishly, had been sitting outside. She was looking stubborn, and when Helen pushed her gently out of the way there was an egg underneath. It would probably be useless now, frozen.

In the mushroom shed, Helen marked Natalie's egg with the green pen. Despite her lack of hope for it, she set it on the kitchen towel with the four others she'd collected.

She was tired. She had listened out last night for the *return*. She had waited until around twelve thirty. She was not used to late nights. By half-past midnight she had been defeated and headed upstairs. She'd checked on Mother, who was still breathing. Her hands were outside the blankets, hard-worn and weathered. 'That's what gardening does, Mother,' Helen muttered, as she had gently tucked her Mother's paper-light limbs under the covers.

She had gone to the bathroom and let the pipes sing a little as she removed her make-up. In bed, she remarked to herself that it was pleasant to have the king-size mattress all to herself. Tim was such a dinosaur when he slept, snoring, or turning, or worse. The cotton sheets luxuriated around her thin body. Tomorrow, first thing, she would wash them: get rid of him for good.

She had closed her eyes but kept her ears wide open, and at around one she had heard them come in; broken bits of laughter and shushing. Gareth's feet seemed heavy with drink. She had closed her eyes and tried to put the 'couple' out of her mind. She had known she needed to get some sleep, known there would be a lot to do the next day.

The shed was still warm against the frost outside. Helen opened the incubator and began to roll the eggs. She wondered how many days of her life she had spent rolling eggs. How many times had she trudged across the lawn to the chicken coop? There were other lives, lives that went on outside of this house, of any house. Gareth had broken free. A charity, that's where he said he worked. Not Alcoholics Anonymous, she was willing to bet. She had hoped he had done a little better for himself. His clothes were expensive enough. Did he think working for a charity would make him a better person? It was too late for that. And this was her life: the eggs, and the marshes and the creeping dark house. It would, no doubt, continue along the same lines until they nailed her into a box. If she had been allowed to escape, she would not have bothered with 'charity'.

Helen felt in her pocket for her phone, flicking on the torch and shining the beam through the egg's shell. They had not slept together, Gareth and Carla. At least, not in the same room, not overnight.

She could see through the egg – the small dark, crimson eye, and the red spiralling frost veins.

She had heard them saying their goodnights at the top of the stairs. She had heard Gareth's door close. She had heard the guest room washbasin growl into life with its low bass tones.

Helen continued to roll the egg gently around in her hands, illuminating it with the soft glow of the torch. Why, she wondered, hadn't the 'couple' both gone to Carla's room? It was something that had puzzled her last night, and she'd returned to the problem this morning. For the life of her, she couldn't work out why. Then she felt a sickening feeling growing deep at the base of her stomach – they had time. They thought they had all the time in the world. Gareth didn't see this as just a quick fling. This was a relationship. Currently it was a small bud, barely two days old, but it was a relationship.

Helen's grip tightened on the egg. She added a little more pressure, then just a little more, before the egg smashed between her fingers. Gently, she opened the lid of the incubator and taking out the eggs, one by one, she crushed them again and again and again.

CHAPTER THIRTY-THREE

HELEN

In the warmth of the kitchen, Helen closed the lid of the widow's chest, put the key back in the lock and turned. Carla had been an easy target. The young were careless with possessions; they had so much. Helen never left her own jewellery beside the sinks. Tim may have failed her, but Helen had managed to Magpie a little something for herself. She felt a small swell of satisfaction for a job well done. Suddenly, she realised she was not alone. Gareth was standing in the doorway. In his hands, she saw that he was holding his overnight bag, and her heart sank. He was leaving.

'You want coffee?' she asked, pushing herself up to her feet.

He made no reply. He came into the room and put his bag down right beside the door. Despite herself, Helen managed to find this vaguely amusing – in case he needs to make a quick getaway, she thought.

'I asked...'

'I heard you. Black,' he stated simply.

She nodded lifting the warm kettle. She would not do bacon. And eggs were no longer a possibility. Toast would have to suffice. 'That was cruel of you last night,' she said, pouring the hot liquid into a cup and spooning in the granules. 'I had supper ready.'

He sat down at the table, rubbing his face in his hands. A day's stubble was already beginning to shadow his jaw.

'Did you wait up for us?'

Helen put the coffee in front of him, then stood back, as if needing to get a better, more encompassing view. He was still half-cut from last night, she thought; his eyes a watery red, his shoes muddy from the walk home.

'What do you do in rural Suffolk till gone twelve, Gareth?'

He shrugged. 'Talk.'

'I haven't seen you in years. Why not talk to me?'

'Because you don't give me straight answers, Helen.'

Suddenly he seemed to realise that something was different. That the tone of the house had actually changed somehow. 'Where's Carla?' He fixed Helen with a hard stare. 'Her room was empty.'

Helen sighed, and moved towards the sink, where her own breakfast things still lay. 'Probably out walking.'

Gareth looked puzzled. 'She got up early?'

'It's not early. It's gone nine.'

But he wasn't convinced. 'Early enough.'

Helen shrugged. 'Maybe she doesn't need much sleep. How would I know?'

'And Tim?' Gareth asked.

'Tim didn't want to stay.'

Gareth's eyes narrowed.

'We had an argument. He's gone to Norwich. He won't be coming back.' She paused. 'So now it's just the two of us.'

'You knew I was in the house.'

Helen gave a short laugh. 'I just told you. I waited up. I was worried.'

'No.' His voice had a hard edge to it, and she realised that a line in the sand was being drawn. 'Not last night. That summer, when I was supposed to be at camp.'

'I don't know what you're talking about.'

She turned her back on him and moved quickly towards the toaster. She would feed him; stop his mouth with bread and butter. How did he know? she kept thinking to herself. How could he have guessed that all those years ago Helen had been aware of her teenage brother hiding out in the attic: hiding for the whole six weeks, watching? Then she remembered the conversation with Carla.

'Always snooping,' she said. 'Has no one ever told you, snooping can get you in hot water.'

He was on his feet and moving towards her.

'You knew I was in the house.'

She was at the sink, hands pressed on its rim. Fingers holding the rolled ceramic edge tight, because if she fell, if she put one foot wrong now, she might never haul herself back out.

'All those visits from the priest.'

She shook her head. 'We don't have to do this.'

'We do, Helen. Look at me.'

But she wasn't going to. She just held on to the sink and stared at her hands.

'Helen!'

'It was a long time ago,' she said quietly, as if the words were being drawn up from another place and time. 'I was very young.'

He grabbed her roughly by the arm, swinging her around so that she faced him. 'You knew what you were doing.' His words were thick with disgust. 'You were in full control, always were. Had me dancing to your tune like a puppet. The beautiful Helen, so superior, so in control, so rotten.'

'Gareth, we're too old for this.'

But he had no intention of stopping. 'I wasn't some voyeur,

232

was I, Helen, when the priest came calling? When he turned up with all those presents, not a voyeur.'

'You saw what you wanted to see,' she lashed back. 'No one asked you to watch.'

'Didn't they?'

'I did it for you,' she pleaded, reaching out one hand towards him.

'No.'

'I knew you wanted me, could see that you were burning for me. Remember?'

'God, Helen! I was fourteen. I wasn't burning for you. Teenagers, they just burn, for Christ's sake. You.' He stared at her with a look of utter betrayal. 'I idolised you.'

'But you couldn't touch me, and you wanted to touch me.'

'I would never have done that. You're my sister.'

'And that tormented you – the fact that I was your sister. I did it for you, Gareth.'

'No. Not for me.'

'We don't need anyone. Can't you see that? It's just you and I, like it always was. No one else matters.'

He looked away, glanced out of the window and saw the rockery, the boulders and weeds pushed out of place; and in amongst the weeds the dying tendrils of poisonous plants.

'Fuck! I didn't hit him, did I?'

Helen felt her face drop as her features scrambled into an attitude of utter panic. 'Of course you hit him.'

'But it wasn't hard enough. That's the point here, the missing piece. I didn't him hit him hard enough.'

'You hit him.'

'No, Helen.' His voice kept hammering into her very brain. 'Not true. Not accurate. He was already dying. That's why he went down so quickly. That's why he went down and never got back up.'

'You hit him.'

'No.' Gareth shook his head. 'We built that rockery. We planted all that crap. You had everything you wanted at your fingertips, all ready to go. You'd had it for years. You must have been itching to try it out. Shit! Mother even helped. That's why, isn't it? That's why the garden never got replanted. That's why she retired to her room.'

Helen was shaking her head.

'She knew.' He spat the words out. 'Planting poisons with your mother? Most women bake cakes with their kids, but she... she had no idea. Not a clue what you were going to do. To her it was just horticulture and she was so delighted you were taking an interest. But you hated all of that didn't you? Hated the garden. Didn't mind using it though, when it suited you.'

Helen leant back against the wall, hoping her legs wouldn't give way beneath her.

'She never got back up out of bed, did she? She could never quite piece it all together. Never had all the facts. But she knew what you'd done.' He looked over at the chest. 'What's in the box?'

'Nothing. I told you.'

'You were looking in it this morning when I came in. Open it.'

She sent the key sliding across the kitchen table. 'Open it yourself.'

He grabbed the key, inserting it into the lock and yanked the chest open. His features fell. 'Is this all that you were worth? A green silk shawl, a pair of Italian shoes, a string of pearls – fake, no doubt.'

'Gareth, this is not making anything any better.'

But he didn't stop. He threw his hands around the insides of the chest as if looking for something. Then suddenly she heard it – the soft jangle. A look of utter panic crossed his face.

Frantically, he pulled everything out. All of the 'gifts' scattered across the cold flagstone floor, until his fingers clutched on Carla's bracelet.

'Where is she?'

'Oh, for goodness' sake.'

'This is Carla's. Where is she? What have you done?' He sank down onto a chair. 'Shit. Your lab?'

'Go on, Gareth.' It was all coming out now.

He shook his head in disbelief. 'You said it was perfume. But it wasn't, was it?'

'You know, Gareth. You know what I did in the shed. Think.'

'No.' His voice broke. He placed his hands over his temples like a cage, as if suddenly he didn't want to remember.

'Too late for that.' She had no intention of letting him off the hook this time. 'I held experiments, remember?'

'Not perfume?'

'No, not perfume. It's coming back, isn't it? You must remember those long summer days. The door to the mushroom shed hanging open on its hinges. You remember what I had strung up all down the sides of the shed?'

'Not flowers?'

She laughed. 'No. Animals, Gareth. Live ones in cages. Dead ones hung on meat hooks.'

His face was beginning to look like wax; a sickly melt of tallowed features. A broken melting man.

'You tried your potions... You tried them out on animals and insects. You experimented.'

'Yes. Remember the promise?'

But he shook his head, perhaps because he couldn't remember, perhaps because he didn't want to. She didn't care anymore.

'I promised you that, if it was yours, I wouldn't touch it.'

235

'I didn't kill Father Wright, did I, Helen?'

'Of course, you...'

'No, you wanted someone in on it, someone to see what was going on, someone to realise how clever you were.' He stopped suddenly. 'Carla?'

Helen shook her head, assuming a mock-serious attitude. 'Not marked. You didn't mark her. Carla was open game.'

'What the fuck have you done?'

'Oh, for God's sake, Gareth. You barely knew the woman.'

He got to his feet but stumbled slightly. 'I have to go to the police.'

He moved towards the door, his bag and his phone.

'You're involved. You are part of this, Gareth. We need to stay together.'

'No.' He shook his head. He took the bag and reached into the front pocket, his fingers closing over his mobile. He was about to dial when he heard Helen's voice, a sad low whisper. 'No.'

When he turned, he saw Helen with a long kitchen knife pointing in towards her stomach, her clothes tight around the blade where it pressed against her skin.

The reaction was instinctive, he dropped the phone and lunged towards her, knocking the knife out of her hands. It clattered across the hard stone floor.

She sank down on her knees.

'What the fuck are you trying to do?'

'Clutch at straws.' Her voice was barely a whisper. 'I am such a coward, Gareth. I wouldn't have done it. I just wanted to know if you'd stop me.'

'Please, no more games.'

'No, it's over. What a mess. All the pieces, they're all there for you now. Are you happier? Really? You can lay it all out, understand it all, but I don't, Gareth. I still don't understand.' She gestured with one arm towards the back door. 'She's out, your little Carla. She's just out. Most likely doing something normal, walking, going to the shop, working up an appetite. She can do all of that because she's not like us – damaged. You must hate me.'

He sank down beside her, taking her gently in his arms.

'No.'

'Well, I disgust myself. There's not a day that doesn't go by when I don't feel utter revulsion. I was just trying to control it. Trying to make some kind of sense of... everything. In truth, I can't see that anyone else's "sense" is any better than mine. Because wanting you helped. And the presents helped. And pretending to be leading things, being at the centre, helped.'

Outside in the garden, a wood pigeon cooed, just like they always had, regardless of circumstance, welcoming in the day.

'Do you know what the church announced recently?' she asked. 'Did you hear the *official* line?'

He didn't answer.

'They said that they could not be held responsible. The relationship between a priest and the church is not one of employment.'

Gareth nodded slowly. 'And if it's not employment the diocese has no liability.'

'The law, it's a slippery beast, more snake than eagle.'

'The courts didn't honour it.'

'No. But imagine having the gall to even put it forward as a proposition?'

He didn't answer. The clock ticked, and for a moment, they just sat on the floor, listening to time dissolving.

'What would make it right? Compensation, it's...'

'Like giving an Elastoplast to an amputee,' Helen finished

his sentence. 'The walls should crumble. That would be justice. They placed men in our homes, trained them, vouched for them, put them in uniforms and told us to trust them. I would like to pull it down, the Vatican, brick by brick by brick. Slide my fingernails into the plaster. Shame it, just like it shamed me. Shame it for everyone. That's how it should be – disgraced.' She smiled sadly. 'You were the only thing that made it all right.'

'The watch?'

She sighed. 'I planted it. I had to know if you were still out there. And... look,' she smiled weakly, 'it pulled you back.'

Somewhere in the big house, the small sound of a bell rang out, but they didn't move. They remained there for a moment, sitting on the hard stone floor, listening to the high-pitched trill threading its way through the cold, dead corridors towards them.

'Mother,' she said simply. Bringing up the edge of her jumper and wiping away the snot and tears.

The bell rang out again.

'That bloody bell.' Helen smiled ironically and pushed herself to her feet. She leant back down, entwined her hand briefly with his and kissed him gently on the knuckles before letting his hand drop away. Slowly, she walked towards the door. When she reached the edge of the room, she turned back for just a moment, reluctant to leave, keen to take another quick look at him. 'Don't go just yet, Gareth. Stay a little longer?'

It would all be okay. Everything was going to be all right now, she was sure of it. She gazed up the stairs through the arteries and veins of the house and began to climb.

~

When Helen came back down the steps only moments later, she was talking, filling the space in the house with her voice.

'It was nothing. It was just...' But the kitchen was empty, and Helen's words were swallowed up once again by nothing but stone walls.

CHAPTER THIRTY-FOUR

GARETH

'And the young woman?'

'Carla?' Gareth asked. 'She texted me. She left early for Norwich. She's fine.'

'So you're saying that your sister was groomed by Father Wright. That she poisoned him, but that you thought for years he had died at your own hands, after you punched him?'

Gareth glanced down at those same hands that had laid the blow. They seemed so much more innocent now. 'That's right.'

'And the body?'

He shrugged. 'I'm not sure. It's a big house, a lot of land. The body could be anywhere.'

'But you're saying your sister, Helen, hid it?'

'Yes.'

'You have no idea where?'

'It's not anywhere obvious.'

'And who have you told about this?'

'Just you. I thought it best. I could go to the police but...'

'But?'

'I'm not sure who's really innocent here. I'm not sure she hasn't been punished enough. I feel I've been punished enough.'

240

He cleared his throat. Took a sip from the water glass in front of him. 'Father Penrose, will you accept my confession?'

There was a pause, a pause in which Gareth's entire life seemed to collapse in on him.

'I will.' Penrose, the man with the kind face, reached forward and took Gareth's hands between his own. 'And can you forgive yourself now, Gareth?'

'I don't know, father. But I'm ready to move on. To take my orders.'

'And it's the States you'd like to go to?'

Gareth nodded. A new beginning.

'Then you know what to do...' Penrose said, sitting back in his chair. Turning his face to the side.

And Gareth did know what to do. 'Bless me, father, for I have sinned.'

THE END

ACKNOWLEDGEMENTS

This project has been gestating for so long that to list all those who helped in bringing it to the table would demand an entire book all of its own. So just a few names: James Holloway (for encouragement), Clare Hawes (reader), Eileen Ryan (reader), my son, Tom (reader), Ian Skewis (editor), Betsy Reavley, Tara Lyons and all the Bloodhound books team (for getting it out there).

ABOUT THE AUTHOR

Shirley writes psychological thrillers. Sometimes they flirt with domestic noir, sometimes they tip over the horror side of the scale, and sometimes they're downright tragedies. She loves science fiction and the elbow room it affords for the realms of the possible. Although her sci-fi has appeared on stage and podcasts, no one has taken that brave step of marshalling it to print. She would love to write comedy and has written and produced comic plays for Radio 4 and the theatre. She'd like to think that even in the darkest corners of the darkest moments of her darkest books, there is a dry sense of humour that can carry the reader through.

After living in Suffolk for most of her adult life, she's recently become a born-again Londoner. It's early days, but so far so good. She teaches screenwriting and Theatre studies at two universities in London and works for The Literary Consultancy as a reader. She has an MA in Philosophy and Classics and is studying a PhD in adaptation studies at UEA.

Shirley is an avid reader. Her literary heroes are – too many to mention, but at a stab – Graham Greene (because she loves armchair travelling), Kurt Vonnegut (because she loves the quirky kindness underlying his books, and the way his ideas explode in the mind provoking universes of thought), Virginia Woolf (for her haunting prose and her advice about getting a room of one's own. Sadly, Shirley has had to say goodbye to her room since the move to the big smoke. She is now Harry Pottering it under the stairs). She also loves George Orwell (impossible not to), Charlotte Bronte for her storytelling and Stephen King for the epic worlds he creates and the sense of humanity (despite all) which pervades them. Although she has had to return *It* to the library because *It* is just too damn scary.

A NOTE FROM THE PUBLISHER

Thank you for reading this book. If you enjoyed it please do consider leaving a review on Amazon to help others find it too.

We hate typos. All of our books have been rigorously edited and proofread, but sometimes mistakes do slip through. If you have spotted a typo, please do let us know and we can get it amended within hours.

info@bloodhoundbooks.com

Printed in Great Britain
by Amazon